MORE PRAISE FOR

"I love a wild psychological ride—and Emiko Jean elevates the genre with this taut, provocative thriller. Jealousy, violence, and revenge are the sharp corners of a novel that holds at center themes of loss, love, and the warm, beating heart of human connection. Alice and Celia are fascinating as twins whose personae play out along a rich dynamic of entrapment, suspicion, trauma, and alienation—and raise always-intriguing issues of sisterhood, duality, and how existing as a double is also a splintering of self. A killer debut!" —Adele Griffin, National Book Award finalist

"Haunting and gripping, *We'll Never Be Apart* is a twisty, thrilling debut that kept me completely riveted. I can't wait to read whatever Emiko Jean writes next!" —Megan Miranda, author of *Fracture*

"[For] readers who enjoy psychological melodrama with lots of action and slightly creepy elements." —*The Bulletin*

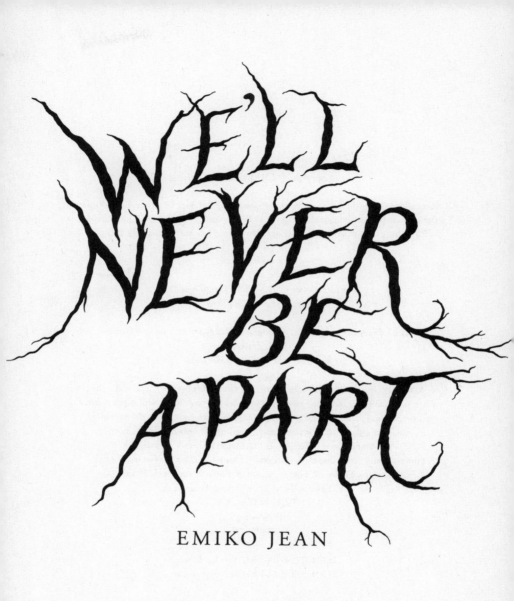

WE'LL NEVER BE APART

EMIKO JEAN

HOUGHTON MIFFLIN HARCOURT

BOSTON NEW YORK

www.hmhco.com

The text was set in 11.5 Adobe Garamond Pro.
Book design by Lisa Vega

The Library of Congress has cataloged the hardcover edition as follows:
Jean, Emiko.
We'll never be apart / Emiko Jean.
pages cm
Summary: Haunted by memories of the fire that killed her boyfriend and twin sister, seventeen-year-old Alice Monroe is in a mental ward when, with support from fellow patient Chase, she begins to confront hidden truths in a journal, including that the only person she trusts may be telling her only half of the story.
[1. Mental illness—Fiction. 2. Psychiatric hospitals—Fiction. 3. Post-traumatic stress disorder—Fiction. 4. Death—Fiction. 5. Twins—Fiction. 6. Sisters—Fiction. 7. Love—Fiction. 8. Foster home care—Fiction.]
I. Title. II. Title: We will never be apart.
PZ7.1.J43We 2015
[Fic]—dc23
2014046785

ISBN: 978-0-544-48200-5 hardcover
ISBN: 978-0-544-81320-5 paperback

Manufactured in the United States of America
DOC 10 9 8 7 6 5 4 3 2 1
4500611330

For Craig,

who really keeps the sun in the sky

and the stars apart

and the water in the oceans.

I wrote this book for you.

PROLOGUE

CELIA

LATER ON, WHEN THEY QUESTION ME, I'LL SAY IT WAS AN ACCIdent. An unfortunate tragedy. But it was neither. When they ask me what happened that night, I'll say, *It was a mistake.* But it wasn't. *I don't remember,* I'll say. But I do.

I, Celia Monroe, remember everything.

If I close my eyes, I can still see Alice and Jason running ahead of me, holding hands, their bodies suspended in a sliver of moonlight as they dashed through the forest. Before everything changed, the three of us were inseparable—Alice and I, especially. We were like the constellation Gemini, mirror images, forever united in the shimmering heavens.

There were no stars the night Alice and Jason escaped from the facility, but even in total darkness, they made it past the barbedwire fence to the other side of an almost-frozen lake and through an overgrown field, where they finally found refuge in an abandoned barn. I crept in when I thought for sure they had gone to sleep, but their whispers made me pause, and my heart beat like a tethered bird's. They vowed quietly to each other to keep running, to head west, toward a better life. A life without me. And suddenly I saw myself for what I was, the perpetual third wheel, soon to be abandoned.

I slipped from my hiding place, and when I found a gas lamp in the horse stall, I thought it must be a sign. Some divine intervention telling me that what I was about to do was right. My hand didn't shake as I lit the match and connected it to the wick. For a moment the warmth that sprang from the glass soothed me.

Alice found me first. Even in the poor light I could make out her face. We were twins, identical from our long brown hair to our too-large eyes. It was the small things that made us different.

"Please don't," she said.

Those two words had become her mantra lately. *Please don't set those leaves on fire. Please don't hurt that dog. Please don't hurt me anymore, Cellie.* I wanted to shout, ball up her words and hurtle them at her. She thought there was something good left inside me. Something she could draw out and bargain with. But that part was long gone, ground to ash by her betrayal.

Jason showed up next. Once, I could have stared at him for hours. His lovely face. The square set of his jaw. The green in his eyes that made me think of walking barefoot in grassy fields. Jason, the boy I loved, who always loved Alice more. He pushed the hair from her shoulder tenderly and murmured something in her ear. The way he looked at her made my stomach feel empty and my body feel small. I spun from them and took a few steps away. I didn't hear him approach, just felt his fingers as he laid them over mine. I studied the tattoo of a unicorn on his wrist, all psychedelic colors and thick, bold lines, a reminder of happier times. "Just let go," he said.

Let go. It sounded like an invitation.

The lamp exploded on impact. Fire spread like roots through the moldy hay and slats of the dry barn. When wind swept through the open window, bringing new oxygen to feed the flames, it felt like I was flying. I'd never been so high.

Alice fought it. I didn't know she had it in her. She screamed and tried to run for the exit, but the fire hissed and the barn buckled. Something collapsed, blocking her way. I watched as she dropped to her knees and tried to claw her way out, but Jason wrapped his protective arms around her, stilling her frantic movements. He knew it was too late.

For minutes that felt like hours, they coughed and murmured pathetically to each other. Then he passed out, leaving my poor Allie to fend for herself. As she drifted into unconsciousness, her eyelids twitched, as if she were lost in a nightmare. I resisted the urge to touch her, to offer her a small measure of comfort while Fate wrote the final period on her life. There was even a piece of me that wanted to weep into her neck, the way you weep into the neck of an old dog right before you put it to sleep.

It wasn't long before the police showed up. Sirens wailed and flashing lights whirled, casting the night into a frenzy of red and blue. When they found me, I didn't fight—didn't bite or spit or claw. I was lifted and then strapped to a stretcher. Through the open door of the ambulance I could see the firemen hauling out their bodies, like trash bags going to the curb.

They placed a plastic sheet over Jason but held off on Alice. Someone shouted, "This one's alive!" They began to work on her wrecked ship of a body, pounding her chest so hard I could practically feel her ribs splintering.

"Die," I whispered into the chilly night air. *Just go.*

But of course she didn't. It would've been so much easier if she had.

1

SAVAGE ISLE

IN MY MIND THERE ARE BLACK-AND-WHITE PHOTOS. THEY FLOAT around, landing softly here and there, resting on top of other memories, dreamscapes and nightmares. Sometimes they bloom color, like the one I'm focusing on now. It unfolds, like a flower opening for the sun, the petals wet and dark. Slowly it bleeds brilliant pigments. Dark sky. Clear rain. Yellow headlights. A boy with curly hair and a crooked grin. Jason in the rain. My favorite memory of him.

"When was your last period?" the nurse asks me. "Alice?" The nurse's voice is like snapping fingers, calling me to attention. The image fades. White paper crinkles as I shift uncomfortably on the exam table. I try to count the hours, the suns and moons, and remember how much time has passed since the fire. It's been weeks, I think. Tsunamis have decimated cities in less time than that. I rub a hand over my chest where breathing is still difficult. The nurse's white ID badge reads NURSE DUMMEL, OREGON STATE

MENTAL HEALTH HOSPITAL. I recognize her face from before, from my last stay here. The face of a bulldog. Round cheeks set over a row of bottom teeth that stick out just a smidge too far. Nurse Dummel clears her throat.

"Uh, I don't know . . ." I say. "I'm not sure. Maybe two weeks ago?" I swallow. Even though it's been a while since the fire, my tongue still tastes of ash. Maybe it always will.

Nurse Dummel types something into a computer. "And how are the burns?"

The burns that travel over each shoulder blade and down past my right wrist tingle. Miraculously, the fire didn't touch my left hand. The skin there is still soft and smooth. "Better," I say.

Although I don't remember the fire, I do have some fuzzy rec-ollections of my intensive care stay. The bitter uncertainty of those days and the bright, bright pain that just wouldn't go away.

"That all?" the nurse asks. "No pain, numbness, or swelling?"

"No. It's just itchy now."

Outside, wind howls and shakes the thin walls of the building. A shudder rolls through me. Oregon State Mental Health Hospital is located on a thin strip of densely forested island. The hospital advertises itself as a peaceful haven where troubled souls recover, but there's nothing tranquil about this place. Even the name of the island, Savage Isle, was born from blood. In the late 1800s, a hundred Native Americans were forcibly relocated here, only to be killed later in a massacre. Old newspapers say there was so much blood that winter, it looked as if red snow had fallen from the sky.

"That's good. You're lucky you can feel anything at all. Some second-degree burns cause loss of sensation." *Lucky.* Am I lucky? That's not how I would characterize the situation.

"You'll need to stay on antibiotics for the next couple of weeks and keep up with your physical therapy." I almost laugh. When I left the ICU, a doctor gave me a pamphlet on hand exercises, explaining that they would help me regain full mobility. *That* was the only physical therapy I received. I flex my hand now. The movement causes a subtle ache, but other than that, everything appears to work just fine.

A white wristband prints out next to the computer. "Left wrist please," Nurse Dummel says, gesturing for me to hold out my arm. I comply, and she snaps on the tight plastic. There are four colors of wristbands at Savage Isle. I have worn them all before. All except for red. Nobody wants a red wristband. Upon admittance, everyone is given the standard white, and after a period of about twenty-four to forty-eight hours on semi-restricted status, they're usually granted a yellow wristband that comes with very few restrictions. After yellow comes green. Green means go. Stay up late, visit home, drink caffeine, get out of Savage Isle.

"All right, kiddo," Nurse Dummel sighs, handing me a pair of ratty scrubs. "Stand up, take everything off, and put these on."

I wait a heartbeat to see if she's going to leave and give me some privacy, but she just stands there, watching me with a hawk's stare. I change quick and quiet and I think of Jason. When we kissed, his lips tasted like fresh spring water and hot tamales. I didn't have the courage to ask about him in the hospital. I feared his fate. Sometimes not knowing is better than knowing. Still, somewhere inside me the truth clanks like a ball and chain . . . *It's not possible he made it out of the fire alive.* I ignore it. Denial is kinder, more gentle. Uninvited thoughts of Cellie pop into my mind, but I push them away. I refuse to waste worry on my twin. Worry is lost on her.

When I finish putting on the scrubs, I throw my hoodie back on, hoping the nurse will let me keep it. I don't like being cold. She doesn't notice, or pretends not to, and gestures toward my shoes. "All right, shoelaces have to come off. This your bag?" She points to the corner of the room where a lavender duffel sits on the floor. It's worn and dirty, the color almost bleached to gray.

I pull my sneakers off and de-thread the laces. The nurse shakes her head a little as she slips on a pair of latex gloves. She picks up my bag and places it on the exam table. In a detached and efficient manner she sorts through my things. A couple of pairs of pants, some shirts, an iPod, toothbrush, toothpaste, some floss, and origami paper, all my worldly possessions.

She holds the origami paper up and raises her eyebrows. I mirror her look, resisting the urge to stick out my tongue like a petulant child and snatch the sheets from her fingers. They were a gift, a gentle reminder to Cellie and me that we weren't always alone. I don't want Nurse Dummel's greasy fingerprints all over them. When she sets them aside, I'm relieved. "You're good to go," she says. "You can pack up everything except these." Nurse Dummel confiscates my toothbrush, floss, clothes, and headphones and dumps them into a plastic bag. I quickly tally the number of items left in my possession—an iPod that's useless without the headphones, some toothpaste, just as useless without the brush, and my origami paper. Nurse Dummel opens the door and gestures for me to follow her. I gather my three remaining possessions and place them in the lavender duffel bag, careful not to accidentally crease any of the origami paper.

Outside the exam room a big guy with a mullet stands guard. He follows us as we walk down a hallway that quickly turns into another. A sterile maze. We pass a sign that says ADMITTANCE WARD C, then another that says PATIENTS ONLY BEYOND THIS POINT. He swipes a badge over a black box and the doors swing open. I shift my duffel bag uneasily. There's a familiar rush of anxiety as we come to a second set of doors. Once again the guy with the mullet swipes a card over a black box and the doors seem to magically swing open. As soon as I step over the threshold, they swing shut behind me with a soft clink.

The place looks the same as when I left it, like something ate the 1970s and then threw up all the furniture here. We're in the common area, the coed area. There's a box TV with two channels, one with good reception. We used to have a DVD player for movies, but some kid peed on it and it shorted out. There are a couple of couches with pillows that look like they're frowning all the time, some cracked green leather chairs, a few imitation wood tables, and steel mesh on all the windows. I think about the time I visited the zoo as a kid, pressed my face between the steel bars of the polar bear cage, and watched the animals pace. Their padded feet were silent and had worn huge, gaping tracks in the dirt. How many months would it take to make such deep grooves? My toes curl in my laceless shoes. The common area is empty, probably because it's close to dinnertime. The smell of beef stroganoff permeates the air.

"Donny will take your bag to your room," Nurse Dummel says. I shrug the duffel off my shoulder and hand it over to the tech. He takes it from me, narrowly avoiding skin-to-skin contact.

The nurse keeps walking and I hurry to keep pace with her long strides. The C ward is shaped like a circle with three arms, the common area at its center. Two of the arms are long hallways that stretch into dead ends—they're all patient rooms. One hallway is for boys, the other for girls. The third hallway houses the cafeteria, the recreation room (where you can glue shells onto wooden boards or ride one of three exercise bikes), classrooms, doctors' offices, and group therapy rooms. The nurse leads me down the third hallway toward the doctors' offices. She pauses in front of a plastic chair just outside a door across from the cafeteria.

"Wait here," she says. She knocks on the door and then enters.

I look at the chair. Its cracked seat looks uninviting and painful. I jam my hands into my hoodie pockets and lean against the wall.

I've just begun to chew the inside of my cheek when there's a buzz, followed by the cafeteria doors swinging open. A steady stream of teens emerges. Their gaits are sluggish and their gazes downcast, like they're afraid to make eye contact. Cellie used to tell me they were like jellyfish. Overmedicated jellyfish. Gelatinous balls whose touch is poison and who always have to move, because if you stop moving, you're dead. Most of them I don't recognize.

Which isn't a surprise. Savage Isle is state funded, so patients are encouraged to stay for as little time as possible. Plus, my last stay here with Cellie was short—cut short, I should say. Barely enough time to make friends or, in Cellie's case, enemies. I study the new crop of patients as they exit the cafeteria. A second buzzer sounds and the jellyfish move a little quicker (a change in the tide), off to the common area or rec room for "free" time. The irony is not lost on me.

The last patient out is a boy. A boy with a measured, unhurried walk. A walk that screams the opposite of jellyfish. He wears one of those baseball hats with no logo, just solid black. He's definitely new. I would've remembered him for sure. His head is bowed, so I can't see his face. Two techs follow close behind him.

"Move it along, Chase," one of them says.

He doesn't turn around. His only acknowledgment is a slight tilt that brings his head up and makes his eyes level with mine. They are blue, the kind of blue that is so light it makes his face look pale. A long scar runs down his left cheek. From a razor-blade? A knife? Something sharp that can cut deep. Despite the scar, he's not bad looking. If he weren't so banged up, he would be out-of-this-world hot. If anything, the gash tempers his beauty, makes him seem real and maybe a little dangerous. He wears a thin T-shirt and jeans that ride low. He's noticed me staring at him. His eyes crinkle at the corners. He laughs, low and sexy, takes off his baseball hat, and smoothes a hand over his mussed blond hair.

My cheeks grow hot with embarrassment, and the guilt I feel is almost as immediate as my body's response. For one split second

I forget about Jason's cinnamon breath, the curve of his smile, and the touch of his callused fingers. All because of this stranger whose eyes make me feel all lit up inside. I bite the inside of my cheek, *hard*. The boy passes me, leaving behind the scent of clean laundry.

The door beside me opens and the nurse reappears.

"All right, Alice, the doctor will see you now."

I push off the wall, keeping my eyes on the boy's retreating back. Just as I'm about to enter the office, he stops, glances over his shoulder, and smiles at me. Intimately. Like he's happy to see me. Like I've just made his day. He smiles as if he knows me. And I get an odd sense of déjà vu. (Jason would say it was a glitch in the matrix.) I can't seem to shake the feeling that he actually looks familiar. That I've seen his face before. That I know him, too.

The doctor's office is cluttered. Shelves and file cabinets, bursting with books and stacks of paper, line the walls. It's like I've been sucked into a vortex and I'm standing in Dumbledore's office. *I wish.* I also wish I didn't know this office so well. But I do. Dr. Goodman stands in the middle of the room. He's young, with thin wire-rimmed glasses. I always thought he looked like the kind of guy who doesn't own a TV. He holds a thick file between his pasty hands. My file.

"Hello, Alice," he says. He waits, as if he expects me to say something. I don't know why he would, based on our past history of awkward, semi-silent therapy sessions. "It's nice to see you again." He crosses the room and extends a hand for me to shake.

I look down at his open palm and my hands twitch inside the

pockets of my hoodie. I like the way the fleece lining feels, soft like a teddy bear. I remove a hand, shake his, and then quickly stuff mine back in my sweatshirt.

"Please, have a seat," he says, motioning to an armchair. He addresses the nurse, who hovers in the doorway. "I think we can take it from here, Ms. Dummel."

Nurse Dummel puckers her lips. I wonder if she knows that her face looks like an asshole when she does that. She gives me a long, lingering gaze before nodding her head. "All right, Dr. Goodman. Donny'll be coming back to escort her to her room. He'll be right outside the door if you need him."

"I'm sure we'll be fine," Doc says. The nurse gives me one more assessing glance, like I'm a downed power line throwing off sparks, then leaves, shutting the door behind her.

I settle into the chair and Doc sits across from me. A heavy silence stretches between us. Doc crosses his legs, adjusts his tie, clears his throat. He picks up a yellow legal pad and a pen from the table next to his chair. "I'm happy to see you, Alice. It looks as though you're recovering well." I wait for him to get to the point. Usually our meetings follow an agenda. Sharing feelings. Exposing secrets. Talking about the past.

"Do you know why you're here, Alice? Do you know why you've been returned to the hospital?"

Images surface. Pictures of my great escape with Jason. Spirals of stairs. Murky water. A red barn at night. But the memory is like water slipping through my fist. My voice is quiet as I speak. "There was a fire."

Doc jots something down. "Tell me about that night, Alice. The night you left the hospital."

I knot my fingers in my lap and stare down at them, still unable to meet Doc's eyes. After a while, my gaze shifts toward the window. Outside, the sky is overcast and gray. A thick fog rolls in behind the steel mesh and it's hard to see anything beyond the hospital grounds. "How come it's always so foggy here?"

The doc glances out the window. "It's because we're so close to a lake. We're in a convergence zone. Does the fog disturb you?"

Why does he have to answer every question with a question? I shrug a shoulder. "No, it doesn't disturb me. I just think it's weird, you know? If we can't see anything but the fog, how do we know we exist beyond it?"

He chuckles, and for once, his hand doesn't move to scribble on the yellow notepad. "That's very philosophical of you, Alice. Perhaps you should walk through it and see what comes out the other side."

I know what's on the other side of that fog. It's water, deep gray water that makes your bones shake and your lips turn blue. I know because Jason and I swam across it. He pulled me to shore and covered my shivering body with his.

"Alice, are you listening?"

"I'm sorry. What were you saying?"

"I was asking you to tell me about the fire." Doc taps the pen against the notepad.

Maybe it's an act of mercy, this lapse in my memory. Maybe my brain doesn't want me to find out what happened. It's rejecting

14

the possibility that my sister, my own blood, could do this to me — to Jason. Too bad I don't need my head to tell me what my heart already knows. "I don't remember," I say.

Doc shuffles some papers around and brings my file to the top. He opens it. "I have the police report here from that night." I stare at my left hand, the one without the burn. I study the bitten-down tips of my nails and the worn cuticles. Cellie used to tell me that the white parts underneath the nail were lies. When she thought I wasn't telling the truth, she'd grab my hands, inspect my nail beds, and claim that the white part had spread. Then she'd accuse me of things. Of keeping secrets. Of wanting to hurt her. Of loving Jason more. "Was Celia with you that night?" Doc asks.

"What does your report say?"

He glances at the paperwork. "It says she was."

I blink and see an image of my twisted twin. The memory comes screaming back. She's standing over Jason and me while the fire blazes around us, the look on her face a cross between pity and revulsion. I feel a million things in that moment. Bad things. Hateful things. All directed at my sister.

Doc uncrosses his legs and leans forward, his nose brushing up against my personal bubble. I press myself back into the armchair. His breath smells like old coffee, bitter and stale. "Do you know why you're here, Alice?"

I shake my head. All I can think of is Cellie. Cellie and Jason. The vision shifts and there's only smoke. I can't see Jason but I can feel him. His hands touch my face and he whispers something to me, but the words don't compute. *"Jason."*

I don't realize I've actually spoken his name out loud until I see the stern expression on Doc's face soften. So far I've managed to hold off on asking Doc about Jason, but now, with this compassionate look he's giving me, I feel my resolve unraveling.

"Alice." He says my name like it's an apology. "I'm afraid Jason didn't make it."

Something that feels like a jagged rock lodges in my throat. For a moment there's nothing in the room but my ragged breathing. Jason. Dead. Gone. So final. I reach for the image of him again. I see him smiling that crooked grin of his, as if he had just hijacked the world and was going to take it for a ride. I see us, two people with the moon at our backs, running with our arms opened wide. In love. Foolish. And living on borrowed time. A sob breaks in my throat. Doc reaches for the tissues on his side table and offers the box to me, but I recoil. I swipe at the tears and force myself to breathe evenly. Raw grief still simmers below the surface, but at least I've stayed the panic attack.

Doc settles the tissues back on the side table. "Would you like to talk about Jason?"

I shake my head. How could Cellie do this? I've known for a long time that she wanted me dead—was plotting my death by a thousand tiny cuts. But Jason? She loved him. At least I thought she did.

"I can imagine this is very difficult." He tries to sympathize, but it comes off as patronizing. "I remember you shared a foster home with Jason a few times."

Twice. Jason, Cellie, and I shared a foster home twice. A hot tear slips down my cheek but I stay mute. I force my features back into a cool façade, a mask I'm used to wearing and have perfected.

Doc taps his pen against his legal pad. "I'd like for you to be able to talk to me, Alice. I know in the past our conversations have been difficult. I understand if you're not ready." He closes the file, shuffles his stuff around, and takes out a black leather-bound book. "There's something new I'd like for you try. As part of your therapy, I'd like for you to journal." He moves to hand me the journal, but when I don't reach to take it, he places it gently in my lap. "I won't read it unless you want me to. But I believe it will help you. I want you to start at the beginning, at your first memory, just write it all out. My hope is that it will bring you clarity and a way to exorcise your emotions. Grief is a powerful thing, and sometimes, if it's ignored, we can become lost in it."

I resent the "we" in his speech. We are not a "we." There is *him* and then there is *me*. Nothing connects us. He leans over again and places a ballpoint pen on top of the journal. My fingers touch it involuntarily. We're not allowed to have pens. In the wrong hands they can become weapons.

As if reading my thoughts, Doc says, "Usually you wouldn't be allowed to have a pen. It's a privilege reserved for yellow- or green-banded patients. But I believe it's the appropriate therapy for you. I also believe I can trust you with it. Can I trust you, Alice?"

I give a swift, jerky nod, mentally cataloging these two new items, adding them to my others. It's a foster kid thing. Tallying your possessions, counting and re-counting them like precious jewels.

"And you'll consider it? Journaling?" Doc asks kindly.

Again I give a vacant nod. My fingers curl around the leather-bound book and I bring it to my chest. I wish I had a picture of Jason. I'd paste it on the inside. Already his image is becoming cloudy.

Doc sits back in his chair. "I'm glad you'll consider it. Now, let's revisit our original topic—why you're here. You've said you don't remember the fire or what happened afterward." He clears his throat and looks directly at me.

I scrub a hand over my face. Everything during that time runs together like a painting submerged in water. Tubes and wires. Buzzing machines and hazy faces.

Doc looks directly at me. "While you were in the hospital, a lot went on." He clears his throat. "During that time you were charged."

Ten invisible fingers wrap around my neck and squeeze. "Charged?"

"Yes. Alice, I'm sorry to tell you that you have been charged with first-degree arson and manslaughter."

<hr />

2

THE GIRLS' WING

"Alice, did you hear what I said?" Doc asks. Worry creases his brow.

"Cellie set the fire," I say, my hands balled into fists. I stand and push the chair back. It scrapes along the floor.

The doctor reaches out a quick, reassuring hand. "I believe you." He glances meaningfully at the door, where I know Donny the Mullet waits on the other side, red wristband within reach. It's a veiled threat. And I don't appreciate it. Not at all. "Please, sit back down."

I sit down on the edge of the seat, my body wound as tight as a bow. My lips are numb and my fingers dig into my palms. "Cellie set the fire," I bite out. I know I sound like a broken record or some stupid bird that knows only one phrase, but I can't seem to stop saying it.

The doctor's eyes soften with what? Sympathy? Pity? Something I've seen before and don't like. "I understand," he says. I don't think he does. "But you . . ." He hesitates a moment, searching my face. "You and Cellie have a history of this type of behavior."

I know what Doc is talking about. Years ago, before the bad blood between Cellie and me, when I was young and foolish and thought I could make her well, I took the blame for a fire she had set. Since that day, we've been lumped together, the pyromaniac twins.

Doc is still talking, but I can process only every other sentence. "The district attorney was very generous in the charges . . . all agree . . . best for you to return to Savage Isle for psychiatric evaluation before the trial . . ."

"Oh my God." This must be some kind of cosmic joke. Disbelief and utter despair run heavy and icy through my veins. Cellie's really done it this time. She's succeeded. She's brought me down. I'd clap for her if it all wasn't so awful.

"We all have your best interests at heart," the doctor says.

I still can't focus on his words. All I can focus on are my breaths. Terrified breaths—and the dark trial looming over me. "When?" I ask.

"When what?" He seems taken aback.

"When do I go to trial?"

"It could be months. I don't think we should focus on that, though. I want us to focus on your recovery. You were injured in the fire. We'll wait until you're healed, see if your memory improves."

A sudden thought occurs to me. "Will Cellie go to trial, too?"

Doc's lips press together and I don't think he's going to answer, but he does. "Yes."

"Is she here?" I fidget with the pen and journal in my lap.

He glances at his watch and sighs. "We're almost out of time."

I don't miss his not so subtle evasion. Questions jumble up in my mind. Where is Cellie? Could she be here? Is she undergoing psychiatric evaluation as well? But we're almost out of time, and there's something else I need, something more important. I think of my social worker, Sara, with her kind eyes that remind me of fireplaces and apple pie. "I want to see Sara," I say, requesting a lifeline.

Doc sets the legal pad aside, leans back in his chair, steeples his fingers together, and breathes in deeply. His voice is steady but not devoid of pity. "Alice, as your attending physician, it is my duty to tell you that you've been involuntarily committed to the Oregon State Mental Health Hospital on Savage Isle to undergo psychiatric evaluation before going to trial. Because this is not your first offense and because you inflicted considerable harm, the judge has decreed a forty-eight-hour no-contact hold. After the forty-eight hours pass, you will be allowed visitors." He pauses, studies me for a moment, and lowers his voice a decibel. "Is there something else I can do for you?"

He's offering me an olive branch. I'm wary, but I take a tentative hold. I hate asking for favors. It feels like you're trading power. But this is worth it because it's for Jason. "I'd like to attend Jason's funeral."

"Perhaps that's something we can work toward."

My grip on the olive branch loosens. I knew it. They always dangle something in front of you. I allow my eyes to frost over. "I see."

Doc shifts in his chair, looks down at the open file in his lap. "There's something else. I want you to know that your departure revealed certain holes in our security here. Since you've been gone, those holes have been patched." Is that another threat? It sounds like one to me. "Are we clear?" I nod swiftly. "In that case . . ." Doc shifts in his chair and grabs a little cup from the side table, along with a bigger cup full of water. "Medication time." He holds them out to me. "They'll help you sleep, Alice. Make the time go faster."

I take the cups from him and easily toss the pill and water back in one swallow. I open my mouth wide and stick out my tongue.

"Okay, Alice, we'll see each other tomorrow, same time, same place. Group therapy in the morning."

I say nothing as I walk out the door and shut it behind me.

In the hallway, Donny the Mullet is nowhere in sight. But the mystery boy is. He sits in the chair just outside Doc's office, his legs splayed, elbows resting on them. Big headphones are looped around his neck. A soft beat emanates from them, and he drums his fingers to the rhythm. He looks up and smiles warmly at me. I glance over my shoulder just to make sure there's no one behind me. The hall is empty. It's just the two of us. Something inside me unfurls and reaches out to wrap around him, a stupid child that whispers: *friend?*

"Overheard some techs talking about you," he says. "How the fire starters are back." He moves his thumb as if sparking an invisible lighter.

I suck in a sharp breath and take a step back. My fingers tense around the journal. Any kindness I felt for him drifts into the sky like a lost balloon. "Don't call me that."

One side of his mouth curls up.

I shake my head and mutter, "Cocksucker," as I pass him.

He laughs. "You got a dirty mouth."

I flip him off and keep walking. Just then, Donny rushes through the hall. Before he can see me, I roll my tongue up into my right lip, spit the white pill out into my palm, and stuff it into my pocket. Behind me, the door to Doc's office opens. "Chase, come on in. We have much to discuss," Dr. Goodman says.

Donny reaches me, the smell of cigarette smoke clinging lightly to his tech uniform. He expels a breath and seems relieved that he's found me. He motions with his head for me to come, and once again I'm trailing behind him, following his mullet down the harshly lit hallways. We make it to the girls' wing, and he pauses in front of a door. He passes a keycard over a black box, and the door clicks as it unlocks.

"You know the drill," he says. "Last bed check is at eleven p.m. Breakfast at eight and group therapy after. There's a schedule on the back of your door." As soon as I'm inside, the door swings quietly shut and I'm bathed in darkness.

The room is sparse. Even though it's dark, I know exactly how it's decorated, with a painting (probably of some serene landscape) that is caulked to the wall (to prevent suicide by art, which may be one of the most poetic ways to go), and twin beds, each with a squeaky metal frame. The bed closest to the window is currently occupied. A shard of moonlight slices through the room, illuminating my roommate's face and bright pink hair. Her arm, which is covered with long, thick white scars, rests on top of her blanket. There's a bathroom in the corner, with a toilet and sink. No shower. The bathroom has a door but no lock. It's an illusion of privacy, and I know in this place there is none. My lavender duffel bag sits on top of a wooden dresser that I'm sure is anchored to the wall. I drop the journal into my bag and fish out my toothpaste. I make my way to the bathroom, but on second thought I twirl back around and retrieve the journal and ballpoint pen.

In the bathroom, I brush my teeth with my finger. It's disgusting and does about an eighth of the job a real toothbrush would do. When I spit and rinse, my mouth still feels dirty. The journal and pen teeter precariously on the sink. I flick on the light, grab them, sink to the floor, and open to a blank page. I write for a few minutes, furiously scribbling until my fingers cramp and the burns on my hand and shoulders itch, almost like something is burrowing beneath the skin.

I rub the back of my head where a headache still lingers. Most of the medication I was given at the first hospital has worn off. I'm feeling more alert, anxious, and a little queasy. The numbness is dissipating, and emotions rip through me like fireworks in the night sky. I think of Cellie and her madness and where it's taken me. In my mind, a red carpet unrolls and all I can see is a future with steel wire mesh framed in windows, a future that was dim before but is even darker now. What little prospects I had left — the hope of going to college, of distancing myself from Cellie — have been extinguished.

All the grief I've tamped down erupts, and I quietly sob. I think of Jason. That I can't remember his last words hurts worse than any physical wound. Were they a plea? Did he quietly beg for his life and mine? Or were they soft and sweet — a final goodbye? Or maybe a promise to meet on the other side?

I let myself cry until there's nothing left but hiccups. I stand and brush myself off. A steel rod settles in my spine. It's then I know what I have to do, for Jason (and for myself). I say the vow aloud, just to make it real. "I'm coming for you, Cellie. Come hell or high water. I'm going to find you. And when I do, I'm going to kill you."

I leave the bathroom and slip out of my scrubs. As I fold them, the white pill falls to the ground. Crying has made the headache worse, and now it's settled into a dull, aching throb. Leaning over, I pick up the pill and study it in the moonlight. I need a few hours without grief and guilt. I pop the pill into my mouth and swallow it dry. I try to keep the noise to a minimum as I climb into the bed. I lay back and wait for the pill to do its work, make the blue turn black. Tonight I'll allow myself to forget. And tomorrow, well, tomorrow is a new day.

In the hazy twilight of my sleep, I replay the day's events. Something that boy Chase said sticks out in my mind. *Overheard*

some techs talking about you, how the fire starters are back. Fire start-
ers. He said *fire starters,* as in plural. Suddenly I know, as if there's
still some chord that binds us, that Cellie is here. She's at Savage
Isle, and Chase knows where she is.

FROM THE JOURNAL OF ALICE MONROE

Doc says I should start at the beginning, at the place where this
all started. I suppose he's right. Because it wasn't always like this
between Cellie and me. There was a time when she was my friend.
My best friend. A time when if she told me she'd murdered someone,
I would have asked her if she needed help digging a grave. So where
does a story that ends in fire and death begin? It begins in the snow
on the coldest day of the coldest winter of the last fifty years, with
two girls on their sixth birthday in a silent house. It begins with a
body.

The first thing I remember is a dream. A dream that tasted like
cake and was filled with confetti, balloons, and gold-wrapped presents. The second thing I remember is waking up to quiet, to hollow,
empty air. Cellie was already up. She'd made her bed in the top bunk
in a sloppy and hurried way that sometimes irritated me. I preferred
things to be a bit neater, with clean lines and crisp folds. I shouldn't
have been surprised. The night before, she'd kept me awake. Too
excited to sleep, she'd chattered on about the next day. Our birthday.

The house was cold, and I shivered through the thin cotton of
my nightgown. When my toes sank into the carpet, it felt as if ice

crystals had kissed each fiber in the rug. For a moment I stayed still and listened to the quiet, trying to decipher a sound from below the stairs or from the snowflakes falling outside our window. But there was nothing, only the sound of my beating heart.

I bounded down the stairs, oblivious to what that silence was telling me. What secret it whispered. Like Cellie, I was too caught up in finding the promised birthday joy. In my haste, I kicked a slipper out of the way and sent it hurdling through the slats in the banister. It landed with a soft thud on the body. Grandpa lay sprawled out on the floor, his head tilted, so that his face caught the reflection of the snow through the window. I stopped, perched on the last stair. One arm was tucked under his stomach at a weird angle, the other arm stretched out, the fingers that clawed the carpet unnaturally still.

"He won't wake up," Cellie said. She sat by the fireplace, her legs drawn up to her chest, her chin resting atop her knees.

I took a deep breath but still felt as if I couldn't get enough air. Cellie whimpered and ducked her head back into the dark cocoon of her legs. I crouched down and touched Grandpa's paper cheek.

"I tried that already," Cellie said.

"Grandpa?" I whispered. He still smelled like Grandpa, a heady mixture of spicy cologne that always made me think of far-off lands. I don't know why.

Cellie grabbed my arm and pulled me away. "I *said,* I tried that already."

"What do we do?"

She bit the inside of her cheek and turned to me, her look

brighter. "We should let him sleep. He must be really tired. Let's open our presents."

Four presents wrapped in gold and silver striped paper rested on the dining room table. We tore into them. Grandpa had bought each of us a new outfit, a game, and a book. We decided that we were hungry, but there was only canned food in the house, and we weren't allowed to use the electric can opener without Grandpa. Cellie found our yellow cake in the cupboard. We ate it till our stomachs hurt and then changed into our new outfits and raced around the house, slid down the banister of the stairs, and watched cartoons all afternoon.

By evening Grandpa still hadn't moved. Not a finger. Not a toe. Not a blink of an eye. His skin felt even colder. Cellie covered him with a blanket, and after we said good night to him, we went upstairs, hand in hand, and tucked ourselves into our bunk beds. We liked our new outfits so much we didn't bother changing out of them. From the top bunk Cellie read to me from one of the books Grandpa had bought us. I closed my eyes to the sound of her voice, so much like my own, so comfortable and familiar, like the feel of a well-loved blanket.

"Cellie?" I interrupted.

"Yeah?"

"Will you sleep with me?"

"Sure," she said, shinnying down from the top bunk. As she climbed in next to me, I scooted over in the bed until my body touched the wall.

"Do you think Grandpa will wake up by tomorrow?" Tomorrow

was a school day, and every Monday was show-and-tell. Taylor Knapp was bringing in his pet rabbit, and I'd never touched one before.

"Of course," she said, her well-loved blanket voice suddenly scratchy, woven through with overconfidence and untruth.

I turned around and rested my head on her shoulder. "I'm glad you're here."

"Me too," she said. "Don't worry, Alice. Everything will be back to normal in the morning. I promise."

Four days passed. Like weeds growing through cement, fear crept in. And with the worry, fear, and panic came bitter cold and hunger. The little ice crystals that had danced outside our windows now waltzed inside and coated the edges of the frames. Every night Cellie and I dressed in our snowsuits and huddled together in the bottom bunk under a mound of covers, but nothing warded off the chill. It would come like a thief in the night, stealing our body heat, robbing us of warmth. Every morning, Cellie would moan. She swore her blood was slush. Still she managed to roll out of bed, go down to the kitchen, and climb onto the counter. She would turn the faucet on to the hottest setting and we'd use the heat from the water to turn our slush-blood back to liquid.

We didn't go to school, and I missed show-and-tell. We also hadn't eaten anything but birthday cake. Cake that had gone stale and turned black around the edges. And then the flies came, dark obscurities that spent the day buzzing between Grandpa's eyelids and the frosting on our yellow cake.

On the fourth morning we lined up all the canned food on the kitchen counter and studied the labels and pictures. Baked beans. Ham. Corn. Hunger clawed and screamed at the base of my stomach. Cellie decided we should make a meal of the glossy photographs. She rolled her tongue around in her mouth and marveled at the different flavors.

"It tastes like Easter!" she exclaimed. "Now you have some." But I couldn't pretend. I licked my lips and my eyes drifted to the cake.

"It's all right, Alice. You can have the last of it." There was one thick red iced balloon left. My mouth watered and at the same time my stomach rolled. So hungry. So sick.

I hesitated. "Are you sure?"

Cellie nodded and folded her arms over her chest. She held herself so tight her skin turned white. I think she might have been physically restraining herself from eating the rest of the cake. "Eat," she said. "Then when you're done, we'll check on Grandpa."

I didn't wait for her to insist again. I dug in, devouring the crusty yellow cake first and the red balloon last. Remnants of frosting clung to the cardboard sheet, and I used my finger to scrape it up. When I was done I grinned at Cellie, but my happiness was quickly extinguished by shame. Her eyes were glazed over and her hands trembled at her sides.

"I'm sorry," I said.

"It's okay," she said, and rubbed her tummy.

A knock on the front door interrupted us.

I moved toward it, but Cellie grabbed my arm, stopping me in my tracks. "Don't. We're not supposed to answer the door if Grandpa isn't home." We stood like statues, weighing the meaning of those words.

"C'mon, let's go play outside. We can put on our snowsuits and make snow angels."

When we stepped outside, icy wind whipped our cheeks and powdery snow swirled up from the ground like mini tornadoes. The yard was a perfect rectangle, and Grandpa had promised us that in the spring he'd plant a garden where we could grow tomatoes.

We ran a couple of laps. I chased her and then she chased me. We pretended to be airplanes zooming through the sky. I was thankful when warmth began to pump through my limbs. Still, my movements were slow and sluggish, and I stumbled more times than I normally would, the hunger in my empty stomach tripping me.

"Home sick from school today?" Our neighbor Mr. Chan peered over the fence, his mustache and hair catching drifting snowflakes.

Cellie and I stared at him from across the yard. Sometimes when we walked down the block to get the mail, Grandpa would stop and talk to Mr. Chan or his wife. They had a little white poodle named DeeDee that I liked to play with. It could do all sorts of tricks. Mr. Chan even trained it to take his socks off.

"Shouldn't be outside if you're sick," Mr. Chan said, peering down at us.

I looked up at him. "We're not sick," I said.

Mr. Chan's brow dipped. "Not sick?"

"Grandpa won't wake up," I said.

Cellie shoved me in the back and I stumbled forward, my body rocking the fence. "Why'd you tell him that?" she whispered in my ear. I wanted to snatch the words out of the air, but it was too late. They'd already landed.

"Won't wake up?" Mr. Chan scratched his mustache. "Maybe I should come over and take a look."

"No," Cellie said. But Mr. Chan was already at the gate to our backyard, reaching his hand over and unlocking it.

Cellie pushed me. "Don't let him go inside." She pushed me again, harder. Before I could yell or raise a useless hand to stop him, Mr. Chan stepped over the threshold of the back door and paused. He crossed himself the same way Grandpa did in church, put a hand over his mouth, stifled a gag, and muttered, "Dear God."

―――――•◦•―――――

CHAPTER

VANILLA CAKE

A BUZZER WAKES ME IN THE MORNING, DRAWS ME FROM A DEEP, dreamless sleep. Rain spatters against the barred window like sniper fire. It drizzles down the glass and makes the trees outside look dreamy and sad. My pink-haired roommate is already up and dressed, moving around the small room. I sit up in the bed, the old metal frame moaning and groaning as I do—a sound that makes me think of ghosts in the walls.

"I was up last night when they brought you in. You were in the bathroom an *awfully* long time," she says, turning toward me, hands on her hips.

I study her small face. With an upturned nose and spiky pink hair she looks like a pixie, something made of mischief and trouble. I swing my legs over the bed and reach for the scrub pants folded on the nightstand. I'm not sure how she wants me to reply, so I stay silent.

She shrugs and goes back to fiddling with whatever she was

doing before. "I saw the pill fall out of your pocket, too." I slip into the scrub pants as she goes on. "You know you can get in a lot of trouble for something like that."

I walk over to my lavender bag and fish out a couple of pieces of origami paper, stuffing them into my hoodie pocket before she can see. "Are you going to tell on me?"

She turns to face me, flushing slightly. "No, of course not. I just want you to know that I can keep a secret."

I shove my feet into my laceless Chuck Taylors. My gaze drifts down to the raised white scars on her arms. They're not from burns. A burn scar has jagged edges. It is careless, messy, like the bite of a vicious dog. Her scars are clean and precise, as if made by a thin blade and a steady hand. "Me too," I say.

Her face turns a deeper shade of red. "Well, good," she says, pulling down her sleeves.

Another buzzer sounds, followed by the whoosh of all the doors in the corridor unlocking.

"Breakfast time. It's Tuesday, so that means . . ." She taps her lips.

"Pancakes—they always serve pancakes on Tuesdays."

She eyes me in an entirely different way. "You've been here before?"

I swallow. "My sister and I were here for a couple of weeks. I'm Alice, by the way."

A short blaze of recognition flashes in her face. For a moment it seems as if she's going to say something, ask me about my pyromaniac twin, my epic escape with Jason, or the mangled flesh on my right hand. The burns tingle and I flex my fingers, waiting for her inquisition to begin. Instead she bites her lip, then smiles. "I'm Amelia."

Amelia and I stroll to the cafeteria together. We stand in line to get our pancakes, and the servers avert their eyes when they hand us our trays. The line moves slowly. The girl in front of me slams down her tray and screams, "I want bacon!" I glimpse a server in the back eating a piece of bacon. Two techs rush over, and the girl is artfully silenced with calm words and a threat of the Quiet Room. She cleans up her tray and softly weeps. I don't blame her for her outburst. Because I don't think it's the bacon she really wants. It's what the bacon represents. A freedom. It's a question of equality, and here there is none.

Amelia and I sit at a round table. Patients spread out among us. Some sit together, others deliberately away from one another. Because they are jellyfish, there is no rest. Some rock back and forth while they eat; some bodies stay still, but their eyes constantly move. Even though our day is rigidly structured, it still feels like there's too much disorder. My palms itch to take out a piece of origami paper and start folding. That's when Chase comes in.

Amelia picks at her food, dissecting the pancakes into little chunks and then even smaller pieces. She pushes tiny bites to the edge of her tray and spreads the food around. I nod toward Chase. "What's up with him?"

She follows my gaze. "Chase Ward. He was transferred here last week. He was in the Quiet Room for the first couple of days. He just got sprung." The Quiet Room is a white padded cell. It has a steel door with a double-plated window for observation. Cellie went to the Quiet Room once and screamed bloody murder until two techs and a nurse came and made her be quiet.

I touch my throat where it suddenly feels raw. "I had a run-in with him last night. I don't think he likes me very much." I want to add that the feeling is mutual.

Amelia takes a tiny bite of her pancake and washes it down with a giant gulp of water, like she's swallowing a pill. She opens her mouth to say something, but we're interrupted by a girl walking past. I recognize her from before, but can't remember her name. She's got curly hair pulled high into a bun and a round face that makes her look soft and sweet. The girl drops a crumpled piece of paper into the pool of syrup on my tray and keeps going. I reach out and tentatively open the note. Written across the lined sheet in big, bold black letters are two words: DIE PYRO.

I crumple the note back up and toss it onto my tray. Pain rips through my skull and then down my arms. Tears of shame and embarrassment burn my eyes. I look around and all I see are faces, faces with big eyes that stare at me, big eyes that couldn't have missed the huge black letters. Damn Cellie. She haunts me everywhere, even in a place that's closed off from the outside world.

Amelia takes the note from my plate and frowns. She turns, and before I know it, she's hurling the dripping, sticky wad at the girl's back. "Monica, you snatch," she yells as the note hits the girl square between the shoulders.

The girl swivels around. "You really want to go?" Her hands fist at her sides, a clear invitation to fight.

Amelia stands and the room goes quiet. Suddenly the jellyfish aren't jellyfish anymore; they're sharks, and they smell blood in the water.

"Is there a problem, ladies?" Nurse Dummel shouts from across the room. Her voice cuts through the tension like a steel knife.

"No problem," Monica says. Her hands unclench. She smiles a smile that's almost as sweet as the syrup dripping down her back. "I was just cleaning up something I spilled."

Nurse Dummel shifts her bulldog gaze to our table. Her eyebrows raise a notch higher.

"What Monica said—there's no problem," I blurt.

Amelia sits down with a loud thump.

Monica picks up the piece of paper and throws it away. Cafeteria conversations start again as if nothing has happened. Everyone resumes focusing on their pancakes, their appetites seemingly increased by the show. Except for one. Chase sits across the way, his eyes level with mine. A smile plays at the corners of his mouth, a smile that is equal parts curiosity, disdain, and amusement.

"Forget about Monica," Amelia says as we stand in line for morning meds. "She's a bitch, and she probably wears dirty underwear."

I smile absent-mindedly while my eyes stay trained on Chase. Ever since breakfast I've been tracking his movements. As much as I hate to admit it, I need his help. I need to ask him if he knows where Cellie is.

Amelia doesn't miss a thing. "You're staring at him again."

"Staring?" I keep my expression blank.

Amelia wiggles her head back and forth in the space between Chase and me. "Yeah, you know, the act of looking intently at something with your eyes wide open." She pries her eyes open to illustrate her point. Her hands drop back down to her sides. "So what's up? You got the hots for him or something?"

I chew my lip, not sure what to say. Should I tell Amelia that I need his help? That I'm using him to get information that'll help me hunt for my sister? Better not. So I stay mute and refocus on the kid in front of me. He wears an Insane Clown Posse tee, and a yellow band wraps around his left wrist.

But Amelia isn't deterred. She sees something in my face, the wrong thing. "Patient relationships are strictly forbidden, Alice." But her face isn't forbidding; instead it's laced with hungry interest and delight.

"It's not like that." I scratch my forehead. "He's hard to read, that's all."

"Like *Atlas Shrugged*?"

I chuckle. "No, more like *War and Peace*."

She shoulder bumps me and grins. "Just remember, Alice, chicks before dicks." I smile and bump her back. Amelia chuckles for a minute, but then her face changes. "Seriously, though, I don't think he's a good idea. He was in the D ward, and one of the girls in my therapy group said . . ."

"What?"

"I'm not supposed to say."

"Christ, Amelia, you can't just leave me hanging. What'd that girl say about Chase?"

"She said, and honestly I wouldn't believe her if she didn't tell me that she went to high school with him and then another girl confirmed it . . ." Her words come out in one long, rushed run-on sentence.

"What'd she say, Amelia?"

"She said Chase is in here because he killed someone."

I imagine that my expression is a cross between disbelief and horror. My mouth hangs open and before I can form a response, Amelia nudges me. "You're up," she says, motioning to the nurse's counter.

"Alice Monroe," a nurse says, and by the annoyance in her voice, I know it's the second time my name has been called. As I walk to the nurses' station, I throw Amelia a look that says *wait here*. I grab the cup from the nurse's outstretched hand. I'm on what I like to call "the Fourth of July," a combination of red, white, and blue pills. The nurse jerks another cup toward my face, one with an inch of water. I grab it from her and down all three pills with one swallow. I open wide, roll back my head, and let her peer into my mouth. "Good," she says; then, "Next."

Amelia is up next, and I try to wait off to the side for her, but a tech comes and ushers me to group therapy. We're broken into groups that are named after birds: sparrows, blackbirds, doves, robins, blue jays, swallows, ravens, crows, etc. I'm in the blackbird group and Amelia is in the sparrows.

The group therapy room is far from peaceful. The harsh fluorescent lights cast a sickening pallor on the speckled linoleum floor and plastic chairs. It makes me feel disoriented and nauseous. I sit in the chair farthest from the door so I can see everyone who walks in. Dr. Goodman is there, along with Nurse Dummel.

Monica comes in and rolls her eyes when she sees me. More patients shuffle in and sit down.

"Good morning, everyone," Dr. Goodman starts. "As many of you can see, we have a new member in our group: Alice." I am not *new*. I've been in the blackbirds before. With the exception of Monica, everyone else here is *new*. "Could everyone help me in welcoming Alice?" There are quick murmurs of greetings, mono-toned *Hi, Alice*'s. And then a much softer whisper, laced with malice, "Welcome, pyro." My eyes dart to Monica, who sits with her mouth shut, but I swear it's her voice. I look around to see if anyone has noticed, but everyone seems oblivious. "Well, that was a very nice, warm—"

The door to the therapy room bangs open. Chase stands in the entryway scanning the group. His eyes land briefly on mine before he settles into an empty chair.

"Well, Chase, thanks for joining us today," Dr. Goodman says.

Chase mutters something, but I can't make it out.

"You just missed welcoming Alice to our group. I think, since we have someone new and it seems that some of us could use reminding"—he shoots a pointed look at Chase—"we should go over our group therapy rules. Would someone care to read them?"

Monica's hand is first in the air.

"Go ahead, Monica."

Monica clears her throat and sits up taller in her chair. She reads from a poster on the wall just to the right of me. "'Speak your truth. Be on time. Accept others' differences. Breathe. Listen. Tolerate. Rest. Recover.'"

"Thank you, Monica," Dr. Goodman says when she's finished. "What Monica forgot to mention is that everything said is confidential. What happens in group therapy stays in group therapy. Now let's pick up where we left off yesterday. Alice, since you're just settling in, you don't need to talk. Just get to know the group. This is a safe place." The doctor leans forward, ready to dig in. "Yesterday we talked about goals. Figuring out what we want. It can be long term or short term. Anything. Chase, since you were the last to arrive, would you like to be the first to share? What is it you want?"

Chase smirks. "I want to be rich enough that every time I enter a room, a dozen white doves are released."

Wow, he's even more irritating than I had originally thought.

"Clearly, Chase isn't up to sharing today." Doc steadies me with a level stare. "It's important to remember how our attitudes can affect the group. It's always okay to feel negative, to not want to share, but it's never okay to damage morale. This is a boundary."

Dr. Goodman asks if anyone else wants to share, and Monica's hand shoots into the air again. Kiss-ass. Bored, I remove a square of origami paper from my hoodie pocket. I can feel Chase's eyes on me. As I begin to fold, I risk a glance up. Sure enough, he is watching me, almost studying me. When our eyes connect he lowers his head, like he's embarrassed to have been caught. The movement gives me a full view of the scar on his face. I go back to folding. By the time group is over, I've made one paper elephant and two paper dogs. And all I think about the entire time is Chase and his scar and how he might've gotten it killing someone.

Lunch comes and goes. Amelia and I sit together. When we start to move from our seats, the lights in the cafeteria dim and a tech comes out holding a massive sheet cake with one candle lit. Unease skitters up my spine. A girl smiles with delight as he sets it down in front of her and begins to sing "Happy Birthday." Other techs and nurses join in and encourage patients to sing as well. Some do. But for the most part it's just the techs and nurses singing. The girl blows out her candle, and the tech takes the cake back to the kitchen and cuts it.

A piece is dropped in front of me, and immediately I am sick. "I don't want it," I say.

"Throw it away, then," the tech says over his shoulder as he continues to dole out the cake.

I frown and inadvertently make eye contact with Chase at a nearby table. "I don't want it," I say a little louder, which gains the attention of the other nurses and techs scattered around the perimeter of the room.

"Christ, Allie, cool it," Amelia whispers harshly. I forgot she was beside me. "You're going to get yourself a stay in the Quiet Room. Give it to me. I'll eat it."

"Have at it," I say, sliding the paper plate toward her. The smell of cake is overtaking the still air. Even though it's chocolate, there are notes of vanilla and almond underneath. A fine sheen of sweat breaks out on my brow. I need to get out of here. Fast. I hightail it down the aisle. The sticky sweetness is starting to coat my skin. When I make it to the cafeteria doors, they're locked. I jiggle the handle, trying to jerk them open.

"Whoa, Alice." Donny the Mullet steps in. "Everybody stays in the cafeteria until it's class time."

"I have to . . ." But the words are lost under a sour, acidic taste. Heart pounding in my chest, I give Donny a weak smile when his palm hovers over the radio hooked to his belt. *It's nothing,* I try to convey silently, but all the patients suddenly have gray skin, and the hum of the fluorescent lights is replaced by black flies buzzing. My head throbs, and the white of Donny's uniform hurts my eyes.

Then everything shifts. Without warning, I'm back in the barn. Now all I smell is smoke, kerosene, and smoldering hay. The burns on my hand and shoulders ignite in a flurry of pain, as if the skin is still on fire. I'm lying with Jason while everything blazes around us. Jason touches my hip, then my cheek, and opens his mouth to speak. Finally, the words that wouldn't compute the other day come back to me in an uneven rush. *Shit, baby. I'm burning up.*

FROM THE JOURNAL OF ALICE MONROE

After somebody dies, people spend a lot of time dwelling on the *what ifs. What if I'd treated her differently? What if he'd never gotten in the car that day?* But those *what if* thoughts never occurred to me. When I found out that Grandpa had died, I didn't even cry. Neither did Cellie. It's not that we were heartless. Far from it. We just didn't understand what "death" meant—and how it would change our lives forever.

But there it sat in the room with us. Amid the Chans' embroidered sofa and dark wood furniture. Words floated around us —*Died. Dead. Body.*—spoken in hushed tones by the policemen who swarmed the house. Mrs. Chan answered their questions in a short and direct manner even though her hands shook and her eyes watered.

"And when was the last time you saw him?" a police officer inquired. The cop was clean-cut, his uniform neatly pressed and his hair closely shaved. He was cold and efficient, and for some reason, this created an aura of instant distrust.

She told him Friday. They'd walked together to get the mail. She called Grandpa devoted. "His daughter, the mother, just showed up one day, her belly so big, and just like that"—she snapped her fingers—"she took off, left him alone . . ." Her voice trailed off, lost in a sniffle and full-body tremor. "When I think about how cold it's been outside," she mumbled. "My husband said all there was to eat was cake."

The police officer said we were lucky someone found us. Another couple of days and who knows what would have happened. There were teeth marks on some of the cans. He asked if we had any relatives in the area. Mrs. Chan shook her head and said we were alone.

Once, Mr. Chan and Mrs. Chan had a daughter. She died on her way home from university. A truck driver fell asleep at the wheel, drifted into her lane, and just like that, she was gone. Grandpa attended the funeral, leaving us at home with a bubblegum-chewing babysitter. Mrs. Chan related the tragic story of her lost daughter to the police officer and then looked at Cellie and me meaningfully. I imagine she thought we could fill each other's voids. That our separate losses could, like a double negative, negate each other and become something positive.

Soon Shawna came, a social worker, the first in a line of three. Shawna sat across from Cellie and me in the living room, but just before she did, she squeezed my shoulder. It was one of the few times I remember being offered physical comfort. Her fingers brushed Cellie's back, but I don't think Cellie felt it. Years later she would throw this in my face—the comfort Shawna had offered me and then withheld from her. She would tell me how it made her feel empty inside, half as loved.

"Hello." Shawna smiled, but the smile didn't quite touch every part of her face, and that made it seem fake, almost painful. Her teeth were a little crooked, and she had the kind of eyes that seemed not the right shape for her face. They opened a little too widely and made you feel uncomfortable, as if she were staring at you. "Do you know what's happened?"

I thought of Grandpa lying in the middle of the living room, his cold cheek that turned a darker shade of gray every day. When neither of us answered, Shawna went on, "You were very brave." She leaned in and told us that Grandpa had died. "Do you know what that means? Do you understand?"

We didn't, not really. The only other time we'd heard of death was when Grandpa told us stories about Nam. Once, he told us about the time he'd dragged a wounded soldier from the jungle. Sometimes he would lift his shirtsleeve and show us the jagged shrapnel scar. Then he would weep and tell us to go play outside.

But it seemed important to Shawna for us to know, so we nodded *yes*. And when she smiled, I felt just like DeeDee the dog must have felt right after she pulled off Mr. Chan's sock.

We stayed with the Chans that night. Mr. Chan retrieved clothes from our house. The room had a double bed, but Mrs. Chan promised she would get us a bunk bed just like we were used to. Lickety-split. We were given a bath and clean pajamas, and when Cellie asked for extra blankets, Mrs. Chan patted our heads and told us we'd never be cold again. Now I think about how wrong she was. This was only the beginning, the first turn of an unstoppable storm. Mrs. Chan kissed each of our cheeks, and her breath smelled musty but clean.

The next morning Cellie woke early, and her excitement was even greater than the night before our birthday. She bounced around on the bed and clapped her hands together, chanting, "Come see! Come see!"

I followed her to the Chans' kitchen, and Cellie twirled on the linoleum floor, gliding like an ice skater in her socked feet. I smiled and we joined hands, spinning together until we were dizzy and fell to the ground, our laughter bouncing off the walls.

Mrs. Chan came into the kitchen and smiled, but then her look fell. "Oh my," she said. Her hand moved to her heart, and she patted her chest like she was trying to keep something from fluttering away. "Oh my." Her eyes locked just above my right shoulder.

On the counter, gleaming under the bright kitchen lights, were perfect rows of canned food. Sometime during the night Cellie had crept from our bed and removed every single one from the pantry, shiny cylinders of peaches, black beans, and chicken noodle soup, all arranged in perfect aisles, one after the other, each can slightly off center, so the label faced the right, just like little soldiers marching off to war with their heads turned toward the sun.

Cellie and I both attended therapy. Our therapist was a kind, bearded man who asked us to paint pictures and build families out of clay. While I only had to visit him once a week, Cellie had to go twice. As the months passed and she didn't improve, she began to go three times a week—I would stay with Mrs. Chan in the waiting room, eating almonds and reading *Highlights* magazine. I hoped against hope Cellie would be better, but she never got the chance; the Chans began to withdraw, to watch us with a different set of eyes.

"Well, what are we supposed to do?" Mrs. Chan said to her husband one night. I paused in the hallway and pressed myself into a dark corner, nightly glass of water forgotten. She stood by the sink and wrung out a sponge.

Mr. Chan shook his head. "This morning I found the leftover chicken in the bathroom. When I asked her about it, she just stared at me and shrugged her shoulders." They were talking about Cellie. She'd been taking food—leftovers, pieces of fruit, loaves of bread—

ferreting them away and showing me where she'd hidden them. Just in case.

Mrs. Chan's lips parted in the way people's do when they're not sure what to say. I liked Mrs. Chan. She was teaching me how to fold origami. Cellie didn't like it; her fingers were too clumsy, always shaking, as if the cold from Grandpa's house had settled into her bones for good. But Mrs. Chan said I was a natural, that I had the hands of a surgeon and the patience of a tree in winter.

Mr. Chan sighed. "I didn't want to tell you this, but she's been sneaking over to the house at night." He walked over and touched Mrs. Chan's hip. "Darla." He lowered his voice. "We're too old. The therapy isn't working. We can't give her the support she needs."

An icy hand touched my shoulder, and I nearly jumped out of my skin. Cellie. She'd crept up behind me, her head tilted in a question mark. I pressed a finger to my lips, folded myself deeper into the shadows, and invited her to join me. Quieter than a whisper she came, laced her fingers through mine, and pressed her cheek into my flannel nightgown.

"Do you think it's possible for us to separate them? Has the doctor talked to Alice about it? Maybe we can make her understand how sick she is? That she needs help?" Mrs. Chan said. Cellie's grip became painfully tight around my hand. "If it was just Alice . . ."

Mr. Chan bowed his head and kissed his wife on the cheek. He sighed as if it was useless. "I'll call Shawna tomorrow."

We went back to our room, jumped into the bed, and huddled under the covers, our heads making a tent. "They're going to try to split us up." Cellie's voice trembled. She wept, and her tears were a siren's cry—beautiful, haunting, impossible to ignore. *Go on, Alice. You can have the last of it.* I found her hand in the dark and rested mine over it. "Don't worry. I won't let them take you away. Where-ever you go, I'll go too."

"Do you promise?" she asked.

My answer was easy and automatic. Because blood was blood and it was thicker than any sickness. "I promise," I said. "We'll never be apart."

———◆———

CHAPTER

4

DEALS

I FALL TO MY KNEES. MY HANDS GRIP THE COLD LINOLEUM floor, trying to find purchase. *I'm burning up.* Donny reaches for the walkie-talkie on his belt. *No.* I tremble.

"I'm okay," I say, rolling back so my butt rests on the floor. Donny's thumb hovers over the call button. "No, please." Ignoring the hungry looks of the other patients, my eyes lock with Chase's across the cafeteria. "No Quiet Room." I don't mean to say that last part out loud, but it just kind of tumbles into the world. *No Quiet Room.* Chase straightens in his seat, and I know he's heard my whispered plea. I wait, breathless, for his smirk or for some other indication of his patronizing superiority, but it doesn't come. Instead, sympathy rolls through his body and lights up his eyes. He stands, as if to move toward me.

Static comes over the radio, drawing my attention back to Donny. "This is the nurses' station. Donny, do you need assistance?"

Donny studies me, and then, after an eternal moment, he puts the walkie-talkie up to his mouth. I smile at him, but I imagine it comes across as creepy and strained. "No assistance needed. I accidentally hit the call button. Thanks for checking-in." The terror in me releases and everything relaxes. Even the fluorescent lights seem less harsh. Still, my stomach clenches and the smell of hay and kerosene persists. I swallow hard and will myself not to puke. I fail. One: I turn away from Donny. Two: I wrap my arms around my stomach. Three: I spew the contents of my lunch (chicken fried steak) all over the floor.

I spend the rest of the afternoon in my room, napping, thanking all that's holy that I didn't have to go to the Quiet Room. Nurse Dummel mumbled something about new medications upsetting my stomach, then gave me a few more pills, this time a "Valentine's Day" combo—a purple and two small pink capsules. I'm grateful that the episode earned me some time alone, even if I'm locked up. Now I get to skip the second round of afternoon group therapy. Double bonus.

Dinnertime rolls around and Nurse Dummel comes to fetch me. By this time I've been awake for a little bit and have already folded two more origami animals, a lion and a bear.

When I've gotten my dinner (spaghetti and meatballs), I spy Amelia sitting at the table where we ate breakfast. I smile and wave, but I don't move toward her. Instead I hunt down Chase. He's in a corner, sitting alone with his giant headphones on.

I make my way over to him and drop my tray on the table. He looks up at me and immediately goes back to eating.

I sit down across from him and clear my throat, but he deliberately ignores me. When he's devoured everything on his plate (I'm wondering if he's going to pick it up and lick it clean), our stalemate ends. *I win.*

"Can I help you?" he finally asks. His voice is deep and strong. Annoyed.

This is the closest I've been to him so far. He's got a five o'clock shadow on his cheeks and looks weirdly old, older than eighteen, which is the maximum age you can be in here. The scar on his face twitches and seems almost too white for his tanned skin. Again, I wonder what it's from. "Hello," he says, waving a hand in front of my face. "Are you retarded or something?"

I flinch. "No. I'm not mentally challenged," I say through clenched teeth. *Calm, Alice. Just get the information you need and go.* "Listen, I think we got off on the wrong foot."

"I think you were pretty clear what foot you wanted to be on when you called me a cocksucker and flipped me off."

"Yeah, well, I was tired . . . I'm sorry." It comes out sounding lame. Because it is. I'm not that sorry.

He laughs and starts to pick up his tray, like he's going to leave. "Yeah, I can tell you mean it."

Shit. Double shit. He's going to leave and I don't have what I need yet. Before I can think, I reach up and grab his forearm. There's an immediate heat that flows through our skin. A pleasurable spark shoots up my spine and explodes like firecrackers.

"Easy, Sparky," he says, prying my fingers from his arm. "I like it rough, but not in public places."

Sparky. Wonderful. He's given me a nickname. I wonder how he would feel if I gave him one, too. Maybe douche canoe. Or turd burglar.

"You're such a dick."

"There's that dirty mouth again. That didn't take very long."

"Look, we haven't really met yet, I'm—"

He cuts me off with a wave of his hand. "I know who you are, Alice. What do you want?"

So rude. I fold my hands in my lap and knot my fingers together until my knuckles turn white. The tightening of the skin makes my burn itch. "When I came in last night you said 'fire starters,' as in more than one." He arches an infuriating brow at me as if to say, *your point?* I remember what Amelia said. *He was in the D ward.*

There are four wards at Savage Isle. The A and B wards are completely voluntary. They house your basic low-risk patients — depressives, drunks, and druggies. A and B warders can leave at any time. The C ward is for involuntary commits — high-risk patients who pose a danger to themselves or others. Cellie and I both have histories as C warders. So it's no surprise that I've ended up here again. In all three wards, A, B, and C, patients can move around and interact with one another. The D ward is involuntary and completely locked down. D-ward patients are confined to their rooms and allowed only an hour or two a day to "socialize." There's no way Cellie is in the A or B ward. Which means she's got to be in D. Where else would they put her? The realization fills my chest like ice water. I think back to my initial conversation with Dr. Goodman. How he so easily evaded my question. He didn't want me to know. Maybe he even guessed my intent before I'd decided on it. She's here and she's close, in the D ward. Dr. Goodman all but confirmed it.

I lift my chin. "My sister is here. She's in the D ward." In the time it takes to blink, my mind runs through the scenarios. Like an architect, I map out the two wards, C and D. At the end of this hall is a locked door, then another. Both require security badges for keyless entry. Then there are flights of stairs, so many that Jason and I got dizzy running down them. Then there's a yard, a field that's only grass, then the D ward, on the farthest side, in a corner surrounded by guard towers, high fences, and barbed wire. My mind hits a brick wall. *Impossible.* It's impossible to breach the D ward. "You've been there."

Chase doesn't deny it. "So?"

"I need your help." Chase knows the D ward, the winding hallways, the entrances, the exits, and the techs' schedules.

He looks down at his shoes. "How come they won't let you two be together?"

"I'm not sure." *Because she tried to kill me, and I intend to return the favor.* "I need to find her, though." My legs tense in their sitting position. He takes a deep breath, and his jaw works like he's chewing my words. "I need to see her."

"I've been there." He shrugs, rolling back his shoulders as if he doesn't want to say the next part. "When I first came here, that's where they put me." Part of me wants to ask him what he could possibly have done to wind up in D ward. But I can't risk pissing him off. I need to convince him to take me there. Plus it's actually better if I don't know. Plausible deniability is my new middle name.

"Will you help me get to the D ward? I'd be willing to return the favor." Favors in the C ward don't come without a price. Last time we were here, Cellie stockpiled candy and traded it for all sorts of stuff: cigarettes, food, even an upgraded wristband.

Something in Chase's face changes, and I feel like the advantage has been passed to me. I've got him on the hook.

"No," he says.

No? Surprise and defeat blaze through me. All I can think of is Cellie's icy hands, stained with Jason's blood. Chase's rejection is humbling. I get up to leave.

"No," he says again, more forcefully.

"I get it," I say over my shoulder.

When he grabs my hand, his thumb moves over the raised skin of my burn. I flinch and pull away. "That's not what I meant," he says. "I meant . . . *No*, I don't want anything from you." He takes a deep breath. "I'll help you."

I am uncomfortable with this. I'm not used to people doing things for free. "Why?"

He takes off his hat and runs a hand through his greasy hair. "You remind me of someone, all right?" I open my mouth but he rushes on. "Don't ask me about it. That's what you can do. Leave it at that. You remind of someone, and I'll help you."

I don't like it. But he's offering to help, and I'm in no position to refuse. "Okay," I say.

"Okay." He spits into his palm and holds it out for me to shake, a triumphant smile on his face, like the devil after he's won someone's soul. I grimace and back away. "C'mon, Sparky. You're gonna have to get over your aversion to fluids if we're going to do this. It's blood in, blood out."

I open my palm and remember a time when Jason traced my lifeline with his finger. It was the first time we held hands. I spit.

Soon. I'm coming for you soon, Cellie.

"How was your first day back, Alice?" Dr. Goodman asks. We sit across from each other. It's still raining out, and in the corner of the room, just above Doc's right shoulder, is a water stain, wetness collects in the middle of it, and drips into a metal bucket. One drop. Two drops. Three drops.

"Alice?" He prompts me.

I map the lines on his face. How was my first day back? I think about the sugary vanilla scent, the taste of stale cake in my mouth, and the sound of flies buzzing. "It was great." My voice sounds a touch too high, falsely bright.

"Nurse Dummel told me that you were ill," he says.

I'm not sure what I'm supposed to say, so I shrug. "Yeah, she said something about the medication not being right."

He scrutinizes me. "Tell me about it."

I choose ignorance instead of confrontation. "I just got really sick all of a sudden."

"Would you tell me if something else was going on?" His voice settles over me, wrought with concern.

"What else could be going on?" I volley back.

"I don't know. I can't see inside your head. But you're on some pretty heavy medications, and there can be all kinds of side effects. If we're going to have a successful relationship, you need to trust me. Part of that trust is telling me what you're feeling. Do you trust me, Alice?"

He's searching, and I know what he wants, so I say the only thing I know that's acceptable. "Yes, of course I do." But I don't. Not really. Couldn't even if I tried. Distrust is second nature to me. Like swallowing or breathing.

"Excellent." He settles back in his chair. "And how's the journaling been going?"

I think of the leather-bound notebook he gave me just under twenty-four hours ago. I've already filled a good portion of the pages. "It's all right."

"Good, good," he says, as if I've conceded something. He picks up his ever-present legal pad from the side table. Pen poised, he says, "Now I want you to tell me about the fire again."

I tell the doctor the same thing I told him yesterday. Cellie set the fire. I know he wants more, that he will keep digging like an archaeologist, trying to unearth all my secrets until they're brushed and picked clean. He asks me about Jason, and that's when the cooperative rope breaks. I take out a piece of origami paper and fold it, making a frog. He feigns interest and asks me about my origami. But I stay mute. He scribbles on his yellow legal pad, page after page. We don't talk for the rest of the session.

Afterward, Dr. Goodman seems exhausted. He hands me two cups. One holds another white pill and the other just a swallow of water. I go through the motions again, show Doc that I've swallowed the pill, even though it's tucked safely in my upper lip.

On my way out I pass Chase. He stares straight ahead but grazes my shoulder. As we collide, he presses a plastic card wrapped in a piece of paper into my palm.

Back in my room, I flop onto my bed. While Amelia brushes her teeth, I wiggle the piece of paper and plastic card out of my back pocket, where I hid them from Donny. The white pill falls to the ground and rolls under the bed. I swing over the bed frame and pick it up, then place it under the mattress with the other pills. Lying back down, I open the note and read it. Scrawled across the lines, in messy boy handwriting, are nine words:

"Third door on the left, wear something dark. C."

I crumple up the piece of paper and examine the plastic card. OREGON STATE MENTAL HEALTH HOSPITAL SUPPORT STAFF. I flip the card over to where there is a picture of a tech. A keycard. He stole a keycard. I chew my lip and wonder how far the distance is between stealing and murder.

The whoosh of the door unlocking draws my attention. Finally the last bed check comes. The door clicks open softly and the beam of a flashlight crosses over my feet, then Amelia's. I lie as still as possible. When the tech is gone and a few minutes have passed, just enough to clear the hallway, I get out of bed, shifting my weight so that it stays off the squeaky parts of the floor. I pick up my Converses and pad across the room to the door. I slip on my shoes, then swipe the keycard over the black box and the door unlocks. I'm out.

The instant I step into the hallway, I regret it. That was stupid. So stupid. I should have poked my head out first and made sure no one was there. Fear climbs onto my shoulders and squeezes my throat. I press my back up against the door and wait for a shout or an alarm to ring in the distance. A bird has flown the coop. But everything stays quiet and still. No one comes. No alarms sound.

Mentally, I map out my path. In order to get to the boys' wing, I'll have to pass through the common area where the nurses' station is located.

I start to walk, small, hesitant steps that are noiseless. The hallway remains clear. I stay close to the wall, trailing one hand along the stucco and over the doors. By the time I make it to the common area, my palms are sweating. Hidden in shadow, with my back pressed to the wall, I listen for sounds of activity. During the day there are three or four nurses milling around the glass-paned counter. At night, the staff dwindles to a skeleton crew, one nurse and one tech. Thank you very much, state budget cuts. Heart pounding, I peek around the corner. A tech is in there, his head bowed while he types something onto a computer screen. A nurse pops into view, her back to the room as she riffles through files. It's now or never.

Two steps and I reach the couch. I take shelter there for a minute, glancing up once more to see if I've been detected. But the tech still types away and the nurse still files. Both oblivious. Two more steps and I reach the entrance to the boys' wing. I stop right outside the third door on the left. A sheet of paper is taped to it. DANGER. NINJAS AND PIRATES AND LASERS AND SHIT. Definitely Chase's room.

I raise my fist to knock but put it down, thinking better of it. *What am I doing?* The gravity of the moment gets into my lungs and sticks there. I press my open palms against the door and bow my head. If I go through with this, if everything goes as planned and we make it to the D ward, will I be able to press my fingers into Cellie's neck? Draw the life from her so I can take life for myself? If I go through with this, I'll be no better than Cellie. Can I really do it? *Yes.* A voice in my head speaks. I may not be better than she is, but I know I will be better off without her. Without thinking, without blinking, I swipe the keycard over the black box. The door lock clicks open. I turn the handle and walk in.

FROM THE JOURNAL OF ALICE MONROE

Grandpa died in the winter and the Chans sent us away in the spring. It was that time of year when the light changes, the snow melts, and daffodils break through the newly thawed earth.

When Shawna came to collect us, Mrs. Chan wouldn't come outside. She stood at the window, curtain pulled back, and watched as we got into an unfamiliar car that had coffee-stained seats. This is something we would get used to. Something we would perfect. How to say goodbye through paned glass. Mr. Chan helped us get buckled in. Before he shut the door, he handed me a stack of origami paper along with a how-to book. "From Darla," he said.

Shawna drove us across town until wood-planked fences turned into chainlink ones. The houses in this new neighborhood wept with neglect. Faded paint. Peeled-up roof tiles. Brown lawns. Shawna stopped the car, turned to us, and said, "This is a transition home. You won't be here for very long." Another thing we would grow used to: our transient nature. We would become like the wind—so easily blown, so easily turned.

It was here, amid old worn-out furniture, pit bulls, and gypsy children, that Cellie started her first fire. She stole a doll from a red-headed girl who was sweet and kind and asked me to be her friend. Cellie took the doll right out of her sleeping fingers and made me follow her out of the house, into the garage, the doll hanging limply at her side.

I don't think Cellie planned to set the doll on fire. She planned on destroying it for sure—on slashing its face or ripping the limbs from its stuffed body. The matchbook on the workbench was an impulse, the closest thing within reaching distance. But when Cellie lit the match and brought life to a flame for the very first time, it was a revelation.

After she lit the doll's hair on fire, Cellie made me hold her hand while it burned. But I didn't watch the doll. I didn't want to see its smiling face turn to ash. Instead I watched Cellie's face. Emotion washed over her like a baptism. Manic glee tipped to calm happiness, then ended in beautiful serenity. For a twisted split second I longed for that peace.

Years later, Jason would tell me about Prometheus. How he stole fire from the gods and gifted it to mankind. How in one single moment humans were able to make light, warmth, pain, and death at the same time. Fire was a necessity. In order for some forests to grow, first they had to burn. In order to create, you had to destroy. And when he told me that story, all I could think about was Cellie and that doll.

When the fire was done, all that was left was scorched concrete and the smell of burnt plastic. Cellie pulled me behind her, back into the redheaded girl's room, where she superglued the girl's eyes shut (the glue was another find from the workbench).

And that's how the firemen found us. Their axes were drawn and their radios blared, but they just stood there, frozen in time and space, mouths hanging open like unhinged doors while the redheaded girl clawed at her eyes and screamed that she'd gone blind.

They took us to the emergency room. All of us. Cellie and I were put in different rooms, and one by one we were questioned. Everyone asked *why*. First the doctor and then the ER social worker. But I didn't have an answer, so they drew a curtain around me. Isolated and alone, I missed Cellie. I didn't feel whole without her. I sat cross-legged in the bed as words filtered through the thin fabric. Words that sounded eerily familiar.

Split.

Apart.

Sick.

And then I remembered Cellie's siren cry when she thought they would separate us and my fevered promise, *Wherever you go, I'll go too.* I knew then what I had to do. I jumped down from the bed and tossed the curtain aside. With more fear than conviction, I confessed what I knew to be a lie. After all, blood was blood.

"I set the fire," I said.

———◆◆———

CHAPTER

WARD D

All the lights are on in Chase's room when I walk in. He lies on his bed with his hat tipped low, and big headphones rest around his neck. The volume is loud enough for me to hear the lyrics "Fuck the Police," by N.W.A. Someone snores loudly in the other bed, a huge Asian kid who I recognize from the cafeteria.

Chase spots me and I pause in the doorway. He sits up and removes the headphones. "I didn't think you were going to show."

I don't say anything, just keep my gaze fixed on his snoring roommate.

"You don't have to worry about Mao Ying." He waves a hand at the sleeping giant. "I gave him something."

"You drugged him?" What would Dr. Goodman say? Drugging someone definitely violates our group's code of conduct.

"Relax." He brushes my worry under a hypothetical rug. "I just gave him an extra dose, and it takes *way* more than that to kill someone. Trust me, I know."

I don't question his certainty or the comment about how he knows. The less I know about Chase, the better.

Chase stands in front of me and takes in my thin, light blue sweatshirt, the ratty scrubs, and my laceless Chuck Taylors. He looks at me as if I have secrets tattooed beneath my clothes. Secrets he wants to know. "I thought I told you to wear something dark."

A smart-ass comment hovers on my lips, but then I remember how quickly Chase had softened earlier in the cafeteria when I'd whispered, *No Quiet Room*. I liked that. "These are my only clothes." The truth. It works. He gives me an understanding nod as he turns from me.

He rummages through a dresser and pulls out a black hooded sweatshirt. "Here." He throws it in my direction. "Put that on. It'll be big, but at least it won't look like you're wearing a white flag of surrender when we run across the lawn." I put the sweatshirt on over my own, and it comes almost to my knees. "You got my key?" he asks. I'm still holding the piece of plastic in my sweaty palm. I hand it over.

"Where'd you get that, anyway?" I ask.

"Ah, Sparky," he says in a condescending tone. "We don't always need to know how the sausage gets made."

He's such a fucking weirdo. Chase goes to the door and swipes the key over the black box. He opens it wide and waits for me to exit. "Ladies first."

Both the boys' and girls' hallways end in emergency exits. These are the fastest ways out of the C ward. "C'mon," Chase says, and leads me to the door with big red letters above it. "Keep a lookout."

I face the hallway, steadfast and vigilant, watching for techs. I don't point out to him that my job is pretty much moot. If a tech comes down the hall, we're screwed. Chase drags a stool over. He stands up on it and reaches the emergency exit sign. He takes out a pair of kid-friendly scissors (probably stolen from the rec room) and quickly cuts a wire. The sign blinks once and then goes off.

Taking my arm, Chase ushers me through the door and we race down the stairs. It's strange—the night I escaped from Savage Isle, Jason and I took the same route. This time there's no alarm screaming behind me, only the heavy sound of our breath, the dull thuds and soft echo of our feet on the cement stairs. We get to the bottom, where there's another door, this one with a black box resting beside it. Chase swipes the key over it. The unlocking mechanism is loud, like the clanking of steel bars opening a prison gate.

And just like that we're outside, thrust into the chilly night air. The door slams behind us. A heavy rain falls, punishing the grass. A green awning protects us from the downpour. I want to spread my arms and twirl. Fresh air has never smelled so sweet.

Chase motions me forward, his hat tipped low. "There's a way in under the fence over to the right." I stare across the expanse of lawn, transfixed by the dark brick building that rises from the ground. It's the oldest building on Savage Isle. The other wards were built in the 1970s. But the D ward was built in the fifties. I can't imagine how many ghosts reside there. Ward D is encased in shadow. A chainlink fence topped with barbed wire wraps around the exterior. "They have bed checks every hour on the hour." He glances at his watch. "So we have just under twenty minutes," he shouts over the pounding rain.

Will that be enough time? I don't know. How long does it take to squeeze the life out of someone? I step off the square of concrete and out from under the awning. The rain hits my body like little pellets of ice, and the wet grass feels squishy beneath my sneakers. My sweatshirt is drenched in seconds. Chase is a few feet ahead of me, and he's hard to see through the rain. Keeping my chin tucked down and an arm over my face, I run to catch up to him.

When we are halfway across the lawn, a flash of lightning streaks across our path. Static crackles and the smell of burnt ozone fills the air. Explosions of light cloud my vision, momentarily robbing me of sight. When the world dims and comes back together, all I can see is the outline of a familiar body. There are the strong shoulders I used to cry on. There is the rough cheek I used to kiss. There is the curly brown hair I used to run my fingers through. And there are the green eyes that will always haunt my dreams. *Jason.*

Jason stands in front of me.

I resist the urge to run into his arms. I'm afraid he'll just evaporate like water on summer concrete. So I stay still, a part of my heart slipping out of my chest and into the mirage. Another flash of lightning splits the night and Jason implodes, bright orange flames engulfing his entire frame. His eyes go wide and he looks at the back of his burning hand, amazed. The burns on my hand and shoulders reignite with pain.

Shit, baby. I'm burning up. A tremor runs through my body, down my spine, and into the soaking-wet canvas of my shoes. *Allie,* Jason says. He takes a step toward me, and I take one back, my foot sinking into the mud. My shoe is stuck, suctioned to the ground. Frantically I try to pull it free, but it won't budge. *Allie,* he says, closer, so close I can feel the heat on my face and taste the smell of his burning flesh. I shut my eyes, put my hands to my ears, and shake my head. *Go away. Go away. You're not real. You're not real.* I shake back and forth until I realize I'm not doing it on my own. Someone's rough hands are gripping me tight. I open my eyes, dazed. All signs of Jason have vanished. I look at the ground, expecting to see scorched grass, but there's nothing there. Only the soft, rain-beaten earth and Chase. Chase is standing in front of me, looking confused. He's speaking to me, but whatever he's saying is lost, drowned out by the roar of a phantom fire.

I focus on his mouth. Focus on reading his lips as they form a single word over and over again. My name. He's saying my name. "Alice!"

"I'm here," I say, soft and far away.

He scans my face, searching for signs that I'm coming undone. The rain is really coming down now. I'm soaked and so is he. Water pours down his face, making his eyelashes heavy and spiky. "Where'd you go?" he asks. His grip on my shoulders loosens. His touch becomes light but firm. The warmth of his hands burns through my two sweatshirts and brands my skin. His breathing is heavy, and little clouds form in the frigid air. "It's colder than shit out here," he says. "Look, maybe this wasn't a good idea. You're soaking and so am I. Maybe it's not the right time."

What is he saying? He wants to give up. "No." I shake my head, and strands of soggy hair whip into my face. "No." It has to be tonight. My resolve is weakening. It has to be tonight.

He stares at me, and it feels as if he's searching for something he'll never be able to see on the outside. "All right. But try to keep up, okay?"

"Okay. I won't lose you," I say, but Chase grabs on to my hand anyway.

He leads us around the chainlink fence to a spot where part of it is warped and ripped from the ground. There's just enough space for someone to crouch under and come out on the other side.

"You go first," he says, gripping the metal in one hand and pulling it up to create a wider space.

I crawl under and Chase follows. To the left there's a concrete path that ends in a metal door with a black box next to it. A sign reads EMPLOYEE ENTRANCE. Chase passes the keycard over the black box, and a light flickers green for a second and then changes to red. A low buzz sounds. He tries it again, and the same thing happens. I shiver. In the shadows, the rain suddenly seems so much colder.

"Shit," Chase says. "This tech must not have D-level clearance. We'll have to wait and come back another time. I'll get us a nurse's card or better yet a doctor's. I'm sure they have clearance."

The words don't register. "What?" I say through numb lips.

"The key." He holds it up in front of my face and enunciates every word. "It's not going to work."

"I don't understand."

"It's not going to happen, Sparky."

"Not going to happen?"

"Yeah. Like I said, I'll get another card. It's no big deal."

"No," I say.

"What?"

"No. I have to get in there!"

"The key doesn't work. We're not getting in there, not tonight," he insists.

"No!" This time I say it more forcefully, my hands balled into fists at my sides.

"Look, we have to go. We're almost out of time, anyway." He closes his hand around my arm and moves, yanking me forward.

I jerk my arm from his hold and at the same time grab the plastic keycard from his hand, turn, and run it back over the black box. I do it again and again and again. The light goes green, then red, green, then red, green then red. I drop the key and start pounding my fist against the box. Pain explodes in my hand, but I keep going until it recedes into a dull ache that travels up my arm and into my shoulder.

"Jesus Christ. You're going to hurt yourself," he says. Thunder rumbles, closer now, and a few seconds later lightning cracks. "We have to go back. The storm is getting worse." I grip the black box, trying to rip it from the wall. He shakes his head at me, his expression part stunned disbelief, part fury. "You're not going to give up, are you?"

Before I know it, Chase's arms are around me, dragging me back the way we came. We get to the fence, and he pushes me into and under it until I'm forced to the other side. I stumble on the ground.

"Please," I cry. A tremor runs through me, stronger than the rumbling thunder in the distance. "I've come so close." I stand, digging my fingers into the chainlink fence. It sways back and forth with the rocking of my body. Cellie is slipping through my fingers. I look up at the building. The brick façade of the D ward is illuminated for one split second. And that's when I see her—a ghost-white face, sunken, hollow eyes, and dark hair. Cellie. She's standing in a window at the top floor. I know she can see me clinging to the fence, crying out for her. For a moment everything goes silent—the ricochet of bullet-like rain, the roar of thunder, the sound of Chase yelling behind me—all is quiet. Cellie presses a pale hand to the window just as Chase wraps an arm around my waist and pulls, wrenching me away from my anchor. I have no choice but to let go or my fingers will be torn from my hands.

"Please." I fight with all my might. Chase loses his footing, slips on the grass, and we fall into the mud. My fingers dig into the soft ground. My cheek rests on the soggy turf, and suddenly I am drained. The fight in me is gone.

Chase kneels beside me, and sympathy pours off of him. "Hey now," he says, brushing a lock of hair away from my face. "We'll try again."

But he doesn't get it. Cellie has seen me; she knows what I'm planning. I had to strike first. She'll come for me now. I know it. It's only a matter of time. Now she knows I'm close, just a few hundred feet away. And she's a master at escaping. Years of foster homes with locked doors, juvenile detention centers, and psychiatric wards couldn't hold Cellie. It's foolish to think that hourly bed checks and a chainlink fence will hold her. I mumble something that sounds like *okay* or *fine,* but it comes out more like a whimper. Chase helps me stand, and we walk back toward C ward. He holds my hand the entire way, and this time, instead of pulling me behind him, yanking me along in a firm grip, he's leading me, leading me with a warm and gentle hand, away from the thunder and lightning and Cellie.

"This way," he says, taking us to the opposite side of the hospital. "I'll make sure you get to your room."

I hold my breath when he swipes the keycard over a black box leading into the building, but the door unlocks. Before I know it we're back inside, walking up the miles of steps to the top floor. It's darker in this stairwell than in the other one. A single light illuminates each flight of steps. We hold hands the entire way. He lets go only to fish the key out of his pocket and swipe it over the black box next to the door at the top of the stairs. The door opens, and we're in the girls' section of the hospital. "What room is yours?" he asks. I point to the door and he slowly guides me to it, as if we have all the time in the world.

When we get to my door, I stop and turn to him. We're still holding hands as we face each other, and something unravels inside me, a tiny flicker of warmth at the very bottom of my stomach that extinguishes the cold fear. *Safe.* Chase makes me feel safe.

"Are you going to be all right?" he asks in a low voice.

I'm not sure. But I don't want to say it and see concern shadow his face. "Thank you," is all I say.

"For what?" he asks.

"For your help." I swallow.

He releases my hand, steps back, and drops his head so I can't see his face anymore. "Don't mention it." He swipes the keycard over the black box and the door unlocks. "I'll see you tomorrow."

I nod, trying to read his face, but he dodges eye contact. I hold the door open as he starts to walk away.

"Hey, Chase?" I whisper when he's just a few feet from me. "Don't call me Sparky anymore, okay?"

He sucks in an uneasy breath. "What do you want me to call you, then?"

"Alice," I say. "Just Alice."

He gives a quick, almost imperceptible nod. "Okay, Just Alice."

Back in the sheltered darkness of my room, I allow myself a few deep breaths, a few unwatched minutes to sort through my feelings. The smell of damp earth and fabric softener drifts up, and I realize I'm still wearing Chase's sweatshirt. Tugging down a sleeve so it covers my hand, I bring it up and place it against my nose. I decide I want to keep his sweatshirt. I slip off my shoes, go to my dresser, and stuff it in the top drawer. I make my way to my bed and kneel beside it, reaching one hand under the mattress. I feel around until my fist closes around one of the tiny white tablets. I pop it in my mouth and swallow it dry. It's bitter and I almost choke, but in the end it goes down the rabbit hole. I curl up in my bed and count the raindrops that hit the window. The silhouettes of the swaying black treetops outside tease me. Somewhere in those trees is the charred ruin of a barn.

<hr />

FROM THE JOURNAL OF ALICE MONROE

After Cellie set the doll on fire and glued the girl's eyes shut, our names were marked with an asterisk. A tiny star that said without words or writing that there was a darkness inside us, as dense and thick as any bone, yet harder to break. Soon we became lost puzzle pieces swept under a rug. We got used to the feel of cheap sheets and the plastic trash bags we hauled our clothes around in.

By that time Shawna had moved on. So Rebecca stepped in. She wore her hair slicked back in a tight bun that showed off the big gold hoop earrings she seemed to never take off. I remember watching those earrings glinting in the sunlight as we drove in the car. The way the light reflected off them made something in my chest balloon. *Hope.* She took us downtown and placed us in a group therapy home, where all the kids slept in tidy rows of metal beds and the fridge was padlocked at night. Our days were rigidly structured, and Cellie told me to make a game of it. We played as if we were invincible soldiers. Prisoners of war, just like Grandpa. At night, from our steel beds with thin mattresses, we'd whisper to each other and wonder if we'd ever have a family again. We dreamed of escape.

At age nine we graduated from the group home. Rebecca was proud of our improvement and took us out for ice-cream sundaes. Over maraschino cherries and sprinkles drowning in melted chocolate sauce, she announced that we would be shuffled again to a big foster family, ten kids in all.

She took us through neighborhoods we knew from before. We drove past the transition home where Cellie set the girl's doll on fire and glued the girl's eyes shut, and then we turned down a street and stopped in front of a house with a sad-looking tire swing hanging from a gnarled tree.

Our new foster parents, Roman and Susan, met us at the door, their arms open, inviting us in from the cold. Rebecca squeezed our shoulders (a distant type of affection that kept her from ever getting too close) and said she would return the following week to check in.

Roman worked as a janitor at the local high school. In the evenings he'd come home with a feral gleam in his eye, crack a beer, and threaten us with a fist he called God's Will. He'd yell at Susan to fetch him things or change the TV channel. During this time, Cellie and I wished we could become ghosts, sweeping through the house undetected. I suspect that Susan also yearned for invisibility, especially when confronted with her husband's fists.

When social workers came on Sundays, Susan would dress, bake, and make us bathe, and Roman read to us from the Bible.

His favorite passages were from the book of Luke. I remember he'd stand in the middle of the living room, his own personal pulpit, and preach. "'John answered, saying unto all, I indeed baptize you with water; but one mightier than I cometh, the latchet of whose shoes I am not worthy to unloose: he shall baptize you with the Holy Ghost and with fire.'" Cellie and I pretended that we were good children, happy children.

It was the worst home yet, but it was also the best because it was there that we met Jason. He was tall for his age but skinny, an electric wire topped with curly brown hair and bright green eyes. A year older than us, he'd been in and out of the system since he was three, when his younger brother had overdosed and died on the prescription pills their mother had left out.

Jason's real name was Valentine. His mom thought it was romantic. But he hated it, so he pinched it in between his fingers and rechristened himself Jason. He picked the name from a Greek mythology book he always carried with him. He had checked it out from the school library and decided he liked it so much he'd keep it.

We took to one another like mosquitoes to blood. I'm not sure what drew us together. Maybe it was because out of the ten kids in that home we were the only three around the same age. Or maybe it was because we knew what it meant to lose someone on a much deeper, more permanent level than the rest of the foster kids. Or maybe it was because Cellie and I refused to make fun of his real name and would only call him by his chosen one.

At night we hid from the heavy footsteps of Roman. Jason would lean over us, his ten-year-old body holding our quaking nine-year-old frames. Deep in the corner of a closet, he'd wrap his arms around us like a comforting blanket. He smelled of clean laundry, a smell that still makes me feel loved and protected. Cherished.

With every boot step, every squeak of an opening door, he would assure us. "It's only the wind. It's only the weather outside. It's only the sound of your grandfather. It's my mother coming to take us home." It worked. Cellie and I would close our eyes and breathe in the smell of clean laundry, and our fears drifted away like a wooden boat in water.

During the day, Jason would tell us about his mom. Whenever social workers came to take him away, his mother would tap her index finger against his, and together they would say, "Keep in touch." Sometimes her words were a little slurred or her eyes a little hazy, but she still said it.

We made the closet our space, and most nights we slept in there. Jason stole a flashlight and held it while I practiced folding origami. Then Cellie got worse. While we all feared Roman, Cellie had trouble containing her fear. Often she would rock back and forth in the closet. I tried to help her, to distract her by making paper lions and pressing them against her chest. But I was helpless, and so was Jason. And the more hopeless we became, the angrier Jason got. Finally his pent-up rage boiled over one night.

Usually Roman picked on the younger kids, the five- and six-year-olds, but that night he was inexhaustible. He trolled the hallway, his work boots shuffling on the hardwood. Back and forth he went, opening a door, then slamming it shut, like playing Russian roulette.

"My tummy hurts," Cellie mumbled. She shook a little and flinched as a door opened and slammed shut. Roman's low laugh echoed down the hallway and filtered in through the wooden slats of the closet.

"I'm going out there." Jason stood, his hands clenched into fists, his head lost in a maze of hangers and clothes.

I reached up and closed my hand around his fist, tried to untangle his fingers, tried to unravel his anger. "Don't. He'll get tired soon and pass out."

But Jason was adamant. Maybe he wanted to live up to his namesake, transform into the ancient leader of the Argonauts and become a hero, a conqueror. Our savior. He marched right out of that closet, out the door, and directly into Roman's path.

The walls shook and voices yelled, and it did sound like something out of Greek mythology. An epic battle with a beast. The whole time Cellie shook and wept, as if the tremors in the walls were originating within her. And me, all I could do was keep folding in the dark, making one paper lion after another, until I had a whole pride, until the walls stopped moving and Jason stumbled back into the closet, broken and bleeding.

The hero had lost. That night I held Jason and whispered in his ear that the pain he felt was that of a warrior. I told him he was brave and strong and his mother would come soon. When he went to sleep in a tight ball, Cellie traded places with me. She stroked the bloody curls from his forehead while I placed the lions in a circle around us. Sometime during the night I woke to Jason moving around the closet. One of his eyes was swollen over, but the other was focused on the lions. He fingered one, picked it up, and held it in the palm of his hand. He looked at me, and I'll never forget the intensity in his one good eye. How bright it burned with pain and anger. "Someday," he said to me, soft and low and very matter-of-fact, "I'm going to burn this place to the ground."

———•◦•———

CHAPTER 6

GROUP THERAPY

THE SLAMMING OF A DOOR JOLTS ME AWAKE. AMELIA STIRS IN her bed as Nurse Dummel enters our room. Once she sees that we're decent, she calls for the techs and tells us to wait outside.

Together Amelia and I stand with our backs pressed against the wall. A string of curse words scrolls through my head, and heat rushes to my skin. I look guilty. Could I look any more guilty? I've broken a lot of rules since my return to Savage Isle: hiding pills, sneaking out of my room after bed check, acting as an accomplice while another patient stole a staff keycard. Ugh. My rap sheet could go on and on, and on.

But there's no possible way Nurse Dummel could know about the pills. Unless, maybe, Amelia ratted me out. But I don't think she would, and even if she did, the evidence is gone; I've now swallowed every last one of those little white capsules.

As for sneaking around the hospital after hours, there's no way the staff could know. Chase wouldn't give me up. If we're discovered, he stands to lose just as much as I do.

So they must be looking for the keycard. This has to be about the card. I hope to hell Chase got rid of it.

The door to our room gapes open like a yawning mouth, and in my peripheral vision I can see the techs as they lift our mattresses, open our drawers, and sift through our clothing, running their hands along the back sides of dressers and nightstands. Obviously they're looking for something—which only confirms my belief that they're hunting for the keycard. When they're satisfied, one yells, "All clear." They shuffle out like a tight military unit. Before Amelia and I can even blink, they've invaded the next room.

"Holy hell," Amelia whispers. We stand in the doorway, a unified front, taking in the damage. It's actually not too bad. Our beds are a little messier than when we bolted out of them, and some of my paper animals have fallen from the dresser onto the floor, but other than that, the techs were surprisingly respectful.

"That was intense," Amelia says.

"Yeah," I agree softly.

After our night in the rain and my mini meltdown, Chase apparently decides he is my super-special friend. At breakfast he plops down next to Amelia so he's sitting directly across from me (Amelia's mouth drops open, as if she's scandalized). He seems his general annoying, happy self—a goofy smile on his face as he silently digs into his eggs and toast. I wonder if his room was searched.

It must have been. They searched every room in the girls' wing. Based on Chase's attitude, he's in the clear.

Chase also sits by me during morning group and at lunch. Still we do not speak. Later he follows me into the computer lab, where we're all required to do one hour a day of online classes, and ever the faithful companion, he takes up residence by my side. Amelia, who sits on my other side, is baffled.

Finally, when we're supposed to be writing expository essays, he speaks, leaning over so far that I can feel his breath on my face. "I'm writing about procrastination, get it?" I glance at the blank screen in front of him. "What are you writing about?"

"Girls and their periods," I say, enjoying the surprise and disgust that wash over his face. See, I can be funny too. He leaves me alone for the next hour.

Dr. Goodman opens group therapy with a poem about acceptance. He then asks us to partner up and talk about acceptance and what that means to us. Of course Chase, my new bestie, turns his chair toward mine, leans back, and crosses his arms. Our knees brush. He assumes we're going to be partners. He assumes wrong.

"I don't feel like talking today." I pull out a piece of origami paper and begin to fold.

"And I accept that," Chase says. "I knew we'd make a good team." A couple of minutes pass, and Chase watches me make a starfish. Monica cries in the corner, and her partner awkwardly pats her on the shoulder. Chase drums his fingers on his thighs and yawns, saying, "I'm bored."

"I'm sorry," I say. Not really, though.

He makes a face at me. "Is that all you do?"

I take out another piece of paper and fold the square in half. "I like it. It makes me feel . . . peaceful."

"Teach me how to make something."

"No."

"No?"

I picture patterned paper crumpling in Cellie's fist. "It's really hard and frustrating."

"Let me try," he insists.

I sigh and level my gaze at him. "What is it you want, Chase?"

His lips twitch. I wait patiently, feeling both expectant and wary while he searches for the answer. Finally he says, "I'm not sure anymore." Cue awkward silence.

I don't think he's going to leave me alone. Across the room Dr. Goodman watches us. I know he'll step in if we refuse to talk to each other. I focus on Chase, the lesser of two evils and all that, and sigh heavily. "Did they find the keycard?" I ask.

His eyes dart to Dr. Goodman, who has now pulled up a chair with Monica's group. "Jesus, keep your voice down."

I frown at him. "Sorry." I lower my voice.

He keeps his eyes on Dr. Goodman. "Would I be here if they did?"

His question doesn't merit a response, but I roll my eyes just the same. Opening the origami paper, I fold it again, so that it's divided into four quarters. Perfect. "When are we going back to the D ward? I was thinking—"

Chase relaxes and slumps back in his chair. "A dangerous pastime for sure."

I ignore him. "I was *thinking* . . ." I flatten the piece of paper and contemplate what animal I should make. I'll try a rabbit. "That I could do something, you know, to get me sent to the D ward."

His smirk fades as he leans forward. "Do something? Like what?"

I shrug, keeping my focus on the rabbit I'm constructing. "I dunno." It occurs to me that I can ask what he did to get himself sent there. But I already have an inclination. "It'd have to be something big, something that would make me unsafe to be around other patients." His hand lands over mine, crushing the paper under the weight. "Shit," I say. "Now I'm going to have to start all over." I try to pry the rabbit from his hand, but he holds tight.

"Alice, promise me you won't do anything stupid."

Goose bumps prickle my arms at the word *stupid*. But then Chase's thumb moves ever so gently over mine, and all of a sudden the air in the room no longer exists. There's only Chase and me, our breaths one symbiotic loop. Chase seems to feel it too. He licks his lips and shakes his head. "Promise me," he says a little more forcefully, "that you'll wait. I'm going to get a different keycard. Soon."

I turn my head and bite my cheek. Chase releases my hand. Frustrated tears burn the backs of my eyes. Weak. I am so weak. I'm failing Jason. I smooth out the crumpled paper but it's ruined. "Fine," I say. Still, I can't look at him. I don't want him to see me cry.

In my peripheral vision Chase seems appeased. "Good." Then he sniffles and coughs a little. "It's dusty as shit in here, isn't it?"

I swipe at my eyes. The sniffle and cough were poor imitations, but I can tell what he's doing and I am quietly thankful for it. Gently, ever so gently, he takes the piece of paper out of my hands. "Teach me how to make something, Just Alice." The way he says it, *Just Alice*, makes me feel like warm soup on a cold day. Then all at once I think of Jason, and the warmth is squeezed out of me.

Shaking it off, I show Chase how to make a butterfly. While we're folding, I tell him about the short lives of butterflies, about how, despite their relatively low status on the food chain, they survive by clever camouflage and subterfuge, about how their paper wings drive some people to zealous heights of over-collection. And he listens.

"Are you *really* enjoying this?" I ask after a while.

He shrugs. "I like listening to you talk."

My tongue feels thick in my throat. I don't think I can speak. Dr. Goodman calls the group back together and asks if anyone would like to share. I don't volunteer, and neither does Chase. But Monica does. While Monica shares her acceptance story, Chase's words roll around in my head. *I like listening to you talk.* A tiny fissure opens in my closed-off heart. I draw in a breath and release it slowly. I'm taken aback. Not because he said he liked listening to me talk, but because I realize I like listening to him, too.

I come awake slowly, my shallow breaths dissolving in the eerie silence of the hospital room. It's night. Something scratches the wall, the *inside* of the wall. The scratching is faint, right above my head, a seesawing noise that sounds like someone's fingernails clawing the inside of a coffin. My heartbeat speeds up. I turn my head a fraction of an inch and look over at Amelia. She rests safe and sound in her bed. Slowly, I flip over onto my stomach and rise up so I'm on all fours, and I crawl toward the scratching noise. I smooth a lock of sweat-soaked hair from my forehead and press my palm to the wall. The scratching stops abruptly. Pipes. It's probably just the heat kicking on in the old building. Yawning, I move to settle back into bed. I glance at the nightstand where my scrubs are folded, where a little white pill rests in the pocket. I can't stop thinking about the vision of Jason all lit up and electric in the dark. His words from the fire linger. *Shit, baby. I'm burning up.* Why would he say that? And why with such happiness? I wish I could remember more about that night. The memory of escaping with Jason, running through the yard, and yanking open the heavy door of the barn is as clear as glass. But everything that came after is a blur, lost in the terrible heat of the fire. When I close my eyes, I can see only Cellie's twisted face. If I take the pill, it will make my mind fuzzy and keep the frantic thoughts caged. I crack my knuckles, hesitating.

There's a dull thump, like a body being dropped in a trunk, and then the scratching starts again, this time in the wall by the window. It's louder, more hurried, frantic, like someone is trying to tear his or her way out. I turn my head to look at the wall, and just as my eyes pin the spot where the noise is coming from, the sound zooms around the room, one long scrape that circles, once, twice then stops. My mouth feels as if it's filled with cotton.

The scratching starts again, quieter, right behind Amelia's dresser. I slip out of bed and edge toward the dresser, careful to be as quiet as possible. The scratching speeds up the closer I get. In a few uneasy breaths I'm there. My hand touches the handle of the bottom drawer. I waiver, suddenly convinced that I'm going to see Jason in there, folded up like some mummy petrified in the Pompeii caves, mouth open in a perpetual scream. There's another long scrape, this time right inside the drawer, and then soft laughter right over my shoulder. A boy's laugh. Jason's laugh. I look behind me but it's nothing, no one, only Amelia still sleeping.

With a shaky hand I take hold of the handle and pull the drawer open.

A hand comes from nowhere and slams the drawer shut.

"What the fuck, Alice?" Amelia stands in front of me, her body shoved between the drawer and me. "That's my private stuff. What are you, some kind of klepto?"

Frozen, I stare at her freckled legs, pale in the moonlight. "I'm sorry. I thought I heard something in the drawer."

She glances down at the drawer suspiciously. "Well, there's nothing in there except for clothes. Do you think they've suddenly come to life?"

I feel embarrassed. "No, no. Look, I'm sorry. Like I said, I thought there was something in —"

Another sound from the drawer cuts me off — scraping,

followed by a scuttling that makes the drawer jiggle in its tracks. "Don't tell me you didn't hear that?"

She sniffs and crosses her arms. "I didn't hear anything."

It's my turn to swear. "Bullshit." Before she can stop me, I rip open the drawer. "Oh my god!" It's a rat. A huge, red-eyed, dirty white rat. I drop the drawer and it bangs as it hits the linoleum floor. The rat rises up and stands on two legs, sniffing the air. I jump back. "Holy shit, there's a rat in your dresser."

Amelia sighs. "Don't call him that." She leans down, picks him up, and cradles him against her chest. "His name is Elvis."

My mouth gapes. "You've named him?" Nothing is registering fast enough. "He's your *pet?*"

She brings the rat up to her cheek. "I found him a couple of hours ago during free time."

I mentally gag. "You can't keep him, Amelia. That's crazy."

She levels me with a look. "That's kind of the proverbial pot calling the kettle black, isn't it?"

Touché. Still, I know she shouldn't keep him. What if Elvis has a disease? He could make her sick. I try to reason with her. "You'll get in so much trouble if they find out." Suddenly a picture of an all-white room with padded walls assaults my vision. The Quiet Room.

"No, I won't. Not if you don't tell anybody. You said you could keep a secret."

"I can . . ." I trail off. Defeat settles on my shoulders. "How do you plan to feed him?"

Amelia smiles, her face lighting up like a child who's just gotten a puppy on Christmas morning. A very, very sick Christmas morning. "I can sneak table scraps in from the cafeteria. He's kind of cute, right?" She dangles the rat in front of me, its eyes shining like silver coins.

"Ugh." I stand up and step back. "He's dirty and disgusting and probably has the black plague. Make sure you wash your hands after you hold him."

"I will. I will." She practically hops up and down as she puts the rat away. Right before I'm about to crawl back into bed, her arms snake around me in a backwards hug. "Thank you." She presses her cheek between my shoulder blades, her pink hair tickling my neck. "Thank you so much."

"Did you wash your hands?" I ask.

She laughs and squeezes me tighter.

Safely tucked under my covers, I try to fall asleep, but memories of Jason hang heavy in the cobwebs of my mind.

FROM THE JOURNAL OF ALICE MONROE

In the summer, Roman and his wife took us camping. All ten foster kids piled into a dilapidated RV he had rented from a guy down the street. And despite our constant fear of Roman and the hand he called God's Will, we loved riding in that RV, all ten of us gypsy kids bouncing around like balls in a pinball machine. Even Susan, his wife, seemed to enjoy herself. A wispy smile played on her lips as we left the city behind and approached the wilderness.

We set up camp and Roman dove right into drinking, which was fine. The public setting kept him from playing his games and allowed us to run free. While the other kids played tag, Jason, Cellie, and I pretended to be explorers, mapping foreign lands like constellations. We drifted away and found a dusty hill to climb. The whole time Cellie kept her hand in her pocket, her fist closed around something. She insisted on leading. I didn't mind. I was more comfortable following, anyway. Jason was also content to walk behind. He stopped every few feet to pick flowers, handing them to me so I could weave them through my hair.

When we were far enough away from our campsite that the voices of the other kids were muted and the sound of the wind in the trees was loud, Cellie stopped. She took her hand out of her pocket and opened her fist to reveal a lighter with a unicorn on it. "I stole it from the campground," she said.

I'll admit, I was curious. Cellie moved her thumb over the wheel, and the flint sparked and the lighter ignited. The flame danced, flickered, and then was extinguished by the wind. She told Jason to get some kindling. She wanted to watch something burn. He did, because he was a boy and he thought it was awesome to light things on fire or blow them up. None of us knew how wrong it would go.

We gathered the kindling, and Cellie wondered out loud what color the flame would be when we lit it. I hoped it would be blue like the sky and Jason thought it would be red. A little trickle of fear danced down my spine. Cellie seemed too excited. Too enthralled.

Cellie pressed the lighter into the pile of dry leaves and twigs and sparked it. The kindling ignited, slower than the doll, but it burned faster, much faster. A brown maple leaf got caught in a gust of wind and drifted a few feet away. A yellowing leaf shot into the air and landed in my hair, where it burst into flame. Cellie giggled and clapped her hands together.

Jason swore and helped me. "It's not funny," he said as he patted my hair out.

There were little fires everywhere, burning the dry brush and eating the trunks of the trees. The smell was a perfumed combination of burning hair, pinecones, and dead leaves. Twigs crackled and popped, sending sparks into the air like fireflies taking flight. When we realized that the fire was spreading too much and beyond our control, we raced down the hill and back to the campground. And nobody knew what we had done. A park ranger came and told us to evacuate. When we got home, Cellie turned on the news. It was the biggest fire Clatsop County had ever seen. Two hikers had disappeared, and one firefighter had already lost his life.

Years later, on his seventeenth birthday, Jason got a tattoo of the exact same unicorn on his left wrist, the ink resting right over an artery. Funny thing was, he'd kept that lighter all those years.

———◦◦———

7

RAZORBLADES AND CIGARETTE BURNS

THE NEXT MORNING THE ALARM IN THE GIRL'S UNIT JOLTS US awake thirty minutes early. Every other day, we're allowed to shower. We shuffle into a large locker room, and we're each given a towel, some soap, and shampoo. You can ask for a razor to shave your legs, but that means extra-special one-on-one attention, so I opt out. We strip under the watchful eye of five female nurses and line up under the showerheads as they turn on the water. We're not allowed to touch anything. Not the tile on the wall. Not the faucet to control the temperature. Not anything. The girls' pale, shivering bodies dance on the other side of healthy and remind me of a black-and-white photo I once saw—of people crammed into a gas chamber during the Holocaust.

My shower is lukewarm and over too fast. But I get all the important parts. I find a spot in front of a mirror and start to comb the tangles out of my hair. Jason had a thing for my hair. He'd run his fingers through it and say, *I love your hair wild like this.* Then he'd kiss me. *Stay wild for me, baby.* He'd made me promise. A spinning grief overtakes me and hurtles me forward. The comb falls from my hands, plastic clinking in the porcelain sink. I put my head down and avoid looking in the mirror.

I count the tiles on the floor, the cracks in the grout. Little beads of sweat form on my forehead. I'm going to be sick again. All that sadness inside me wants to come out.

"Alice." A voice over my shoulder.

The spinning stops, I take a deep breath, exhale slowly, and swallow back all that black sorrow.

"Alice?" Nurse Dummel is beside me, my name on her lips a question. She clutches a see-through plastic bag with my regular clothes in it. I take the bag from her and murmur a *thank-you,* my hands still shaky. She looks me up and down, and I resist the urge to bare my teeth at her like an animal cornered in the jungle. "Put the towel and scrubs in the plastic bag and leave them over there." She gestures to the grimy wood bench behind me and leaves.

Monica sneers over my left shoulder. My eyes find her reflection in the mirror. I didn't see her come in with the rest of the girls. She's skinny, scary skinny. Her bones jut out all over the place, like someone took a spoon and scooped out her skin. Her towel looks as if it could wrap around her twice. It's weird that I never noticed before. Probably because her face looks all right, not all hollowed out and creepy looking. A little tendril of pity sprouts, and I almost feel sorry for her, and then she speaks. "You still stink, pyro." She fans a hand in front of her face. Before I can call her a snaggletooth or a twunt, a nurse yells a five-minute warning.

I quickly exchange my ratty towel for a pair of worn jeans, trying to forget about Monica. And how much I hate her. As I'm pulling on a thin tee, my hand brushes the cool, bumpy burns that span my shoulders. I know they're there. The skin is itchy and tight, impossible to miss. But I've avoided looking at them, afraid to see physical evidence of Cellie's madness. I suppose it's time to assess the damage.

I take a deep breath and turn toward the mirror.

The twin burns look the same as the one on my hand, blotchy, uneven—mangled, angry flesh. But to my surprise, there are two areas, one on each shoulder, where the skin is smooth and almost completely unblemished. I cross my arms so that my hands grasp the opposite shoulders. The half-moon marks fit almost exactly into the size of my palms. Could they be from where Jason held me? Did he try to protect me from the fire? I can practically feel his weight on me. I feel sick at the thought. That Jason perished so I might live.

The morning passes without another run-in with Monica. Even in group therapy she stays quiet, only speaking when Dr. Goodman makes us go around and say what we want. And today he makes *everyone* participate.

The question goes around the circle.

An Asian kid says, "I don't want to be angry anymore."

A boy with dreads says, "I want to forgive my family."

A girl with brown hair says, "I want to be an architect."

Monica's turn comes. "I want to be hungry." The sincerity of her answer surprises me. It surprises the whole group, and Dr. Goodman squirms in his seat. "Very good, Monica." He adjusts his tie and scribbles something in his notebook—probably *breakthrough*.

Chase, who sits beside me, goes next and easily deflects. "I want James Earl Jones to read me bedtime stories."

Dr. Goodman frowns but doesn't say anything to him. Again he scribbles in his notebook, this time pressing the pen hard into the paper.

"What is it you want, Alice?" Dr. Goodman asks.

There are lots of things I want. I want Jason back. I want Cellie gone. I want Amelia to have a real pet. I want to see my grandfather one more time. But I'm not ready or willing to share. So I deflect, albeit not as charmingly as Chase. I turn my head and gaze out through the steel mesh in the window and focus on the gray sky and the green treetops that dance in the wind. I say the first thing that comes to mind. "I want to go outside."

I examine the lunch tray in front of me, filled with what looks like roast beef smothered in gravy. But I'm not sure. I get closer and take a sniff. It doesn't smell like roast beef. I opt for the roll, the lone survivor in the gravy flash flood.

Amelia plops down beside me. "Look what I swiped from the

showers today," she says with ill-concealed glee. She holds out her hand, keeping it hidden under the table. In her palm rest two Bic razors. "Now we can shave our legs in our room, and nobody will watch us. It'll be a little awkward because we'll have to use the sink or the toilet. But isn't it great?"

I look at the razors, at the pink handles resting over a puckered scar from a cigarette burn. The bite of the roll I just took lodges in my throat, and I have to swallow hard to keep from choking. "Are you sure you should have those?"

Amelia's eyes brim with tears. She closes her fist around the razors and shoves them back into her pocket. "I'm not going to hurt myself."

Shit. I've hurt her feelings. I've hurt my only friend's feelings. "Look, it's not because I think you're going to hurt yourself." *I hope not.* "It's because you already have." I pause and shudder a little on the inside. "Elvis, and now this? I just don't want you to get in trouble."

Amelia takes a deep breath and smiles at me reassuringly. "It's fine, Allie." She treats my worry as if it's something flimsy, something made of paper in the wind.

I decide not to press her and offer her a white flag instead. "Monica called me a pyro again this morning in the shower."

Amelia shakes her head. "She's such a muff eater."

My laugh cracks across the cafeteria. The sound gains the attention of the patients, who freeze, suddenly uncomfortable with my happiness. The only person, aside from Amelia, who doesn't seem alarmed is Chase. He stands in line waiting for his tray of mashed potatoes and mystery meat. He gives me a two-fingered salute followed by a grin.

That day marks the end of my forty-eight-hour no-contact hold. I am antsy, eager for my social worker Sara to come. Visiting hours are late in the afternoon. Usually right after class time. Anyone who doesn't get a visitor has to go back to their room. But Nurse Dummel calls my name, and I'm escorted with others into the visitors' area.

The visitors' area at Savage Isle is nice. It's one of the few rooms that have been redecorated since the hospital opened. The walls are painted a warm taupe, and groups of overstuffed couches line the walls. A coffee machine and tea station sit in the corner.

Monica has visitors today. She has a whole family here to see her. My dislike for her grows. She squeals with delight as she runs toward them, hugging a little brother, embracing a mother. Sara sits in the middle of the room, her narrow frame taking up as little space as possible. I walk over to her and stand nervously in front of her. She is young, maybe mid-twenties, and pretty. Wisps of blond hair frame her petite face, and she wears a gold cross around her neck that she plays with sometimes when she gets nervous. Right now, she's pinching it between her white-tipped fingernails. She became our caseworker a couple of years back. I've always had an okay relationship with her. She's kind, and sweet almost in a naive way. I think we were her first two cases, Cellie and I. Of course, Cellie hated her from the beginning.

"Alice," Sara says in one breath, and smiles. She examines me and reaches out a hand to squeeze my elbow. "I'm so happy to see you're all right."

"Hey, Sara," I say, sinking into a chair. The coolness from the faux leather seeps in through my threadbare jeans. I wonder if Sara notices my brand-new shiny yellow wristband. Nurse Dummel gave it to me right before I came in.

"I came and saw you in the hospital a couple of times. Do you remember?" Sara asks, her expression searching.

I blink and try to think back to my hospital stay. Unbidden, there's a memory, a memory of someone's cool hands touching my cheeks and quietly weeping. But I'm not sure who that person was. It was most likely Sara, but I don't want to ask if she came and cried by my bedside. Other than that, everything that happened in the hospital is still a blur, hazy shades of red and black.

"I'm not sure. Maybe I remember?" I don't know why it comes out in the form of a question.

She doesn't look disappointed. Instead she nods in gentle acceptance. "How are you?"

"I'm all right."

Sara reaches over and puts a hand on my knee, silently encouraging me to go on. The coolness of her fingertips brushes through one of the holes in my jeans, and in that moment I know. I recognize her touch. She *was* the one in the hospital, the one whose soft cries woke me from the dark. Why would she weep for me? An emotion I can't describe slices through me.

I sigh. "I miss Jason." Finally the dam breaks and I allow myself to think of him. His curly hair, his green eyes, and his sweet face that always looked at me the way Sara looks at me now. Cellie loved him, too (as much as Cellie's ever been able to love anyone), and then when Jason and I grew closer and Cellie and I further apart, her love slowly started to die, wilted like a flower left out in the sun too long. I loved Jason so deeply. I try not to think about what would have blossomed between us if he were still alive, if that love hadn't been slashed short. What happiness would have grown from it?

Cellie snatched that away from me, as she's done with so many other things, and deep in my bones I know it will always be this way, unless she's gone, wiped from the earth. There's not enough room for both of us.

"Alice," Sara says nervously. "I need you to tell me about the night you left. Why did you do it? You were doing so well here."

I caused her to worry when I escaped with Jason. It's one of the many things I regret about that night. My gaze circles the room and stops at a couch in the corner where Chase's huge Asian roommate and his family currently sit. The same couch where Jason and I sat when he visited me, where I sobbed in his arms and told him that I couldn't take it anymore, that Cellie was tormenting me and wouldn't stop screaming during the night that the doctors were plotting against her. The same couch where he assured me with quiet conviction that we should run away together, escape. That he could take me somewhere far enough away that Cellie would never find me.

"I'm sorry, Sara. I don't know why I did it." But I do. I just don't think she can handle it. Sara seems so soft, and part of me wants to protect her. I'm sure she's seen the inside of a mental hospital, but she's never had to spend the night in the Quiet Room or shower with the door open or listen to the dizzying hum of fluorescent lights because nobody wants to talk.

By the look on her face, my evasive response doesn't quite placate her. Still, she accepts it and says, "All right. We don't have to talk about it if you don't want." That's something about Sara; she doesn't press the issue, knows intuitively when to move on, when I've given everything I can give in that moment. She regards me tenderly. "Is there anything you need? Clothes? Toiletries?"

Mentally, I shake my head at her offer. Those things would be nice, but I need something bigger. "I need your help," I say.

"Okay." *My lifeline.*

"Jason. I need to know what they did with his"—the word makes hurdles that my mouth can't jump—"body."

She sucks in an uneasy breath. I think maybe she thought I was going to ask about something else. About the charges and the court case. But the truth is, I don't want to talk about all that. There are more important things and time is limited. Sara and I get only one hour once a week. One hour to make a plan to bury my best friend. I used to count my life in moments, but now, in here, I measure my life in minutes, by the hands of a clock and the sound of a buzzer.

Sara hesitates a moment, seems to gather her thoughts. "Right," she says slowly, drawing the word out in one long breath. She tells me the state will bury him and gives me the date of the funeral. It's tomorrow. We hug goodbye, and Sara clings to me an extra minute more than is necessary.

"Jason's funeral is tomorrow," I tell Dr. Goodman. We sit in our usual places: Dr. Goodman in a wing-backed chair, a yellow legal pad perched on his knee. Me, across from him, as curled and pressed back into the chair as I can be.

He raises his eyebrows at me. I'm sure he was expecting another freeze-out this evening. When we sat down he pulled out some huge medical journal and started reading it, didn't even try to ask me any questions this time. Interesting. He puts the book down on a side table and picks up a pen. "Would you like to go?" he asks.

I nod my head.

Dr. Goodman writes something. "That would be a considerable undertaking, Alice. We'd have to get the judge's permission."

I want to ask why, ball my hands up into fists, and wail. It was Cellie's fault. It's always been Cellie's fault. I've never done anything wrong. Just because we share the same face doesn't mean anything. I picture Jason's body in the casket, being laid to rest with no one there. I cross my arms over my chest, trying to hold in the hurt that threatens to spill over. "Fine."

"I'm not saying it can't be done, Alice." Why does he always have to say my name in such a perpetually concerned tone? "But the judge will want to know that you're making progress. And I'm afraid based on the last couple of days . . ." He trails off.

"But I haven't done anything in the last couple of days."

"That's the key, Alice. You haven't done *anything*. You share the minimum in group therapy, and today is the first day you've spoken more than twenty words to me. I need you to participate in your recovery."

Mentally, I build myself a hole and crawl into it. I take out a piece of black and white striped origami paper and fold it into an angelfish. Doc goes back to reading his medical journal. I wish I hadn't wasted so much time talking to him. Then I would've had time to make another angelfish. Then I would have two angelfish and they could kiss.

When the session ends, Dr. Goodman holds the door open for me to exit. "Remember what I said, Alice. *Participate*."

Donny escorts me back to my room. We're just rounding the corner to the girls' wing when a scream splits the hum of the fluorescent lights. The ear-piercing cry echoes through the hallway, bounces off the walls, and makes my heart stand still. Without thinking, without breathing, I go toward it. All along the wall, doors open and curious patients peek out. Their faces become a blur of white as my footsteps hasten. Donny shouts behind me. It's coming from my room. Briefly, I think that Cellie must be in there. She's returned and is demanding to see me.

I'm afraid, and I know it's crazy to be going toward her, but I'm even more afraid of not answering her cry. When I get to the doorway, Cellie isn't there after all. But my relief is short-lived. A lump rises in my throat. The stifled and strangled cry comes from Amelia.

From the Journal of Alice Monroe

Rebecca, our old social worker, caught a glimpse of bruises on Cellie's upper arm, and she asked to look at my back and Jason's chest. When she saw the fresh black-and-blue marks the size of meaty fingers, she squeezed our shoulders and told us we'd never have to go back to Roman's again. Jason said goodbye to Cellie and me, stretched out his index fingers and pressed them against ours, promising to stay in touch. But we knew we'd probably never see him again. His mom wanted him back, wanted to try again with her only remaining son.

Time went by. Our tumbleweed existence continued. The foster system liked to keep siblings together, and for that I was grateful. And I had so few things to be grateful for.

We stayed for a while with a lesbian couple, Pam and Gayle. They had a bunch of dogs and a kitchen decorated in a rooster motif. Cellie giggled the first time she saw all those red roosters and whispered to me, "They sure love cocks." They had two kids already, adopted them right out of foster care. At night, while Cellie fitfully slept across from me, I'd clasp my hands together and pray that they'd also adopt us.

Pam and Gayle's yard stretched into a field, and Cellie would spend days out there running around with the dogs. She fit in more out there than at school. We'd been to five schools in under two years, and she'd always had a hard time blending in. At all of our schools Cellie and I were placed in different classrooms. Something else I was grateful for. I promised Cellie we'd never be apart, but that didn't mean we always had to be together, attached at the hip. Sometimes she would come find me. I'd be sitting in class, and suddenly I'd see a patch of dark hair right outside the door. She'd pace outside until I asked the teacher for a hall pass to go to the bathroom. We'd duck inside the same stall and I'd ask her what she wanted. Most of the time it was to complain.

"I don't like it here, Alice," she said one day.

"The school day is almost over. Maybe we can ask Pam and Gayle to get pizza tonight." She looked hurt and blinked furiously, trying to keep her tears at bay. "Look," I said. "I have an English test next period, but I suppose I could skip last period."

Her face brightened. "Maybe we could go over to Highland Park?"

I chewed the inside of my lip. She always wanted to go to Highland Park, the middle school where we would've gone if we still lived with Roman. I knew she was hoping we'd see Jason again. She looked for him all the time, at bus stops, through the windows of well-known foster homes and social worker offices. "Sure," I said. "Go back to class now. I'll meet you by the boys' bathroom after fifth period."

She smiled and skipped away. But Mr. Winters held me up after English class. He wanted to talk about my essays. He said I had an aptitude for writing and asked if I would consider an advanced placement class for high school next year. I smiled, but the rush of victory was quickly drowned by worry. I glanced at the clock. I was late to meet Cellie. Scooping my books into my backpack, I took off toward the boys' bathroom. Students scurried out of my way as I passed them in the hall. They always gave Cellie and me a wide birth, afraid the rumors about us were true, that we'd lived with our grandfather's dead body for days on end and the stench of death we carried about us might somehow rub off on them.

I expected to find Cellie pacing, murmuring to herself and pulling at her hair. But she wasn't there.

I checked the girls' bathroom, looked under each of the stalls, and quietly called her name. No sign of her. It was then that I smelled it. The average person might have dismissed the odor as something that had gotten caught in the wind and would soon disappear. But I knew what she had done.

Every fire has a special smell, depending on what's used to spark and feed it. Like a recipe, all the ingredients come together to create an aroma and a taste that are unique. When Cellie set the doll on fire, it smelled of sulfur mixed with chemicals, plastic, and fiber. The forest fire was like a perfume, wet earth drying out, pine and sap boiling. This smell, on this particular day, was a whole new scent—paper and hair. But with all the fires, the underlying notes were the same, hauntingly familiar. Sadness. Rage. Fury.

I found her in the boys' bathroom, sitting next to a smoking metal garbage can. She rocked back and forth, the same way she did in Roman's closet. A book of matches hung loosely from her fingers.

"Cellie?"

She looked up at me.

"What have you done?" It was the first time I had ever asked her that. *What have you done?* Perhaps I should have asked her *why* or *how come*. Maybe she would've answered, and we could've dealt with it, boxed it up, and put it away.

"You didn't come," she said simply. "I thought you'd left me."

My mouth hung open. I can admit it now: I was angry with her. But under that anger was sadness and sweet forgiveness. I could never leave her. But I didn't have time to tell her that. A flame jumped up and caught onto the paper towel that hung from the dispenser right above the trash can. It was the fastest I'd ever seen anything burn. Just like that, fire erupted in the bathroom. Thick black smoke rose to the ceiling like an ominous cloud. I coughed and waved my hands in front of my face. Fire alarms sounded and sprinklers went off, and just as quickly as the fire had started, it was put out. My hair was drenched, my shoes soaked.

"Shit, Cellie," I said, gaping wildly at the damage done to the bathroom, damage that had taken only minutes to occur. "We have to get out of here." All I could think about was what would happen if she got caught, where they'd send her. Foolishly, I didn't think of myself. How bad it looked for me, to be soaked and covered in the remnants of black smoke and ash right along with her. I grabbed her hand and we ran out the bathroom door toward the nearest exit, our sodden shoes leaving an easy-to-follow trail. The school was being evacuated, and behind us a tidal wave of students walked single file to the nearest exits. They must have seen us. But we kept running. Out the back doors, down the side of the building, toward the athletic field. We kept going until we ran directly into a security guard.

I stopped short a few feet shy of his glinting badge and bulging navy uniform. Cellie skidded into me. She pinched the tender flesh on the back of my arm. I could feel the bruise blossom under my waterlogged T-shirt. I rubbed the spot and glared at her.

Officer Davis looked at us suspiciously, and I saw the foregone conclusion drawn all over his face. "Where do you think you're going?" he asked.

Cellie rolled her eyes. "There's a fire alarm. We're evacuating per school regulation."

Officer Davis made a little sound of disbelief. He radioed for help, and we were escorted to the other side of the building. The principal came, then the firemen, and finally the police. We were taken to the emergency room, where we were checked for injuries. And when the doctors asked me if anything hurt, I wanted to say *only on the inside*. But I kept quiet and so did Cellie. When we refused to talk, kept our lips sewn shut, we were cuffed and escorted out to a waiting police car. When we had been driving for a while, I finally got up the courage to speak. Through dry, cracked lips and with a shaky voice I asked, "Where are we going?"

The police officer didn't answer. He didn't bother to turn his head or look at us in the rearview mirror. We weren't even worth the eye contact.

Silver cuffs jingled around Cellie's wrists. "I did a bad thing, Alice," she said.

"Yeah." I couldn't look at her. I felt her hands slide over mine. Her skin was dry and cracked, her nails bitten down to the quick.

"I'll make it better," she said.

A tear slipped down my cheek. "I'm not sure you can."

THE QUIET ROOM

AMELIA STANDS BY HER DRESSER, THE BOTTOM DRAWER PULLED all the way to the end of its tracks, spilling from the frame like blood from a slit wrist. Her body is hunched and she cradles something in her arms. She cries again, this time lower and more mournful. A sound like the shriek of an animal with its foot caught in a trap.

"Amelia?" I say tentatively and softly in the doorway.

She turns to me, eyes wild. "He's dead." She moves her hand so I can see what she's holding. Elvis lies in her arms, his little body limp and broken.

"Shit, I'm sorry, Amelia," I say.

"I hate this place. Everything turns to shit here," she bellows, stomping her foot like a child throwing a temper tantrum. "See what happens when you care for something? See what happens?" She holds up the rat and its head flops over her hand.

A chorus of footsteps sounds behind me. Suddenly I'm being pulled and pushed aside. Five huge techs, Donny leading them, enter the room, closely followed by Nurse Dummel and Dr. Goodman.

"Amelia, it's Dr. Goodman. What's happened?" He eyes the rat. When she doesn't respond and continues to sob, Dr. Goodman goes on. "I'd like to give you something to help you calm down." He motions Nurse Dummel forward. She leans over and he whispers to her, "Ten milligrams of diazepam." His eyes flick to me standing in the doorway. "And close the door."

Nurse Dummel nods, radios the nurses' station for the drug, and softly shuts the door in my face.

Through the door I hear Amelia. "No," she says, loud and feverish. "I don't want anything to calm down." And then, "Don't take him from me. Don't take him."

A nurse rushes down the hallway, a syringe held upright in her hand. She doesn't notice me as she opens the door. Through the crack I briefly see Amelia, her back pressed to the wall, shaking her head like a feral animal, holding on to that damn rat like a lifeline. The door closes and I'm shut out once again.

On the other side of the door, there's a scuffle. The louder Amelia screams, the quieter the five plus people in the room get. I stay by the door, frozen and trapped, unable to leave, but at the same time wanting to run away so badly. For a moment my head feels as if it's detached from my body, and everything seems like a memory—a washed-out echo and an imprint of the past. Patients begin to crowd the halls, their hungry eyes devouring the commotion.

The door opens, slams, and ricochets against the wall. A couple of techs walk backwards, holding Amelia's legs. Two more walk sideways, holding her arms. Another keeps her torso steady, and Dr. Goodman holds her head.

"My parents will sue, you son of a bitch. They'll sue all of you," Amelia cries, thrashing and kicking the whole time. A nurse comes from the side and hurries in front of them. A couple of doors down the hallway, she swipes her keycard over a red box. The door automatically swings open wide. The interior is padded and coated in white.

They get her into the Quiet Room and the door closes with a soft whoosh. The thick walls muffle her cries, cries that started strong and unbreakable and have ended in a sort of whimpering that is swallowed by the eerie silence of the hospital.

The techs and nurses huddle around Dr. Goodman and listen while he gives them instructions. By this time the patients have scurried back to their rooms, not wanting to draw attention. When the techs disperse, Nurse Dummel pulls up a barstool next to the door, where there is a shuttered window in the upper half. She clicks it open and quietly watches Amelia. I slip back into my room. It looks as if a storm has passed through. Amelia's mattress is overturned and the bedsheet is crumpled on the ground. The dresser drawer has landed halfway across the room. The origami animals I have so lovingly and painstakingly made are tipped over, crushed, some with dusty footprints on them. I take the time and carefully clean up everything. I don't want her to come back to a room like this.

I make Amelia's bed, push the drawer back, and safely restore our menagerie. Some of the animals can't be saved, but I can't stand the thought of throwing them away, not when I love them so much. So I hide them behind our dresser in the hole in the wall where Amelia and I have been keeping our razors ever since our room got searched.

After I'm done, I go to the door and press my ear against it. I wait. When the unmistakable sound of Nurse Dummel's quick strides disappears down the hallway, I step out of my room. I walk down the hallway. When I get to the Quiet Room, I rest my cheek against the cool metal door. "Amelia," I whisper, even though I'm sure she can't hear me. "I'm here." I sit on the floor and then lie down so that I'm facing the crack under the door. I slide my palm along the cool linoleum floor until my fingertips are inside the room. "I'm here," I say again. I close my eyes and drift off to sleep.

Nurse Dummel makes me go see Dr. Goodman. I don't say anything when she asks what I'm doing in the hallway. Nor do I ask about the haunted sort of grim expression that shadows her face when she sees where I'm lying. I don't knock when I get to Dr. Goodman's office; instead I sink into the plastic chair just outside his door. I'm anxious to get back to the Quiet Room in case Amelia wakes up. I want to be there for her.

The door opens, and two security guards followed by Dr. Goodman emerge. Dr. Goodman shakes each of their hands. "Thank you, gentlemen," he says. "Please keep me apprised of the investigation."

"We will," says a guard whose body is the opposite of slim. "Let us know, as well, if there are any other incidents or anything else goes missing."

Dr. Goodman nods his head and murmurs, "Will do." He stands there for a moment, hands in his pockets, contemplating. He looks down and his gaze registers me in the chair. "Alice, you're here. Why didn't you come in?"

I shrug, stand, and jam my hands into my hoodie pockets. "I wasn't sure I could." I follow him into the office.

"Of course you can, Alice. My door is always open." He sits and picks up his yellow legal pad. "Please." He gestures to the seat across from him. I sit. He clasps his hands together, laces his fingers. We stare at each other. "How are you doing, Alice?"

"Is Amelia all right?" I blurt.

Doc frowns in disapproval. "Alice, you know I can't discuss other patients with you." He crosses his legs. "Are you worried about Amelia?"

Inside my hoodie pocket I crack my knuckles. "I guess."

"Did you know about the rat?"

It's on the tip of my tongue to say, *Dr. Goodman, you* know *I can't discuss other patients with you.* Instead I look him directly in the eye. "Of course not," I say.

"You know, Alice, it wouldn't be a bad thing if you did know about the rat. I would understand."

"Understand what?" I ask, confused.

"Sometimes, when we think it's in the best interest of someone, we may choose to withhold things."

I bite my cheek and lower my chin so my hair falls in a curtain over my face. "What is that supposed to mean?"

"What do you think it means?"

"I think it means you're trying to get me to admit to something I don't know anything about." The air between us changes.

"All right, Alice." His tone is placating. "Let's change the subject. I have some good news for you." I blink at him. "I've spoken with the judge just this evening." I straighten up a little in my chair. He scratches the back of his head. "Well, Sara and I both spoke with the judge, and he's agreed to grant you a four-hour release to attend Jason's funeral tomorrow."

Happiness gurgles in my throat and a smile touches my lips.

"I have to admit, Sara did most of the persuading. I'm not sure how, but she managed to. I thought it might be better if you stayed. But I can see her reasoning. We convinced the judge that it would be beneficial to your therapy. You'll be in Sara's care the entire time. She will have to sign you out and back in. And unfortunately, you'll be searched again when you come back."

He goes on telling me about hospital policy and protocols, but I don't hear what he's saying anymore. All I can think of is Jason. *Jason,* who kept the sun in the sky and the stars apart and the water in the oceans.

Donny walks with me back to my room and I'm locked in for the night. Amelia's still in the Quiet Room, or she may have been moved by now. After the Quiet Room, patients usually go to seclusion, so I probably won't see her for another twenty-four hours. The room seems vast, empty, and lonely without her. I run a finger over the paper animals. Taking out a piece of gray paper, I fold it into a mouse. I lay it on her pillow and turn out the light. I don't bother to get undressed or brush my teeth. I just huddle under my covers and pull them up over my head. Closing my eyes, I wait for sleep and hope I won't dream.

From the Journal of Alice Monroe

The first time Cellie and I were institutionalized, we were sent to Pleasant Oaks, a privately run mental health hospital that received state subsidies for treating foster kids. We spent three days there, but it felt like an eternity. The facility, a converted Victorian mansion, made me think of gingerbread and dollhouses. If only the kids inside had been as welcoming as the building's façade.

Rebecca brought our things from Pam and Gayle's; they had decided that we might not be "the right fit" for their family. I blamed Cellie, and it showed. We didn't talk much, and Cellie kept following me around, apologizing. We stayed in separate rooms and met individually with psychiatrists who prescribed all sorts of medications. I perfected the art of compliance. How to nod my head when I really wanted to shake it violently back and forth. How to open my mouth for pills when I really wanted to clamp it shut.

We were older than most of the patients at Pleasant Oaks, yet nearly everyone we met, even the younger children, seemed more deeply disturbed than we were. A seven-year-old boy with a patch of hair missing and a dead tooth said he would nibble on our toes and make soup out of our hair. Cellie pushed him down and said, "Not if I get to you first."

After that encounter, I stuck close to Cellie. I accepted her apology, since all I ever wanted was to forgive her.

I loved her.

When we were released, Cellie promised Rebecca (and me) that she would be better. But that promise was impossible for her to keep.

Rebecca took us to a new living situation. A group home. A woman named Candy ran it and lived onsite with us. As Candy's name suggested, she enjoyed sweet things. Well, any food item, really. She was more wide than tall and had to ride around on a scooter when we shopped at the grocery store. Candy smoked menthol cigarettes and watched soap operas all day. Cellie used to say she looked like Jabba the Hutt's less attractive sister and kind of spoke like him, too. Candy insisted we call her Mama.

On our first day there, Mama sent Cellie and me down the street to get her some food at Carl's Jr. "Don't forget the hot sauce," she said, handing us a twenty.

We skipped out of the house. Out of the twenty-dollar bill she'd given us there was enough for us to get milk shakes. We drank them on the way back, our fingers bumping along the chainlink fence. Summer was coming, and we liked the idea of what the warmth would bring.

When we got back to the house, the Carl's Jr. bag clutched in my hand, Candy was where we had left her, sitting on the threadbare black and yellow bumblebee couch.

"Here we go, my boy, this is Mama's favorite," she said. An hourglass appeared on the screen. She turned up the volume on the TV and leaned back before seeing Cellie and me in the doorway. "There you are. Did you get my food?" A box fan spun in the window, mixing Candy's cigarette smoke with spring air and the smell of the barbecue shack down the street. Tendrils of hair blew into my neck and stuck there.

A low chuckle emanated from the recliner. I crossed the room to hand the bag to Candy, the chuckled ceased, and I felt a prickling on the back of my neck. "Alice?" the voice from the recliner asked.

I turned and dropped the bag of food. *Jason.* He unfolded himself from the recliner and stood, stretching to his full height. Our five-year separation had been kind to him, well, physically at least. He was bigger, much bigger than the last time we'd seen him. Broad and thick, he could have easily taken Roman now. But his hair was still a familiar mess of curls, and in them was a glimpse of the boy I once knew. Above his right eyebrow was a small scar, courtesy of Roman. "Jason!" I exclaimed, and then I was running toward him, leaping onto him.

His arms snaked around me and he laughed, tucking his chin into my neck. "I thought I'd never see you again," he whispered. For a moment we just stared at each other, and then Cellie cleared her throat behind us. She hovered in the entryway, her eyes wide and curious.

"Cellie?" Jason asked. He smiled at her, opened an arm, and motioned for her to join us. She came to him, softer than I had. He enfolded her in one arm and me in the other. We stood like that for a while, with him covering our bodies just as he had before, sheltering us from the echo of angry footsteps and a fist called God's Will. For the first time in years, I felt like I'd come home.

———————•◆•———————

9

JELLYFISH

I IGNORE THE OPENING OF THE DOOR. IT'S LATE, THE LAST BED check having come and gone hours ago. For once, the rain has stopped and it's quieter than a ghost ship. I'm already awake, hyperalert and vigilant. Earlier in the night, I'd fallen asleep, huddled under the covers. Though it felt like I'd been asleep for a long time, the moon was still in the same position when my eyes popped open. The burns on my shoulders and hand ache, and my thoughts race like dogs at the greyhound track—thoughts of Jason. His funeral. His unicorn tattoo. The door to my room closes with a soft click. A person loiters in the entryway. I go completely still, hoping whoever it is will take the hint and leave. No luck. The person comes closer and stands at the foot of my bed. Maybe it's Amelia, back from the Quiet Room. That thought has me moving. I shuck the covers away. "Amelia?" I peer into the dark.

The silhouette at the end of my bed is most definitely *not*

Amelia's. Broad shoulders, a black hat, and a baggy sweatshirt eclipse my view of the wall.

"What'd you just call me?" Chase asks.

"I thought you were my roommate."

"Your roommate?"

I sit up and wipe nonexistent sleep from my eyes. "Yeah, she went to the Quiet Room yesterday, and I thought you might be her."

"What'd she go to the Quiet Room for?" He walks over to Amelia's empty bed and picks up the origami mouse, inspecting it.

"Don't touch that," I snap. "It's for Amelia."

Chase holds up his hands like I'm pointing a gun at him. "Sorry."

"What are you doing here, anyway?"

"I was bored."

I narrow my eyes at him. "I'm not here to entertain you, Chase."

He grins, and I ignore the surge of pleasure that runs through me as he sits down on my bed, positioning his back so that it touches my thigh. "Want to get out of here?"

What is he asking? My mind fills with winding stairs. An expanse of green lawn. A lightning storm. My body winds tight with anticipation. "You want to go back to the D ward?"

"Nah, nothing like that. But I thought we could go exploring." He dangles the plastic keycard in front of my face. "You know, see where this might lead us?"

I grab the keycard. "I can't believe you still have that."

He scoffs. "Like I'd get rid of it . . . You know how hard it was for me to lift? I mean, not that hard, because I'm super awesome. But no way would I get rid of it. Whaddaya say, Alice? Want to get out of here?"

It's tempting. I chew on my thumbnail and my stomach grumbles. I barely ate a bite of dinner, too consumed with thoughts of Jason's funeral. Now my appetite is rearing its ugly, embarrassing head, right in front of Chase.

He laughs. "You're hungry. C'mon. I'll take you to the kitchen."

I stare at Amelia's bed, at the little paper mouse. Since I can't fall back to sleep and I'm apparently starving, Chase's offer seems like the next best option. "Okay," I say. And I won't have to think about Jason and his unicorn tattoo and what that means.

We're almost to the kitchen when I realize the gravity of my mistake. Jason's funeral is in the morning, and if I'm caught, I won't be allowed to go. I may even wind up with an all-access pass to the Quiet Room. I let my stupid hunger and childish desire for company get the best of me. The knowledge that I've put every truly important thing in jeopardy is paralyzing.

Chase pauses outside a big black door with a sign that reads KITCHEN — STAFF ACCESS ONLY.

"Still hungry?" he asks.

Suddenly I'm not. My belly is too full of panic and regret.

"Alice?"

But it's too late to turn back now—even though that's *exactly* what I want to do. Turning back would cause Chase to ask questions, and I can't bear the thought of telling him the truth. That Jason's funeral is only a few hours away. That I don't know if I'll survive it.

"What are you waiting for?" I ask.

He snorts and swipes the key over a black box. The door unlocks. We're inside and it's black. Pitch-black. I break from Chase's side and trace the wall with my hands, searching for a switch. I find one and flick it up. Suddenly the room is bathed in harsh light. It's an industrial kitchen. Stainless steel counters run along the walls, interrupted by two huge refrigerators and an equally huge dishwasher and oven.

"Shit, warn me next time you're going to turn on the light." Chase squints and rubs his eyes.

"Sorry," I mumble.

He opens the door to the fridge and peers inside. "What are you in the mood for?" For some reason, bacon dances behind my eyelids. I can almost taste the salty flavor. Chase rummages through the contents of the refrigerator, removing giant packs of generic cheese (the kind you buy with food stamps and tastes like cardboard), some funky-smelling deli meat, and iceberg lettuce (which looks surprisingly fresh, all things considered) and places them on the stainless steel island. A piece of what I think is fruit rolls off and drops to the floor with a thunk.

"What's this?" I pick up the unfamiliar food. It's oval-shaped, like some kind of weird prehistoric egg. The green, red, and yellow color of the smooth, soft skin reminds me of the changing of autumn leaves.

Chase turns from the fridge and gives me a get-the-fuck-out-of-here sort of look. "You've never had a mango before?"

I shake my head.

Chase finds a butcher knife in a nearby drawer and sinks its gleaming, serrated edge into the flesh of the fruit. Amelia's warning rings in my ears. *He killed someone.* I stare at the knife in his hand, at his fist closed around the wooden handle. He doesn't seem like the violent type. In fact, I really don't think he could hurt anyone. Then again, maybe he did hurt someone, someone who hurt him. That I can understand.

The fruit slices easily. The flesh inside is a brilliant orange. "Here." He holds a square of mango between his thumb and pointer finger. Juice drips down, making a path over his knuckle.

I take the mango from him and pop it into my mouth. All thoughts of bacon are forgotten. My lips pucker at the tangy taste. It's a heady combination of orange and apple infused with pineapple. I can feel the sugar somersaulting through my veins. I want more.

He laughs, low and husky, and slips a piece of mango into his own mouth. "It's good, right?"

"It's . . . all right," I say.

"You're a shitty liar, you know that?"

I shrug, purse my lips. And smile. A real smile. One that I feel all the way down to my toes. Happy. I'm happy. How long has it been since I've felt this way? "It's kind of awesome," I say.

And all of a sudden I'm ravenous.

I devour almost the entire mango in the short time it takes Chase to throw together a simple sandwich. I've just shoved the last piece of gooey-delicious awesomeness into my mouth when Chase turns to me with a goofy grin on his face. "You're a messy eater."

I swallow hastily and wipe my mouth with the back of my hand.

"You missed," he says.

I wipe at my face again, but he just shakes his head and goes to get a paper towel from the dispenser by the sink. I can feel my cheeks heating up. I bet they're bright red. Now he's staring at me, his expression serious. The look he's giving me is scary and exciting —more exciting than scary—speaking to a part of me that only Jason could ever speak to.

"Here, let me."

I wince a little as he wipes some of the sticky juice from my cheek. His hands on my face are like a hurricane. A storm of nervousness and anticipation begins to churn inside me. He's close enough to kiss me. Jason was the first and only boy ever to kiss me. I wonder what Chase's kiss would feel like. Would it be like Jason's, rough and hard, with a glimmer of conquer behind it? Or would it be softer and sweeter, without pretense? Somehow, I think the latter.

Laughter sounds from outside the door. We come apart like

grass split by a bolt of lightning. Chase flicks the light switch and the room plummets into darkness. Muted voices come from the other side of the door. Whoever is there has stopped right outside the kitchen.

Even though we're no longer touching, I can feel Chase across from me, our fear ballooning between us. I squeeze my eyes shut, waiting for the inevitable beep of the lock and whoosh of the door opening. But it doesn't come. The voices fade, and then they're gone. We're safe. For now. Chase waits a few seconds more and then turns on the light. "We should probably clean up," he whispers.

"Yeah," I mumble. While Chase returns the food to the refrigerator, carefully arranging everything so it's just as we found it, I wipe down the counters.

Chase moves behind me, brushing my back as he walks to the kitchen door. "Ready for the next adventure?" he asks.

Am I ready? *Yes. I am.*

"I think some of the techs come up this way to smoke," he says.

We're back in the stairwell, but this time we're going up, up, up. There's a black metal door at the top, but this one is different from the others. It's got a bar across it and a big sign that reads CAUTION EMERGENCY EXIT ALARM WILL SOUND. The door is propped open with a wooden triangle, wedged at the base. Chase opens the door and gestures for me to go ahead. *Ladies first.* I step outside, but I'm not prepared for the rush of frozen wind that blasts my cheeks. I stuff my hands into the pockets of my hoodie to ward off the chill. Still, the night is clear and beautiful, with a thousand stars winking in the sky and the crescent moon hanging low and bright. My grandfather and I used to go on walks at night. We would gaze up at the stars and bask in their glow. That's when I thought I could be anything, an astronaut, a doctor, a dancer on a star — then Cellie ripped it all away.

Chase closes the door carefully, making sure the wood stopper stays trapped in the threshold. The roof is littered with antennae, chimneys, and other stuff I don't recognize, stuff that's probably part of the building's internal organs. A couple of rusted lawn chairs are off to the right, and there's a bucket filled with murky water and floating cigarette butts. To the left, another square rises from the roof and a ladder leads to the top. I make a beeline for the ladder. I want to get as close to the stars as possible.

I climb. My face is wind-stung and the cold of the ladder's metal bars bites into my fingertips. I climb faster, place my foot on the last rung, and hoist my body up over the ledge. The D ward looms in the distance, dark and silent. I study it, waiting for a sign of life in the windows, but everything is calm. From here you can see all of Savage Isle, the A and B wards, the water, the city lights that twinkle in the distance. We're even standing above the thick gray mist of the fog line. Another breeze comes, cuts across the rooftop, and pastes my jeans to the backs of my knees.

Chase's hand touches my shoulder. I whirl around and the wind whips my hair into the side of his face.

"What are you thinking about?" he asks.

I study the white oblong scar on his cheek. "I like it up here."

He gives me a soft, sad sort of smile. I wonder what I said to make him look like that. "Me, too. You want to sit?"

There aren't any chairs up here, so I assume he means we should sit on the ground. It's dry, but I bet it's really cold. "Sure," I say. We sit at almost the exact same time. An involuntary shiver ripples through me.

"I hate it here." Chase stares off into the distance.

"It's not so bad, once you get used to it."

"I don't think I'll ever get used to being cooped up."

A question hovers on the tip of my tongue. The question I've been waiting to ask since we met. *What did you do to get locked up?* Chase breaks the silence. "You've been here before, right?"

"Once. With my sister." I trace the cracks in the roof with my finger.

Maybe he senses my reluctance to talk about my past stints at Savage Isle, because he quickly changes the subject. "What'd your roommate get Quiet Roomed for?"

I don't want to talk about Amelia, either. Her story isn't mine to tell. Plus we're friends. And friends keep each other's secrets. So I ignore his question and ask one of my own. "What about you, have you ever been to a place like this before?"

His scar twitches. "No. I've never been to a place like this before. And, God willing, after this, I'm never coming back."

I chew my lip. Chase doesn't seem like he belongs here, in the aquarium full of jellyfish. Like right now, he sits completely still.

He doesn't fidget or sway. His eyes are focused on the horizon. Steady. So steady. "You're not a jellyfish," I say.

"Huh?" He peers at me through the darkness.

"It's something my sister and I made up last time we were here. This place is like an aquarium, everyone swimming in circles, never stopping. All the patients are like jellyfish."

"But I'm not a jellyfish?" A wry smile appears on his face.

"No, you're not a jellyfish. You're definitely something else."

"What about you? Are you a jellyfish?"

I think about jellyfish and the dangerous toxins they inject into their prey. "I don't know," I say honestly. "I hope not."

Chase palms his head and his fingers ripple his hair. "What happens if someone wants out of the aquarium?"

There's no way out. But I don't want to tell him this. Not when he still has hope. Hope to break the surface and taste the salt in the air.

Chase stands up, as if all this is too much for him. He walks to the edge of the roof, where he picks up a piece of gravel and hurtles it as hard as he can over the side, into the bottomless black night. I think he would cry out if he could. Silence always hurts more.

I go to him, not sure of what to say or do. I want to absorb his rage. Take away his sadness. Smooth the scar on his face. Fix him. But I don't know how. I couldn't fix Cellie. I can't even fix myself. I extend my arm, just a little, until the side of my hand grazes his.

"Why'd you leave?" he asks.

He's asking why I escaped with Jason. I'm not surprised he

knows. He insinuated as much the first time we met, *Overheard some techs talking about how the fire starters are back.* So I tell him. I tell him about Cellie and her fires and the one that killed Jason and about the charges against me. He doesn't ask for more information about Jason, but I know he feels the tremor that runs through me when I mention his name.

"We'll find your sister," he says, and it sounds like an oath, a sacred promise. What started as a deal, a bargain for each other's services, has suddenly changed. Because now he's talking to me like a friend, a real friend. Like he's committed to something bigger than himself. What I don't tell him is the reason I need to find Cellie. I'm sure he assumes it's to get her to confess, to repent and then atone. I don't think he would understand the real reason. He'll find out soon enough. He'll probably be there when I wrap my hands around her skinny throat. That'll be the hook that unravels our tenuous friendship. He won't be able to look at me in the same way. And I won't blame him. I wonder if he might even try to stop me. What would I do then?

"What would you do if you could see Jason again?"

I lower my lashes. "If I saw him again?" It's an impossible thought.

"Yeah, if you had one more minute. Just one. What would you do?" Chase steps closer to me, and I think I can hear his beating heart. I close my eyes and pretend it's Jason's heart. So strong. So alive. I pretend the smell of clean laundry is really cinnamon and cigarette smoke.

"I wouldn't do anything. Because he's . . ." I can't say the word *dead*. "Because he's gone." It's no use thinking what could have been. Hope is a four-letter word.

Chase moves slowly, almost hesitantly, until both of his arms are around me and I'm enveloped in a tight hug. I go stiff. In foster homes, human affection is rare. I used to crave it, like an alcoholic craves the bottle, but now affection makes me feel awkward and uncomfortable. Chase rests his head on top of mine. "I'm sorry, Just Alice. I'm sorry he's gone."

I pull away from him and look up into his face. I don't want to talk about Jason anymore. Self-denial can be such a beautiful, powerful thing. I need to steer the situation in a new direction. I say the first thing I can think of. "Who's your favorite Muppet?"

His eyes widen a little, confused, but then he decides to just go along with it. "Animal," he says.

I picture the drummer Muppet with the crazy hair. It fits him. "Who's yours?"

"The Swedish Chef, obviously."

He grins and rolls his eyes. "*Obviously . . .*" He steps back and lets go of me. Mission accomplished, the serious moment broken. So why do I feel like I've missed out on something?

Chase runs a hand through his hair again and mutters something about how we should get going. I agree in a noncommittal way. We should get going. But I know neither of us wants to. Especially me. I could stay up on the roof forever—or at least all night—bathing in the moonlight, illuminated and free.

From the Journal of Alice Monroe

Over the summer we got to know Jason again. Most days we hung out on the roof of Candy's house. The hot tiles poked our legs and the sun scorched our faces, but it was better than being inside, where the smoke from Candy's cigarettes clung to everything.

Jason's mom had died a couple of years back, following his younger brother on the overdose train. Now Jason was just like us, another lost puzzle piece swept under the rug. He'd bounced around a few times, living in different group homes until he finally landed at Candy's. He told us it wasn't so bad there. And we agreed. Because we knew there were worse places. Way worse.

Some nights Candy would take out her accordion and play sad love songs on the porch, making all the dogs in a two-mile radius howl. The neighbor next door said he was going to call the cops if he had to listen to "Moon River" one more time. From the roof we would watch them argue, Candy and the neighbor. It was better than any movie I'd ever seen, and I'd think to myself, *If I died right now, I'd be happy.*

When the neighborhood grew tired and lights flickered off down the block, we'd stay up on the roof. Jason lay between Cellie and me, and occasionally he'd brush his hand over mine. It was then, in those moments, during a summer of record-breaking heat, that my heart slipped out of my chest and into Jason's. I didn't love him. Not yet. To be honest, I wasn't sure I was capable of love, having experienced it so rarely. The love Grandpa had shown me felt like it belonged to another lifetime. Everything from my childhood felt stale, worn away. But I did feel something for Jason, something deep and wide—gratitude, maybe, or devotion or loyalty. During our last stay at Savage Isle, before my epic escape with him, I would replay those nights on the roof of Candy's house in my mind. Our faces lifted toward the sky and the heated wind against our backs. Up there, we were untouchable.

Rebecca, our social worker, got pregnant and decided to retire. The last time we saw her, she introduced us to her replacement, Sara. They came to Candy's in separate cars, and I couldn't help but notice that Sara's car was the nicest in the neighborhood. The nicest I'd ever seen. It was shiny silver, and even from the porch I could tell it had a sleek leather interior. A bumper sticker advertised that she had graduated from the private liberal arts college on the other side of town.

As Sara climbed the porch steps, she fidgeted with the cross charm on her necklace. I could tell she was young and nervous, unaccustomed to neighborhoods like this. I imagined her wanting to turn around and run away. The sound of a daytime soap opera filtered through Candy's flimsy screen door as we came out to meet her.

"You must be Alice," Sara said. She smiled brightly and extended her hand for me to shake. I glanced at Cellie, who was making a show of scowling. She shook her head at me. A warning. I knew she was pissed about getting a new social worker, but that didn't mean she had to reject a gesture of kindness. Sara's nails were clean and manicured. She had perfectly styled hair, and she smelled like expensive body wash, the kind you buy in a department store. I ignored her hand but gave her a warm smile. Rebecca motioned for us to sit on the beat-up outdoor chairs, but Cellie quietly refused.

Sara looked anxiously at Rebecca, who stepped in, her huge belly creating a wall between us. Cellie snickered and lit up a cigarette, a new habit she'd picked up from Jason. Generally speaking, Rebecca was pretty cool with Cellie's bullshit, but today she wasn't having it.

"Um. Hello? Pregnant here." Rebecca pointed to her ginormous belly, then coughed and waved a hand in front of her face at the ballooning gray smoke. She plucked the cigarette from Cellie's mouth and stomped on it.

Jason appeared in the doorway, shirtless. He stretched his arms, the skin of his stomach taut, his abs rippling. "I can't believe you're not going to be around anymore, Becky," he said. Sara's cheeks turned a brilliant red.

"Don't start with me, *Valentine,* or I'll call Charlie and suggest that he check your school attendance record from last year." Charlie was Jason's social worker, and Rebecca didn't like being called Becky any more than Jason liked being called Valentine. Cellie snickered. "And you, missy," Rebecca spat, pointing her finger at Cellie, "don't think I don't know you've been ducking out on your counseling appointments." Cellie was required to attend therapy once a week. I thought she'd been going. She left at the right time to catch the bus and returned an hour or so later. Now I saw how stupid

I'd been. Of course she'd been skipping. I had no trouble imagining her loitering around town. Up to no good. Her hair a little wild. Her heart a little dark.

Cellie's bottom lip curled, and I thought, suddenly, of an angry cat doused in water.

Sara cleared her throat, desperate to ease the tension. "I was thinking we could all go to lunch, anywhere you want."

I gave Sara an encouraging look.

"You could join us if you'd like, Valentine," she offered.

Jason's eyes got hard. "That's not my fucking name." He spat and disappeared back inside the dark house.

We went to the barbecue place down the street. Cellie and I rode with Rebecca, and Sara followed close behind. I ordered the pork ribs with coleslaw. Cellie ordered the same and then accused me of copying her.

After the bill was paid, Rebecca said goodbye to us and Sara drove us back to the house. She went the speed limit the whole way and kept both of her hands on the wheel, perfectly positioned at ten and two o'clock. At Candy's, we found Jason up on the roof. He had just rolled a joint and was about to spark it. I flopped back and rubbed my hands over my face. "Well, that was a disaster."

"She sucks," said Cellie.

"You didn't even give her a chance."

"She's not like us, Alice. Did you see her car? She's not from the Eastside."

I didn't mention that we weren't always from the Eastside. Grandpa's house wasn't in the best part of town, but it was nice enough, and if he'd lived, we might have attended a decent high school, one where there were plenty of extracurricular activities and less than ten percent of the student body was on free or reduced lunch. Maybe, just maybe, we would have applied to the same private liberal arts college Sara had graduated from.

"So?" I threw my arm over my eyes, blocking out the sun. Jason lay down next to me.

"So, I'm sad Rebecca's gone," Cellie complained.

"I know something that'll take your mind off it . . ." Jason said. He took a long drag off his joint and then offered it to me. I waved it away.

"What'd you have in mind?" Cellie perked up.

"Follow me."

He climbed down from the roof and we followed him down the sidewalk and through the winding streets, chasing the wind and the summer breeze. Along the way, he told us to pick up some rocks. We complied without ever asking why. The three of us walked until the sun started to set and orange light shaded the sky. Finally Jason stopped in front of a house. It took me a few minutes to recognize it. Cracked, peeling blue paint. A warped chainlink fence. A ripped screen door. In the honey glow of the sunset it looked like some sort of tomb, a mausoleum full of broken childhoods. The back of my head pulsed. I thought I heard angry footsteps, a closet door shaking, and then the sound of a fist meeting flesh. Roman's house.

"I found it by accident one day," Jason said. We sat on the curb across from Roman's house, waiting for the sun to dip below the horizon, for the neighborhood kids to abandon their jump ropes and go inside. "I was out walking right after my mom died, and all of a sudden I was here. They don't get foster kids anymore, but they still live here. He's probably in there right now."

Jason's words prickled my skin. *He's probably in there right now.* Of all the faces, all the people Cellie and I had met, Roman's face always stayed fresh. His gray and brown beard that would catch spit and food. His grease-stained T-shirts. The gap in his teeth on the right side of his mouth. The hand he called God's Will. I played with the rock in my hand and wished I had picked up something larger, something heavier, something the size of a fist.

As we sat on the curb across the street, waiting for some sort of sign, Jason and Cellie smoked cigarette after cigarette. We didn't talk. None of us wanted to reminisce about our nights spent in a closet, when Roman trolled the halls and played Russian roulette with our childhoods. Besides, we all knew what we were feeling, anyway—sadness, impotence, rage—it flowed through our bodies and then into each other's, and somehow, in some way, it was oddly comforting to know that we were all feeling this again, together.

When the lights went out in the house, Jason stood up. He tossed his rock up in the air, caught it, and then hurled it right into Roman's living room window. Giddy, Cellie and I jumped up and followed Jason's lead. I know it's corny, but as that rock left my hand, I literally felt a weight come off my shoulders; the fear that had been riding on my back all these years was suddenly lighter, more manageable. Some of my power had been returned to me. The sound of shattering glass woke the neighborhood, and lights blinked on one after the other like dominoes falling down the block.

Jason grabbed our hands and we fled. Behind us a door slammed open. Foolishly, I turned around. Sure enough Roman was there, watching us run away, his shadow long and distorted and dark, stretching across his untamed lawn. Cloaked in the night as we were, I don't think he could really see us. Probably wouldn't have recognized us anyway. But for a moment, time stood still and I was a little girl again, hiding in a closet, making paper lion after paper lion.

Afraid, I stumbled over a crack in the concrete. Cellie pulled me up, and Jason shoved us both behind his back. Always the protector. Even though Roman wasn't chasing us, Jason picked up a rock and threw it at him. With a metallic sound, it grazed the beer can in Roman's hand. I'll never forget that moment. The rage in Roman's eyes, the adrenaline coursing through my veins, the squeaky sound of our sneakers as we ran away. It was such a thrill.

Cellie and I went to sleep early that night, exhausted from the day's drama, but I woke in the small hours of the morning, when the sky was still pitch-black, and discovered Jason crawling beneath my bedcovers. He'd come to me like this before, and I didn't mind it. I liked it when he spooned me. My body fit perfectly into the shape of his.

"Alice," he said into my hair.

"Yeah," I said dreamily, bringing his knuckles up and tucking them under my chin.

I felt his mouth curve into a smile against the shell of my ear, and when he spoke, there was a quiet hum of excitement vibrating in his chest. "I'll hurt him worse next time."

CHAPTER
10

VIKING FUNERALS

THE DAY OF JASON'S FUNERAL IS BRIGHT. THE SUN BLOSSOMS high and yellow in the clear sky. It's cold, a bitter cold that makes such a pretty day seem cruel. There will be no church service, not even a short memorial by the graveside.

Sara comes and signs me out. Dr. Goodman brings a police officer. The police officer outfits me with an ankle monitor that gets strapped to my right leg. It's light but too bulky to wear under my jeans, so it rests on the outside. Donny, Dr. Goodman, and Nurse Dummel escort me outside, which makes me feel like I should be wearing an orange jump suit, a straitjacket, and a facemask. Dr. Goodman looks especially worried. I climb into Sara's car, which smells like pine trees, leather, and vanilla. I have to crack a window to keep from choking. We drive to the edge of town.

I've been this way before, with Cellie when we buried Grandpa. We had taken the bus as far as we could go and walked along the frozen river, our footsteps harsh and unforgiving on the frigid land-scape. The day of Grandpa's funeral it snowed, a beautiful white blanket that bleached the world of color. There's no snow today, but it's just as cold. And that seems worse.

I stay pretty quiet during most of the drive, and Sara doesn't push me to talk. A couple of times she reaches over and squeezes my hand or my knee. When we get to the cemetery, she parks at the gate.

"Do you know the way?" she asks.

I nod. Dr. Goodman gave me directions to the plot, courtesy of the cemetery director. "Do you mind waiting here?" I ask. "I think this is something I need to do alone."

She bites her lip. She seems nervous to let me out of her sight.

"Look, I know your ass is on the line if I run. I promise, I won't. Just give me thirty minutes. I'll give you the directions, and you can come for me after. Plus . . ." I gesture to the blinking ankle monitor.

She mulls it over for a minute and then finally says, "Okay. You can go by yourself."

I thank her and get out of the car. Right away the cold seeps through the canvas of my shoes, gets into my socks, and nibbles at my toes. I hug my sweatshirt tight to my chest, as if I could ward off the icy chill by huddling inward. I walk a few steps and pause by a pillar with a carved lion on top of it. The cemetery is bare and bleak, the grass brown even though it's rained off and on the last couple of days. Gray tombstones dot the lawn and roll up through the hills. I can feel Sara's eyes on me, boring into my back. I turn and give her a short wave. She returns the gesture, her face a little grim.

When we buried Grandpa, Cellie walked through the cemetery with me, our joined hands swinging between us. This time I walk alone. I start up the winding road. Digging into my hoodie pocket, I retrieve the directions Dr. Goodman gave me. My toes grow numb. I curl and uncurl them in my shoes, hoping to push some blood back into them. Once I'm out of Sara's sight, I stop at a holly bush and pry some branches from it. They're pretty, with little red berries and evergreen leaves.

I walk until I see a tractor with a backhoe. A few feet away there's a hole in the ground, with a casket lying next to it. There aren't any flowers. The state sprung for a plot of land and a cheap wooden casket. That's all. I glance down at the sprig of holly leaves in my hand, hoping it's enough. The gravedigger is here, dressed in a green jump suit. He leans against the tractor, smoking a cigarette. He drops it and stomps it out when he sees me.

"Wasn't sure if anyone was going to show," he says, inspecting the red-blinking ankle monitor strapped to my leg. "I was just about to finish up."

"I'm here." I don't take my eyes off the casket. My hand clenches the holly branch and the little thorns pierce my skin. My heart crashes like waves against rocks.

"You want some time alone?" the gravedigger asks.

"No." I reach out a reverent hand to touch the casket. Jason's in there, resting peacefully, I hope. I lay the sprig of holly on top, the way I've seen people do on television. It doesn't give me any comfort. I didn't think it would. Still, I want Jason to have the best. "Go ahead," I say. I know what's coming next.

The gravedigger sighs, makes his way over to the lowering device, and begins to crank it. The coffin hovers just above the ground, then moves slowly to the right before descending into the hole. I watch, oddly detached.

Then there's a guttural cry that I barely recognize as my own voice. I leap onto the casket. "No," I cry, hugging the cheap coffin as it swings above the hole. Even though I know Jason is gone, I somehow can't let go of his body. I want to rip the lid off the coffin, touch his face one more time, feel the warmth of his cheek under my fingertips, feel the flush of his face, smell the breath of his voice.

Strong, dirty hands drag me back, away from the casket. "You're going to break my winch," the gravedigger says.

I struggle against his fierce grip. Sadness and fury rage inside me. The gravedigger drags me back a few feet, my heels digging into the soggy earth. When we're a safe distance away, he drops me, and I crumple into a heap, exhausted. Through my sobs, I hear the gravedigger walk away and start the winch again. There's a soft thump as Jason's casket hits the slushy bottom of the hole. This isn't right. Jason should have had a Viking's funeral. His body should have been lovingly wrapped in linen, placed on a boat, and set adrift in the ocean, where flaming arrows from the shore were shot to catch the boat on fire. He should have been cremated at sea. Not left to rot in some cheap grave. When I open my eyes, all I can see are the gravedigger's green kneepads. He's crouched in front of me again.

"Shame no one else is here to bury your young fellow," he says. "I've been doing this a long time. Seen a lot of grief. Sometimes it helps if you write it down. Write the person a note. A goodbye letter. Say all the things you want to but never got the chance."

That's when I notice the piece of blue paper and chewed pencil in his dirty hand.

"Here, take 'em," he says. "I only got the schedule of plots to be dug, but you can use the back to write something."

I reach out and take what he's offering.

The gravedigger stands. "You take your time. This is my last dig today. I'll wait over there." He points to a mausoleum down the hill. "When you're finished, give me a wave and I'll help you bury your fellow."

The gravedigger leaves. I smooth out the piece of paper and use my thigh as a writing surface. Then I think better of it. There's no way to explain how I feel in words. I fold the paper over so it makes a triangle and then I rip off the excess. Now I have a square. Perfect. I fold it into a crane, a symbol of peace. Something I think Jason didn't have in this life. Something I hope will follow him into the next. I stand and wave the bird at the gravedigger. He nods and walks toward me.

"You done?" He eyes my unusual choice.

"Yeah." I rub one of the wings between my fingers.

"Well, go on, then." He nods toward the hole. Slowly I make my way over to the gravesite. I hold the crane aloft and then release it. For a moment it catches the wind, floats, then drifts down until it meets the top of the casket. A couple more tears slip down my cheeks. "You can start again," I tell the gravedigger. "I won't freak out this time."

"All right then," he says, making his way over to the tractor. He sits in it and starts it up. The tractor comes alive with a rough jerk. He shifts the controls and the backhoe lifts, scooping up the perfect amount of soil. Dirt spatters on the hollow wood, and the sound is more difficult to listen to than the silence that accompanied me on my walk through the cemetery.

I relax my eyes and let my focus soften until the sky and trees blend together like the heavy brushstrokes of a van Gogh painting. I pretend that the sound of the dirt is only the rain, only the sound of my grandfather coming to take Jason home. As if on cue, dark clouds cover the sun. The sky opens and an ugly, gray sleet begins to fall. *Yes,* it's only the sound of the rain, of the weather, of our families riding the storm clouds to carry us away.

———————

FROM THE JOURNAL OF ALICE MONROE

On the Fourth of July, the whole neighborhood gathered to make a bonfire under the bridge, just down the street from Candy's house. Candy even managed to get up off the sofa, huffing and puffing like some old dragon with emphysema. One of the younger kids had to carry her accordion for her.

Right as the sun dipped below the horizon, we made it to the bonfire. Candy settled herself on a pair of milk crates, unhinged that accordion, and began to play "Moon River." Until the booing and hissing and throwing of garbage started. Then she changed to "Paint It Black" by The Stones. Other musicians joined in as well, bringing an odd assortment of instruments into the song: a four-string guitar, a harmonica, even a violin. There was laughter and dancing and cheap, illegal fireworks. I was happy. A girl from down the street offered me a shot of tequila. I took it in one swallow, and just as quickly it blazed a fiery trail in my veins. I liked how it touched every atom inside of me, made me feel alive. I took another shot from her. Then another.

Jason and Cellie had disappeared. They'd been up to something all day, talking seriously in corners, plotting something, I was sure of it. But I didn't care. I wanted Jason and Cellie to be close. Then she wouldn't think of him as a threat.

I took another shot. Mickey, the boy who lived next door in a two-bedroom house, had offered it to me. He had a Mohawk, a lip piercing, and ten siblings. When he grabbed my hand, pulling me closer to the fire, I didn't struggle. "C'mon, Alice. Just one dance," he said. Looping my arms around his neck, I closed my eyes and got lost in the beat. Everything felt so good. So warm. But then Mickey was pushed away from me. My arms dropped to my sides. Jason stood between us. His eyes were cold and dark, glinting like black diamonds in the firelight.

"Find another partner," he said.

The way he said it, Mickey knew to back off and walk away. Immediately.

When Jason turned back to me, I felt the weight of his stare settle on my shoulders. "How much have you had to drink?" he asked.

I shrugged. "A few shots ... I feel all tingly." I grinned and tugged at his shirt. "Please don't be mad."

He snorted. "Yeah, well, you're going to feel like shit in the morning."

I rolled my eyes. I didn't care. The tequila steamrolled through my body, making it feel limber and numb. I wanted to take more shots. I wanted to do them with Cellie and Jason. "Where's Cellie?" I asked.

The bonfire lit one side of Jason's face while the other was cast in shadow. It looked as if he was wearing a mask. "I'm sure she'll show up soon."

"Dance with me," I said, and without waiting for his consent, I put my arms around his waist and drew him toward me. Even though the song was fast, we moved slowly. Jason held my hips and I pressed my cheek into the blue of his shirt, rubbing my nose against the soft fabric.

Usually I loved the way he smelled, like cinnamon and cigarettes, but that night he smelled like something different, something new, something that made the hairs on the back of my neck stand on end. "You smell funny."

"I have a surprise for you," he said, ignoring my observation.

I felt my face light up like a Christmas tree, the excitement and curiosity and tequila eclipsing my concern. "What is it?"

"Come on. I'll show you." He wove his fingers through mine and led me away from the fire and into the dark. We stole through the night. The streets hummed with the sound of streetlights and the bugs getting zapped in them.

When we turned onto Roman's street, I shook free of his grasp. "I don't want to go back there," I said.

Behind us fireworks exploded in jets of color over the black arc of the bridge. Iridescent blue, red, yellow, and green sparkled in the sky. I wanted to go back to the party, light a sparkler, and spell out my name, create some indelible proof that I had been there—that I existed at all.

"C'mon, baby. Don't be difficult. I just want to show you something." Jason reached for my hand again, and because I didn't want to walk all the way back to the party on my own, I allowed myself to be led by him.

We made our way to Roman's house. The neighborhood was quiet and still. Most of the families were out by the bridge or had already turned in for the night. Roman's house was dark. Even the street lamp outside had been extinguished.

I sucked in a breath and came to a stop. It was then I recognized the smell, the one that clung to Jason's shirt and now settled in a cloud around Roman's house. Gasoline. The grass and the wood shingles of the house were wet. It hadn't rained in days.

Laughter, like a child's, came from the back of the house. Jason was already walking up the driveway. "C'mon, baby," he beckoned. I charged past him, instantly sobering, the warmth of the tequila draining from my body, a profound coldness settling in.

I found Cellie crouched in the backyard, a pile of wadded

newspapers and dry grass at her feet. A book of matches was in her hand.

"Don't, Cellie." She looked up as if I'd startled her. Jason went and stood by her side. "I don't want this," I said to him. He looked confused, utterly baffled.

"I told you not to tell her," Cellie said. "She's weak."

Jason defended me. "Shut up, Cellie," he said, then to me: "I don't understand, Alice. We did this for you. Do you want him to hurt more kids?"

"He's not hurting any kids. The state took them all away. He'll drink himself to death soon enough, anyway." I tried to reason.

Jason lowered his gaze and I could barely hear his voice. "What about what he did to us? *To me*. Don't you still see him at night? In your dreams?"

Of course I do, I wanted to say. I saw Roman's face every night in the plaster of the walls and in the quaking floorboards. But I shook my head. "What he did to us was awful, especially to you. But this isn't the way, Jason. We have to forgive, to forget, to move on. The only power he has now is the power we give to him. You don't want to do this. I know it. This isn't *you*."

His upper lip curled. "You don't know shit about me." And in that moment, I didn't. I couldn't recognize the hard lines in his face or the malicious flash in his eyes. Cellie struck her match first, inhaling deeply at the explosion of sulfur. All the bones in her body seemed to relax. She handed the matchbook to Jason, and he struck one as well.

"Please," I begged.

But they didn't listen. Maybe they couldn't hear my voice above their own anger and sadness. I could feel it coming off of them, radiating in waves, their desire, their strong compulsion to burn something down. Because in their heads they were still fighting him, still locked in that epic mythological battle. Together they held the matches aloft and dropped them.

11

CODE RED

I LET SARA HUG ME WHEN I CLIMB BACK INTO THE CAR. SHE holds on to me tight even though I'm wet from the sleet. I'd been in the cemetery for more than my allotted thirty minutes, and I'm touched and grateful that she trusted me enough to wait, didn't sound the alarm as soon as the clock ran one minute over. I allow myself to weep into her neck, which almost feels like home. I pull away before she does. She starts up the car and turns up the heat.

"You loved him a lot." She cranks the wheel and pulls out of the cemetery.

"Yeah." I can only get out that one word.

"I loved someone like that too, once."

"Like how?" I wipe at my nose. I'm not a pretty crier. My cheeks get puffy and my eyes turn red.

"Bottomless, consuming. In high school, when I was about your age. Our circumstances weren't nearly the same as yours. But our breakup was painful." Sara sighs and seems lost in a memory of her own. "First loves are always special." She pats my knee. "You've had a rough afternoon."

I lean my head against the cool glass of the window. I think about Jason and the night of the fire in the barn and his happy smile when he'd said *Shit, baby. I'm burning up.* It triggers something in me. I've seen that smile before. The type of smile that starts manic, then tips to glee, and ends in a wash of tranquility, the kind of smile that is equal parts pleasure and pain. Everything suddenly weaves together like the heavy braiding of a rope.

I remember the way he loved watching Roman's house burn. I remember the forest fire and his unicorn tattoo. And I remember, for the first time, that Jason liked fire just as much as Cellie did. I can't believe I didn't see it before. Or maybe I did and chose to ignore it because I wanted to love and be loved so badly.

By the time we get back from Jason's funeral and I've been reprocessed, dinnertime has come and gone. Nurse Dummel says she'll get me a sandwich from the cafeteria, but the last thing I want to do is eat.

All this time I was blind to Jason's darkness, so blissfully unaware, and now everything is flooding back to me like a burst dam: the way his eyes glazed over with pleasure at the sight of a fire, the way he licked his lips, hungry for the heat. Sometimes he'd even put out a cigarette just so he could relight it.

I go to my room. I have a little time before my one-on-one with Dr. Goodman, and I need to sort this out, chop it up into little pieces, and figure out how I could have missed something so important.

I lie on my bed. My stomach churns and my head begins to throb. It's too quiet in the room. And I don't like it. Amelia still isn't back. The paper mouse on her pillow remains undisturbed. I stare at it until my vision blurs. My headache makes everything pulse, as if the air has a heartbeat. I stand up and steady myself against the wall. My face is too hot and the room is too cold.

I make it into the bathroom and splash cold water on my face. I lean against the sink and grip the porcelain. A lock of hair falls in my face and Jason's words come unbidden, *I love your hair wild like this.* It's all too much. I squeeze my eyes shut. My hair. A shackle that binds me to Jason.

Before I know what I'm doing, I've hauled myself out of the bathroom. Kneeling on the bedroom floor, I rip the middle drawer from my dresser and dig through the hole in the wall. It doesn't take long to find what I'm searching for. A pink-handled Bic razor.

I go back to the bathroom. I take a lock of my hair and hold it away from my head. Cellie never wanted me to cut my hair. She wanted us to look the same, and she insisted that long hair was the prettiest. And once, when I tried to cut it, she had painfully grabbed my hand and called me a deceitful little witch.

Wielding the razor like a saw, I hack at the lock until it slips through my fingertips and falls to the floor. I don't think about what I've just done or what it means. All that matters is that Jason's memory and his words are fading. I continue on, crying ugly tears from somewhere deep in my body, a place I didn't even know existed. It takes a long time.

When I've finally finished I look in the mirror. My hair hangs in jagged edges around my shoulders. The new cut makes my face look more angular and my eyes seem bigger. I smile softly and touch the reflection in the mirror. I like the way I look now. Different from Cellie. Distant from Jason.

A beep comes from behind me, followed by the soft whoosh of my bedroom door opening. Donny's voice calls out, "All right, Allie, time to see Dr. . . ." He pauses, his mouth registering shock, then disbelief. I must look like a madwoman, standing in a pile of my own hair. *What have I done? What have I done?* The radio is off his belt in an instant. He's that well trained. "Code red, code red," he says into it.

I want to move toward him, grab his forearm, and tell him that it was a mistake. Cellie's the impulsive one. Not me. This isn't me. I'm not crazy. But there's no time.

The response is almost immediate. In seconds the room is flooded with techs and nurses. Even Dr. Goodman is there, rushing in behind them. I'm overcome with fear, paralyzed by it. And underneath all that fear is helplessness. Everything I thought I knew about Jason was a lie. The crushing weight of the truth leaves me without an ounce of fight. There's no negotiation like there was with Amelia. No soft voices urging me to come out of the bathroom. No quiet invitation to talk it out. Something jabs into my arm, and I think it would hurt if everything else didn't hurt so much more. I go limp and clutch my heart as I fall to my knees.

A part of me wants this. It's punishment for turning the other cheek to Jason's darkness and Cellie's madness. I deserve this.

A numbing heat runs into my neck and down my sides. It feels like I'm drowning, but the sensation is not entirely unpleasant. They've given me something—some heavy drug that will banish the black by plunging me into it.

Then there will be silence.

Then there will be *nothing*.

From the Journal of Alice Monroe

The fire was quick and violent. I only had a second to shield myself from the backdraft. Up to this point, the fires Cellie had set were natural burns, slow burns, but this one was explosive. It burned at the velocity of a scream.

Instinct kicked in and I ran through the dry grass and into the back alley behind the house. It dawned on me that for the first time, I wasn't running *with* Cellie and Jason. I was running away from them.

I continued until the roar of the flames faded. I stopped four or five blocks away, when my legs refused to go any farther. I stumbled and fell, scratching my knees on the asphalt. Little rocks and dirt tore into my palms. I sat up slowly and leaned against a rickety fence. Fireworks still lit up the sky, but they were partially obscured by a huge black cloud of smoke. Sirens wailed and someone shouted. From this distance, it sounded like they were yelling underwater.

It took another couple of minutes for me to catch my breath and regret what I'd done. I had run away from Cellie and Jason in fear and panic. Left them behind. What if they got caught? Or worse, what if they got stuck in the blaze? I had to go back. Make sure they were safe. I owed it to them. Owed it to myself. I wouldn't abandon them like so many others already had.

I circled back, this time approaching Roman's house from the street rather than from the back alley. A mass of fire trucks and police cars was already there. Yellow crime-scene tape cordoned off the area. I dodged through the crowd, anxiously searching for Cellie and Jason. Two firemen were trying to hack through the walls, but the blaze was too big, too hot, and they had to turn away. All they could do, all anyone could do was try to contain it. The whole neighborhood had shown up to watch.

Arms slipped around my waist and I jumped. "Shhh," Jason whispered. My body responded to his soft reassurance. Despite my conflicting emotions, dark gratitude crept in.

"Where's Cellie?" I asked him.

"I sent her away. She's safe. I thought we could be alone for a while." He held me from behind and rested his chin on the top of my head. "Don't be mad," he said, tucking a piece of hair behind my ear. "I did it for you and Cellie. For us. We're free now. It'll be so much better, you'll see." He kept talking, kept murmuring in my ear while we watched the house burn. He told me he'd take Cellie and me to California after graduation and we'd always be warm. He told me that he would buy us a house with a bathtub and closets big enough to sleep in. He told me he'd do anything for me. *Anything.*

I closed my eyes and inhaled gasoline and ash. The backs of my eyelids were washed in an unnaturally bright orange. Jason kissed the hollow of my collarbone but then abruptly pulled away. I opened my eyes. Roman's wife, Susan, stood next to us. She wore a white nightgown covered in soot. The hair around her face was wild, electric, forming a halo in the heated wind.

"I remember you two," she said, her voice haunted and dreamlike. I thought maybe she was in shock and didn't realize what was happening. Then I realized that she knew *exactly* what was happening.

"He's still in there," she said flatly. "Do you think he'll make it?"

I opened my mouth but was too stunned to say anything.

"Ma'am, we need to take you to the hospital." A firefighter approached us and wrapped a blanket around Susan's shoulders. "Please stop wandering away."

Susan let the firefighter take her arm. But before he led her away, she leaned toward me. Her cheek grazed mine, and I felt grainy ash rub onto my skin. Her breath was sweet and warm and conjured images of candy and a rock baking in the sun. She whispered so only I could hear, "He was asleep in his chair."

I remembered that armchair, its scratchy patchwork fabric. He would throw beer cans at us from it when we blocked the television.

Susan's lips curved into a smile against my ear. "I walked right past him."

———•-•-•———

CHAPTER

12

SECLUSION

I'm numb. Everything is a blur. A white haze of techs, nurses, and doctors shuffles in and out of the seclusion room. They fill me with medication until I'm full and pump me for information until I'm drained.

"Alice," Dr. Goodman says. My vision is hazy, and it's like I'm seeing his reflection in a fun house mirror. "We need to know where you found the razor."

I mumble something incoherent and try to turn away from him, but my limbs are heavy, too heavy for my body, my bones too dense for my skin.

"It's very important that you tell us, Alice. Where did you find the razor?"

I moan and close my eyes. Even in my overmedicated state, I hesitate to betray Amelia. But her name lingers on my tongue. It's only a matter of time before it accidentally slithers out. "Amelia," I say, and it tastes like bitter treachery.

Doc pulls away and speaks to Nurse Dummel at the foot of the bed. Their conversation is muted, but there are threads of discomfort and concern. I can hear only a few words. "Search the room."

I fight sleep—a dark tidal wave that wants to pull me under—for as long as I can, but eventually I succumb. When I wake up again, Doc sits beside me. He checks my IV line and flips through my chart.

"Alice?" He says my name, then calls out behind him, "She's waking up."

It feels as if my heart is shedding a two-hundred-pound weight. My vision blurs and then narrows. Everything in the room is coming back together. I try to lift my arm but something holds it down. My wrists have been bound to the bed.

"Alice," Doc speaks. "The medication you were on is wearing off. Breathe deep. Be calm. You're in a safe place."

I do as he asks because I don't really have a choice. Even though his voice is gentle, there's an underlying threat to it. *Breathe Deep. Be Calm. Or Else.* I flex my toes and move my legs, relieved that they aren't shackled like my wrists. The blood in my veins feels as if it's reanimating, as if it's been set on slow motion and all of a sudden someone has pushed play.

"How are you feeling?" Dr. Goodman asks me.

I take in my surroundings. The room is bare, nothing on the walls and no furniture aside from the bed I'm in and the stool where Dr. Goodman is sitting. There's a small window at the very top of the wall, and I can just make out a square of sky. Dark gray clouds are converging. Raindrops pelt the window, fat and heavy.

Donny is standing in the corner, leaning against the wall with his arms crossed.

"Alice, how are you?" Dr. Goodman asks again. They must teach this technique in psychologist school—ask the same question over and over again until you get a response. Waterboarding for the mind.

"Thirsty." My voice is hoarse and it hurts to talk, though not half as bad as after the fire. Still, my throat feels raw and uncomfortable.

"We can take care of that." Doc nods to a nurse who I didn't notice before. She brings a small cup of water to my lips and I murmur, "Thank you." As she tips the cup to my mouth, there's a flash of scarlet in my peripheral vision. I've been red-banded. Super.

While I sip, I take stock of the rest of my body and notice that they've removed my street clothes and dressed me in ratty scrubs again. When I finish the water the nurse hurries away, like I'm going to spit or start throwing knives at her.

"Do you know how long you've been in here?" Dr. Goodman says. He's got my chart in his lap, even though I'm sure he's got it memorized by now.

I search the room again, this time for a clock or a calendar, but there's nothing. Then my eyes land on Donny. He's holding up two fingers. At first I can't understand why he's making the peace sign, then I get it. Two. Two days.

"Two days." Out of the corner of my eye I see Donny shake his head. He mouths the word *hours* at me. I quickly try to cover my mistake. "A couple of hours, I mean."

Dr. Goodman swivels around and looks at Donny. "We were all very concerned about you, Alice," he says, turning back to me. "Do you remember what you did? Why you're here?"

I don't see any reason to make small talk. We both know what he's doing. Dr. Goodman is here to assess me, to evaluate my current level of psychosis and determine if I'm fit to return to the general population.

"I cut my hair," I say.

"Yes." He goes silent. I don't know why he always waits for me to fill these conversational lulls. "I'd like to help you understand why."

I lay my head back on the pillow and stare at the ceiling. I wish I had a piece of origami paper. My nose itches. Involuntarily my hand moves to scratch it, but the restraints hold me in place.

Doc sighs. "I don't believe you meant to harm yourself, Alice. Although you did impulsively alter your appearance, and some psychologists would categorize that as a breakdown."

I categorize it more as a break*through*, but something tells me to keep my mouth shut.

"Still, it's against the rules to have razors without staff supervision. And anytime a patient is caught with a dangerous object, necessary precautions must be taken."

Doc asks me if I'm hiding anything else.

I shake my head no.

He asks me if I'm ready to go back to my room and be with the other patients.

I nod my head yes.

He asks if I'm feeling sick.

Again, I shake my head no. My stomach feels queasy and I still feel a little sluggish, but I attribute that to the amount of drugs cartwheeling through my system. Doc says something to the nurse about releasing me. He wants to send me back to my room, but he is going to restrict my privileges.

The nurse unbuckles my restraints and I rub my wrists where there are red marks. She offers me a wheelchair and I fall clumsily into it. My legs are watery, and I'm not sure I can stand just yet. Donny wheels me to my room and helps me into bed. I lie on my side and face Amelia's bed. The mouse is gone and the bed has been slept in. Amelia must be back. I wonder if she got in trouble for the razors. I look over to my dresser, where my little paper zoo is supposed to be, but it's gone. So is my stack of origami paper. I close my eyes and curl into a tight ball. Sour darkness has crept in. It fills the space where Jason used to be. Now there's only dust, dry dust that fills my throat. One of these days I might just let it choke me.

———•··•———

FROM THE JOURNAL OF ALICE MONROE

Some kids from the neighborhood told me that the cops found Roman's body among the black and charred ruins, his hand still clutching a beer. Uniformed men carried the body out in a bag, but the thick plastic couldn't contain the smell of toasted skin and sour beer. The odor got into the trees and hung around the neighborhood for days.

The day after the fire, Jason got his first tattoo. While the scent of gasoline still clung to his T-shirt, we went to Tiger Lily, a tattoo and piercing parlor where the owners didn't check IDs and in exchange customers didn't check the cleanliness of the needles. The floors were sticky, and it reeked of cigarettes and other things people smoke. It was the kind of place where hepatitis and gonorrhea meet to have parties.

Jason slipped the tattoo artist some cash and told him what he wanted done. Then he pulled off his shirt and lay across the table. I stood in the corner while Cellie flipped through the tattoo books. A giant guy with inked sleeves offered Cellie and me a beer. I shook my head but Cellie nodded, giggling as the guy handed her a cold one from the mini fridge.

"Thanks." She tipped the neck of the open bottle toward him. He did the same and their bottles clinked together in cheers.

The giant guy lifted a blond eyebrow at her. "You wanna see my tattoo booth?"

"Lead the way," Cellie said. She turned and followed him, vanishing into a back room. I started to go after them. I was worried about her.

"Alice." Jason called to me.

I chewed my lip and hesitated, my eyes refusing to leave the doorway Cellie had disappeared through.

"It's okay, baby. Leave her be. Come hold my hand." He reached for me. I didn't take his hand but I moved so I was close to him. I watched the needle work into his skin, turning pink flesh into black ink. I thought about the three of us in that closet all those years ago. I worried that Jason had somehow hung up his soul in there, and since then he had never really figured out how to put it back on.

When the tattoo artist was done, Jason stood, flexed his broad shoulders, and showed me the tattoo. The words *God's Will* were scrawled between his shoulder blades in an Old English–style font.

Over the next year, Jason got more tattoos. They were all trophies of the fires he'd set. A thicket of trees spanned his lower back. A unicorn covered his wrist. All the familiar images were wrapped in fire, the flames lovingly intertwined like the arms of a mother.

Jason got a job working construction under the table. He managed to scrounge up enough cash to buy a beat-up Oldsmobile from a woman down the street who needed the money to bail her kid out of jail. The car was a clunker and made a strange wheezing noise whenever it braked, but it provided us with a freedom we had never thought possible. During the summer, we'd load up the trunk with blankets and drinks and head down to the river.

The river was a yawning eighty-three-mile tributary that stretched from old-growth forests to agricultural fields. When it got hot enough, locals would gather at its rocky beaches with makeshift rafts and coolers of beer. Every summer the coast guard would issue warnings about the dangerous current, and every summer some drunk kid would decide to go for a swim or jump off one of the rocky cliffs and drown.

Jason sprawled out on a blanket and rested on his stomach while I rubbed sunblock on his back. I traced the letters of his God's Will tattoo and thought about our time at Roman's house, how Roman would preach on Sundays, his hands always curled into fists that came crashing down like fire and brimstone.

"Do you believe in God?" I asked.

He turned his face toward me and closed his eyes, squinting against the bright sun. "No. I don't believe in anything. Not anymore."

His answer made me sad. "Nothing?" I finished rubbing in the lotion and wiped my hands on the blanket.

He popped one eye open and smiled at me. "Well, maybe not *nothing*." He grabbed my wrist. "I believe in you and me."

I eyed Cellie, playing in the water. She was looking for crawdads. Jason had said that if she caught enough, we could boil them. He said they made a funny noise in the water, like screaming. Cellie had already found two and deposited them in our cooler. She turned to me and waved, but her happiness quickly dimmed as soon as she saw that Jason and I were holding hands. She'd been a little more clingy than usual lately. After setting the fire at Roman's, she'd stayed closer to me. I thought she was worried about Jason's reappearance in our lives and how close to him I had become. Sometimes she'd pull me aside and remind me of my promise all those years ago, that we would never be apart. I'd do my best to reassure her, stroke her hair or pat her arm, but I was starting to feel like she didn't believe me. And Jason's words, *I believe in you and me,* were worrisome because I wanted him, *needed* him to consider Cellie, too, when he thought about us.

"And Cellie, too. Right?" I asked him.

He brushed some hair back from my face. "Of course, baby. You, me, and Cellie. Always."

———————

CHAPTER

13

COMATOSE MIX

I DON'T FEEL LIKE TALKING. IT'S BEEN TWENTY-FOUR HOURS since I've been released from seclusion, and I've stayed in my room the entire time. Aside from getting up to go to the bathroom, all I do is sleep, and when sleep doesn't come, I lay in bed and watch the rain hit the window. Dr. Goodman comes and says I am being uncooperative and only hurting myself. I tuck my chin and let my eyes flutter shut. He can't even imagine how much it hurts.

Just as I thought, Amelia has come back from the Quiet Room. But she's not the same. She sits across from me and seems lost. She is a wisp of smoke, a husk of her former self. All that pixie energy has fizzled and gone flat. She reminds me of Susan, Roman's wife, already dead on the inside. While I watch the rain, she watches me. She's waiting for me, I know it, waiting for me to come out of . . . whatever this is. But I don't have it in me, not right now. Not yet. Maybe never.

Someone enters the room. I don't look up to see who it is. I can't even muster interest or concern. But based on the slow, hesitant footsteps, it's not a tech, a nurse, or Dr. Goodman. Their strides are always self-assured and mission driven. A smell of fabric softener precedes the person. It's Chase, using his handy key to come check up on his super-special friend. Me.

"You can't be in here," Amelia says, but he ignores her.

Chase comes and stands in front of me, so that his thighs are at my eye level. One hand is jammed in his pocket and the other holds his giant headphones and his iPod. I squeeze my eyes shut and press deeper into the pillow.

"I dig the new look," he says. "It's very Bettie Page."

Amelia snorts at the end of the bed, and I imagine an eye roll along with it. There's the sound of angry footsteps followed by the door slamming. Chase and I are alone. For a moment the pitter-patter of rain fills the room. I wish he would go away.

"Don't feel like talking? That's all right, I understand." He pauses for a moment, and I can feel him studying my profile. "I just came to bring you something. My sister, she got into moods like this. I made her a mix. It's mostly awesomely bad eighties hits. It always helped her, made her smile." There's the feeling of someone's skin close to mine—a slight change of temperature in the air and then the cool plastic of cushioned headphones resting over my ears. "Just make sure you hide it if they come in and check on you." He pulls away, but before he does, the music begins. He touches the red band on my wrist, gently. Then he's gone.

When the music has been playing for a while, when the room

stays still and no one enters for a long time, I let my hand drift over and close my fingers around the iPod. Clutching it, I bring it up and hold it against my chest where it hurts the most. I look down at the screen and click backwards to see the playlist. It's titled "Maya's Comatose Mix, Music to Emotionally Break Down, Cry, and Be Depressed To."

Another song starts and a tiny fissure, a hairline fracture, starts to form in my closed-off heart. Light begins to pour through a pin-hole in the dark. Stupid Chase and his epically bad taste in music. A small, very small smile touches my lips. I turn up the volume and let Styx's "Come Sail Away" drown out the shadows and take me into a merciful sleep.

I ignore the surprised looks as I walk down the hallway the following evening. I listened to Maya's mix for hours, the songs playing while I drifted off to sleep and when I was eventually drawn from it. When I woke, my stomach grumbled, and for the first time in the last three days I was hungry for food, for company, for life. The clock on the wall indicated that it was free time. So I got up, stuffed Chase's iPod and headphones into my hoodie pocket, and left my room.

A couple of techs line the walls a few feet away and eye me as if I'm a bomb under a car or the pedophile next door. I run my hand through my hair and pull up my hood.

I get to the community room. Patients are scattered all over; some of them rock back and forth, some pace, and some sit in pairs playing games or chatting with each other. I scan the room, searching for a black hat or a wave of pink hair. No Amelia. But I see Chase. He's sitting on the couch that appears to be perpetually frowning, watching *Back to the Future*.

I go and stand in front of him so that I'm blocking his view of the television. I withdraw the iPod and headphones and throw them into his lap. "You have shitty taste in music."

He catches them. A slow smile, part relief and part happiness, creeps across his face. He looks up at me. "There's that dirty mouth again." He pats the seat next to him. I sit down and pull my legs up to my chest. I play with the grommets on my shoes. I wish I had origami paper, but Dr. Goodman took all of my sheets. He said they were getting in the way of my progress, that I use them to deflect and shield myself from others.

There's an explosion on the television, the crackle of electricity, and a man with white hair shouts, "Roads . . . Where we're going, we don't need roads."

"This movie sucks," I say.

"Well, aren't you just all sparkles and unicorns today."

The word *sparkles* makes me think of the Fourth of July bonfire—brilliant colors, Roman's burning house, and Jason's sick happiness. I bow my head in my hands. Before I can stop it, I'm quietly weeping, big, soft, silent tears that leak through my fingers and run down my arms.

"Hey." Chase turns to me. "Hey." He pulls my hands from my face. "Your hair will grow back, and you know I dig the new look —I've always had a thing for pinup girls."

Despite trying not to, I give him a watery smile. But he doesn't understand. I'm not crying because of my hair, that's the least of it, a piece of sand in the desert. "I think I'm falling apart," I say, and the honesty of the admission startles me.

He shrugs like it's nothing. "People come undone all the time, Alice. We're all unraveling here. You've just done it in the most spectacular way. In fact, you could be our queen," he jokes.

I smile, but it's wan and distant. "Queen of the Undone?"

"It has a certain charm to it, don't you think?"

My smile fails and the dark tide pulls me under again. "Nothing makes sense anymore. That night in the field, when we went to the D ward, I thought I saw Jason . . ." I trail off. I don't tell him the rest, because it's too embarrassing, too humiliating to say how Jason was a thief, a criminal, an arsonist. It's even more embarrassing that despite all that, despite my new knowledge, I still miss him and love him. I'd do anything to have him back for just a day, an hour, a minute.

"Maybe it's your grief you're seeing," Chase suggests.

I wipe my nose with the back of my hand. "Really?"

"Yeah, I think. Sometimes I think I see things. Like my sister —she's dead, and I think I see her all the time, especially here."

My mouth gapes. This is the most Chase has ever shared with me. His sister. Maya. Dead? "Your sister Maya?"

He shifts uncomfortably in his seat. "You remind me of her, you know. A little bird with a broken wing."

I smile. "You know you're kind of a sick bastard. You're into me because you dig 1950s pinup girls and I remind you of your sister?"

He smiles back. "Don't forget your dirty mouth and fascination with paper animals."

"You're such a fucking weirdo."

"Takes one to know one."

We go silent again and watch the movie.

"I don't need you, you know." I'm not sure why I say it, where the words even come from. They just kind of bubble up and float into the air. I imagine that Dr. Goodman would say something like I have a pathological need to push others away, to not get close to anyone, hurt them before they can hurt me. Maybe he's right. Maybe I am part jellyfish, and all I have is poison running through my veins.

Chase doesn't look at me, doesn't even deign to move his head in my direction. "That's not true. I'm the wind beneath your wings," he says jokingly. Then he grows serious. "Besides, even if you didn't need me . . . maybe I need you."

***

From the Journal of Alice Monroe

Thanks to Jason, Cellie's new favorite pastime (aside from setting fires) was catching bugs. Sometimes she'd catch two different species, like a bee and a grasshopper, and then she'd shake the jar, agitating the bee so she could watch them fight. It was in these moments that I thought my emotional life might be less connected to Cellie's and more connected to the bugs she tortured.

At night, when the house was quiet and Candy had fallen asleep on the couch, the three of us would sneak out onto the roof and stargaze.

"Ooh, I hear crickets!" Cellie said one time. She scrambled off the roof, using a dead maple tree as a ladder.

Jason chuckled at her exuberance. He lay next to me, his gaze pointed at the blackened sky. Light pollution from the city obstructed most of the stars, but we could see some, and Jason told me that the stars that burned the brightest were the strongest ones. They were like us, he said, light shining through all the bad shit that humans created. He leaned over me.

"I'm so glad I found you again," he said. He touched my face, and I felt it all the way through me, to the ends of each strand of hair and the tips of each of my toes.

"Me too," I murmured, allowing my fingers to explore his face as well, to lightly graze the scar from Roman over his right eyebrow. I kissed his cheek, and there was a sharp intake of breath from both of us.

"I won't lose you again," he said as he traced my eyebrow. He said it in such a way that I thought it might literally kill him if we were ever separated. I could hear Cellie in the backyard, her small movements as she stalked her prey through the grass. She couldn't see us, because we were on the other side of the roof. The shelter from her watchful eyes made me feel safe and wild.

Jason buried his head in my hair and kissed me right behind my ear. Every one of his movements was an electric current running through me. He rose up so he was looking into my eyes. "You're so pretty," he whispered. His hand drifted down and splayed along my hip, brought our bodies so close that even the barest sliver of moonlight couldn't penetrate the small space between us. My hands combed through his hair, and his hands swept under my thin T-shirt. A million tiny flames sprang to life inside me. Every sense became heightened, the smell of dying grass from the yard below, the sound of the wind through the cottonwood trees, the feel of his skin against mine. I ached for him. We kissed, meeting each other halfway. It was as if we were trying to bridge the gap in all that time between us, make up for everything we'd lost. And I knew we were both thinking the same thing. It was such a waste, our being apart. His lips broke from mine, quickly traveling to my jaw, my neck.

The maple by the roof shook, and it was like a seismic shift. We tore away from each other. Cellie's voice quickly followed. "You should see how many I caught," she said, hoisting herself from the tree to the roof.

Jason grinned and leaped to his feet. He took her hand and helped her up the rest of the way. I rose up on my elbows. Cellie caught our labored breathing, and suspicion darkened her eyes. "What's going on?"

"Nothing," Jason said, not missing a beat. "Show me what you caught." Cellie waited a minute, her eyes still narrowed, and pointed at me. Jason picked up the jar and examined it under the moonlight. "Wow," he said. He put the jar down and lit up a cigarette. "You caught a bunch." He looked at her as if she had just lassoed the sun.

She bloomed under his attention, like a child with a piece of art-work on display. He asked what she was going to do with them, and she said she was going to wait until morning, leave them up on the roof, and then watch them fry as the sun rose.

We stayed up on the roof a little longer, until our eyes were heavy with sleep. The whole time Cellie sat between us, carefully watching. It was like she knew. She knew what I was feeling—that a beam of happiness as soft and shiny as the moonlight had found its way in. She couldn't wait to carve it out.

We climbed down from the roof and went to our rooms. When we were safely tucked in across from each other in our twin beds, Cellie spoke, her tone harsh and unforgiving. "You know he's just playing with you, right?"

I didn't know anything of the sort, but I didn't say so. I just stared at her, watched her face as she cut me down and sliced me up.

"You can't actually believe that he would want you or me. He feels sorry for us. But that's all."

She turned her back on me to face the wall. Anger and sadness ran through me, her words shredding my tiny ribbon of hope. Tears formed in the corners of my eyes and spilled over my cheeks. I sniffled.

Cellie sighed and got up from her bed. She touched my hair. "Don't cry, Allie. You have me, isn't that enough?" She climbed back into her bed, tossed and turned, and went to sleep.

It wasn't enough. It would never be enough. And Cellie wouldn't ever understand that because, to her, I was enough. Aside from setting fires and watching bugs squirm, I was the only thing she wanted. I tossed off my covers and crept barefoot out of the room.

Before I knew it, I was back up on the roof. The jar was exactly where she'd left it. The crickets chirped noisily, almost frantic, like they knew all about their impending doom and wished to sing one more time. One last song.

I picked up the jar and walked until I was a couple feet away from the roof's edge, where the browning, dying maple tree rested against the house. I unscrewed the lid of the jar and dumped the crickets out into the thicket of branches. *Cellie will be furious,* I thought.

Just as I was about to go back inside, a soft mewling stopped me. I searched it out. In the bushes up against the cracked yellow paint of the house was a small long-haired kitten. I scooped it up and peered into its dark eyes. It was mangled and flea-bitten, and it looked more criminal than cute. But it was mine. At the back of the house, across the lawn, there was a small rusted toolshed that nobody, except for Jason, ever used. I knew he'd never tell. Holding the kitten close, I made my way over the dry grass and into the shed. I deposited the kitten there, making sure there wasn't anything it could get into. I wished I could stay longer, let the kitten curl into my side and drift off to sleep, but Cellie waited.

That night, I tried to dream of crickets and the soft purrs of kittens. But all I dreamed of was Cellie. Cellie and her terrible love.

14

THE DOCTOR'S OFFICE

CHASE AND I WATCH THE MOVIE FOR A WHILE, SITTING IN COM-fortable silence. Sometime during it, I'm not sure when, his hand finds mine. We're sitting like this, with our fingers linked, when Donny comes to tell me it's time for my one-on-one with Dr. Goodman. I follow behind him and watch his mullet sway as he walks. When we get to the door, Donny knocks for me and Dr. Goodman opens up right away. He smiles warmly and pushes his glasses up from the bridge of his nose. "Right on time."

Like I had a choice. I shuffle into his office, hood still drawn tight around my face, my hands jammed into the pockets of my sweatshirt. On his desk I spy my stack of origami paper and a plas-tic ziplock bag containing my folded animals.

"Welcome back." He gestures to our usual positions and I fold myself into the chair, wishing I had the paper between my hands. "How are you feeling, Alice?"

How am I feeling? That's a complicated question. I'm not sure how to answer it. I pick through the emotions ranging from black sadness to grim hope. "Better," I lie. I'm not worse. Just the same.

He crosses his legs and reaches for a yellow legal pad. "I'd like for us to talk about what happened, what brought you to the point where you decided to cut your hair."

I shrug. "Just felt like a new look."

He scrutinizes me. "It's kind of an impetuous decision, don't you think?"

I ignore the question. "Can I have a piece of origami paper?" I rub my hands together, anticipating the smooth surface and sharp creases.

"In time, Alice. Right now I want you to focus."

I clench my fists.

"Let's talk about what happened leading up to the event. You went to Jason's funeral. How was it?"

"There wasn't a funeral." Only a gravedigger and a six-foot pile of dirt.

He writes something on the notepad. "Did anyone show up besides you and Sara?"

"No." I peer out the window at the steel mesh and the gray fog. "Sara didn't even come."

"Sara didn't go with you?" He sounds surprised.

"She parked by the gate. I asked her to stay in the car."

He sighs and lays down the pen. "Do you want to know what I think? I think something happened that day, something significant.

176

I think, perhaps, you recalled something you had repressed. How's your memory, Alice?"

Dim and cloudy around the edges. "I don't know."

He leans forward. "Did something happen during the funeral, Alice?"

"I'm not sure." I start to crumble, decay under his perpetually concerned face.

"I can help you, if you let me."

I don't think he can. I don't think anyone can. Maybe I belong here. Maybe this really is my punishment. *How could I love someone who was so bad?* Doubt washes over me and fills my lungs. No, nobody can help me. I rub my eyes. "Can I go back to my room now? I'm tired."

He leans back in his chair, coolly assessing me. "You're free to go whenever you wish."

I get up from the chair and wipe my palms on my scrubs. When I get to the door he stops me. "Alice." I turn around. He holds two paper cups aloft. I go to him and take the cups from his hands. The nightly white pills make me sleepy. In the mornings when I wake after taking them I feel disoriented, queasy, and I have to remind myself of where I am, who I am. In one fluid motion I pop the pill in my mouth. Usually I tuck it in my upper lip, but this time I take the swallow of water and let it slide down my throat. And in the morning I won't mind if I can't remember. Because that's the point. Tonight, I want to forget.

When I get back to my room, Amelia's already asleep. She

sleeps a lot now. When she's not asleep, she's distant. I'm scared to talk to her, afraid she's angry at me about the razors. I climb into bed and stare out the window. The moon is full, its face glassy and bright. I wish I could howl at it.

"What do you think she's in for?" Chase points to a chubby blond girl in the corner. It's Monday. Four days since my freak-out. I'm still red-banded, forced to wear ratty scrubs, and Amelia and I still haven't spoken. We orbit each other, existing in the same space but never interacting. Chase hasn't left my side.

An intern social worker is leading us in arts and crafts. We're supposed to be making collages, but Chase and I are playing a game instead. We're trying to guess why people have been committed to Savage Isle. So far we have one ax murderer, one phantom pooper, and someone who keeps jars of spit under his bed. Chase seems to have an odd fascination with bodily functions today.

I chew the inside of my cheek and try to form a hypothesis about the chubby blond girl. "I don't know. She looks pretty normal." I use my kid-friendly scissors to cut out the eyes of a model in a magazine. "But looks can be deceiving . . . I got it! I bet she's a barfer." I stick my finger down my throat to emphasize my point.

"No. You got it all wrong. You're looking for the obvious. You've got to look below the surface. She's got sexual deviant written all over her."

"Sexual deviant?" I cock my head.

"Yeah, you know . . ." He waggles his brows at me suggestively.

I open my mouth for a comeback, but Chase's huge roommate draws my attention. He sits at the next table over and quietly mutters at his collage. He raises his voice, slams his fist down, and says, "I hate fucking forks." A tech comes over and places a hand on his shoulder to calm him. I watch for another minute and then go back to gluing the eyes into my collage.

"That's fucked up." Chase gestures at my collage. I look down at what I've created, a face of a woman with huge offset eyes. It looks like a schizophrenic Picasso painting, and that makes me laugh, on the inside of course.

I smile, sweet and buttery. "I made it for you." I thrust the picture at Chase.

He chuckles and starts to say something, but we're interrupted.

"Alice and Chase. How are my two favorite patients?" Dr. Goodman stands in front of us, his hands jammed into his pockets.

Chase stiffens a little in his seat and avoids eye contact. *"Asshole,"* he mutters under his breath. I wonder what Chase's deal is with Dr. Goodman. He's got a serious case of the hates for him.

"I'm sorry, Chase. I didn't catch that."

"I said, *swell.*"

Doc turns toward me, effectively walling Chase out. The reflection of my collage glints in his glasses. "Alice, we're not going to be having our regular one-on-one this evening. We will be meeting, but Sara and your attorney are coming to visit, and they want to go over some things with us. Donny will be able to show you the way. But since we aren't going to be able to talk one-on-one today,

I wanted to check-in and see if you'd like to chat about anything beforehand."

I shake my head, careful to avoid Dr. Goodman's eyes. I tell him I'll see him later. He gives my collage one more lingering look before moving on to someone else.

Chase watches Dr. Goodman's retreating back. "What do you think that's about?"

"Don't know, don't care."

Chase looks like he wants to ask more questions, but since I'm in no mood to discuss the good doctor, I decide to distract Chase instead. "Tell me a secret," I say.

His eyes flicker with surprise, but then warmth seeps into them. He uncurls his fists. All the curiosity seems zapped from him. It worked. He gives me half a smile. "A secret?"

For some reason my palms start to sweat a little. I rub them on my scrubs. "Yeah, tell me something nobody here knows."

He contemplates this for a minute, his Adam's apple bobbing up and down as he swallows meditatively. "I'm, like, really awesome at baseball."

"You're humble, too." I instantly regret my sarcasm. "I'm sorry," I say.

He nods, seemingly appeased. "I could've gone pro."

"What happened?"

He spins his finger, indicating the hospital around us.

I chew the inside of my cheek, unsure what to say. "I'm sure plenty of baseball players have criminal records." I meant to offer the statement as comfort, but it comes out all wrong. Instead, it sounds as if I'm fishing for information. Which maybe I was, on some subconscious level.

His mouth opens and then shuts. *He thought I didn't know.* I'm ashamed at my lack of tact, even more so when he looks sad and bows his head. "Yeah, I guess they do," he says in the faintest of voices. He shakes off his sadness and gives me another trademark smile. "Now you. You tell me a secret."

It seems unfair to deny him. "I've never seen the ocean."

He snorts in disbelief. "We're, like, two hours from the coast. You've never been to the beach?"

I shake my head at him. Once, Jason, Cellie, and I skipped school to go, but we didn't make it all the way there. I can't help thinking how things might have been different if we'd made it to the coast that day. I ask him to tell me another secret, but this time I'm more specific. I want to know what he's most afraid of.

He fingers the scraps on the table. "I fear . . ." He swallows and then clears his throat. When he speaks, it sounds like his mouth is full of paste. "I fear never being able to forgive myself."

We keep going like this. Listing our fears to each other. But we don't prod, ask why or what makes it so. Which makes it more comfortable. We share things on the surface and dance around the darker parts. Carefully we avoid things like the exact reason why Chase is at Savage Isle and my true plan to exact revenge on Cellie.

The intern social worker claps her hands and starts to speak. She applauds us for all the work we've done and says she hopes we've found our time with her helpful.

When we start to clean up, Chase's hand stops mine. "You

going to let me keep that, or what?" His eyes drift to my horrific collage.

I look down at the piece of paper, at the small face of the woman and her too-large eyes — eyes that originally belonged to a different face. I shake my head at him. "It's ugly."

He looks at me like I've disappointed him. "Haven't you ever heard that beauty is in the eye of the beholder?"

I want to tell him he's an even worse poet than he is a comedian. But he seems sincere, so I bite my tongue; still, I don't give Chase the collage. Instead I crumple it up and bury it in the trash.

Despite what he said, I know better. The collage is ugly. And there's enough ugliness in this world.

From the Journal of Alice Monroe

"You're never going to find it." On the shore Cellie laughed, mocking me. Through every ripple in the river I could feel her sick joy. Waves lapped against my face as I tried to stay afloat. Overhead, the sun was just beginning to rise, etching the gray sky with hazy bursts of pink and orange.

Jason stood next to Cellie on the shore. "What did you fucking do?" he said. He was mad, as mad as I'd ever seen him. The chords in his neck stood out, and a muscle ticked along his jaw.

I held my breath and went back under the water. It was cold, so cold that my teeth hurt from banging against one another, and I couldn't feel my legs anymore. Still, I propelled my body down and furiously searched the sandy bottom. Cellie was getting worse, and lately her rage, her chaos, her madness had been directed at me. I pretended I didn't know why, but I did. She was angry that Jason and I were becoming a couple. The closer Jason and I got, the more volatile Cellie became.

I couldn't tell what hurt more, my body from the physical exertion of swimming and diving—or my heart.

I stayed under for as long as possible. My eyes stung from the dirty water, but I kept them open, scanning the bottom for something that didn't belong there. My lungs burned and the carbon dioxide in them begged for release. I was forced to the top. My body broke the surface and I inhaled a huge breath. Jason shook his head and crouched by the river, his combat boots meeting the waves. He lit a cigarette and watched me carefully.

"Please help me," I yelled, sucking in a mouthful of water, almost choking. My body was getting tired, and the special blue dress I'd worn that day, the first day of our sophomore year, kept getting tangled in my legs, threatening to take me under.

"This is ridiculous. You're not going to find it," Jason said. Still, he put out his cigarette, slipped off his shoes and shirt, and joined me in the water.

"He's right, Alice. You're never going to find it," Cellie taunted. She made no move to help, just sat on the shore, sifting sand through her pale toes.

While Jason swam toward me, I dived back down. I couldn't afford the time it would take to wait for him. It was hard to see in the murky water, so I relied on my hands to do most of the exploring. I reached for another rock, but instead of cold granite my hand met a soft burlap sack. The relief was instant but fleeting. It had been too long. Too many minutes had passed. Still, I reached for the sack, my fingers searching, just to make sure this was what I'd been looking for.

I swam to the surface and held up the sack. It was sickeningly heavy. "I found it," I yelled. It had been cinched with a thin piece of rope. My numb hands fumbled with the knots, trying to get them undone, but it was impossible to tread water and work at the knot at the same time. Once or twice my head slipped under as I continued to hold the sack aloft.

"You're going to drown yourself." Jason grabbed the tops of my thighs and wrapped my legs around him. "I got you." I worked at the knot, my teeth chattering as he swam us back to the shore. When we got to a place where he could stand, he began to walk. I tried to slip off of him but he held me tight. "No," he said. "Just hold on, baby."

By the time he set me down on land, I'd untied two of the three knots. My hands shook as I undid the final one. I couldn't tell if the tremor was a reaction to the cold water or a response to what I knew I'd find inside that burlap sack. The knot unraveled easily.

Jason picked up his pack of cigarettes from the pocket of his discarded shirt. He tapped one out and lit it.

I opened the sack and reached inside. My fingers met sodden fur. There was no movement, no subtle sign of life. It was too late. I pulled out the ball of fur. The soft, long-haired cat I'd found and secretly kept in Candy's toolshed for almost a year seemed small in my hands.

"No." I brought the cat to my chest and pressed my cheek to its head. A sob racked my body. I didn't expect to find it alive, but I had hoped.

Cellie snickered behind me. "Poor Alice. It struggled a lot."

Jason shrugged his shirt back on. "This is really fucking sick, Cellie. You couldn't just let her have the cat?"

Cellie's face changed, crumbled like old paper in a book. Her lower lip trembled. "I'm sorry. It was supposed to be a joke. I'm sorry." She crossed her arms over her chest. "Please don't be mad at me. I'm sorry."

I rocked back and forth. I held the cat close with one hand and with the other dug into the soft, sandy earth. Cellie grazed my shoulder. "Don't touch me," I yelled, throwing a handful of sand at her face. She was surprised because I'd never done something like that before. Her shocked expression was enough to break me. But something inside of me had cracked open and I felt wild. I scrambled to my feet. I picked up handful after handful of sand and threw them at her. All the while I clutched the cat to my breast, wishing I could pump the life from my own heart into its body. "You ruin everything. I hate you. You're ruining me," I cried, hurtling handfuls of sand in her direction.

Covering her eyes with her hands, Cellie backed away. "I said I was sorry, Allie." But she wasn't. I knew her words were hollow. Meaningless. Empty air.

Jason grabbed me around the waist. For a moment I struggled against his hold, but then I turned into him and sobbed into his shoulder. "She's ruining me!"

"Shhh," Jason said, running a hand through my soaked hair. "Cellie, you should go."

"Don't make me leave. Allie?" She tried touching my shoulder again but I recoiled, pressed myself farther into Jason's body.

"I'll find you another cat," he whispered.

There was a crunch of sand and Cellie was running down the beach, into the woods, and out of sight.

Sand and sorrow clung to my body. Jason sat and cradled me on his lap, rocked me back and forth while I cried. The whole time he ran his fingers through my hair, ran his thumb over my pulse, tried to smooth away all my rough edges. He licked the water from my face and sucked droplets of the dirty river from my lower lip.

We buried the cat in the forest next to the riverbed. Our drenched clothing made our movements stiff, but we managed. My blue dress was ruined. It didn't matter. I'd never wear it again, anyway. It would always serve as a bitter reminder of the day.

When it was done, Jason and I walked from the woods, hands intertwined. I didn't know where he began and I ended. It was then I realized three very important things. One: I loved him like a fever —hot, bright, and maybe a little dangerous. Two: I loved him more than I loved Cellie. Three: someday Cellie might try to kill me like she had killed that cat.

15

COMPLICITY

RIGHT AFTER DINNER, AT EXACTLY SIX THIRTY, DONNY COMES for me. We walk down the hallway, past Dr. Goodman's office, all the way to the end, where there is a meeting room. I haven't been in this room before. It's small and windowless. A radiator hisses and gurgles on the far wall. Donny follows me inside and takes up residence by the door.

Sara and Dr. Goodman are already here. With them is a man I don't recognize, a man who is the embodiment of messiness, from his wrinkled suit to his unkempt hair. All three of them sit on one side of the table. On the other side there's a solitary chair, which I assume is for me. Nurse Dummel stands in the corner. A capped syringe peeks out from her front scrub pocket and she holds a radio in her hand, thumb hovering over the call button. All in all it's pretty crowded. I feel their stares on me like a noose around my neck.

"Alice." Sara stands and smiles. She opens her arms to me and

I move toward her, but Dr. Goodman motions for her to sit down and she obeys. I frown at him. Sara seems anxious, even more worried than usual.

"Have a seat, Alice," Dr. Goodman says.

The chair scrapes across the floor as I pull it out and take a seat.

"Before we begin, I'd like to go over some rules for our meeting. For the safety and security of our guests, there will be no touching. If at any time I feel that this meeting is becoming unsafe for any of us, it will end, and we will postpone until another time, when you're more fit. I'd also like to say, for the record, that I believe it's too soon to discuss this matter. But your attorney, Alice"—Dr. Goodman nods to the man sitting beside Sara—"is convinced this matter is of some urgency, so I've allowed it. Do you understand the rules of the meeting?"

I nod and so does everyone else, even Nurse Dummel.

"Excellent." Dr. Goodman steeples his fingers. "Alice, do you remember Robert Cohen, your court-appointed attorney?"

I give Cohen a small smile. "I'm sorry, I don't remember you."

Cohen extends a hand for me to shake. My eyes flick to Dr. Goodman, and Cohen withdraws his hand, runs it through his hair. "We met in the hospital," he prompts, as if that'll jog my memory.

Dr. Goodman answers for me. "Alice doesn't remember very much from her hospital stay. Part of her therapy here is helping her to regain that memory."

Cohen nods in understanding. "Yes, well, it looks as if you're recovering quite nicely." Unbidden, the burns on my shoulders start to itch, and I resist the urge to scratch them beneath my shirt. The radiator kicks on and a small bead of sweat forms on Cohen's upper lip. He pops open the gold clasps of the briefcase that rests in front of him on the table. "Anyway, I guess we should get down to business." He pulls out a thick pile of bound papers. "The district attorney has made a very generous offer regarding your case." He slides the papers over to me.

I take the papers and move them in front of me. I give him a puzzled look. "I don't understand."

"Yes, well." Cohen shifts in his seat. He takes a stained handkerchief from his pocket and wipes perspiration from his forehead. "I apologize. I'm doing a crummy job of explaining this . . ."

Dr. Goodman cuts him off. "What Mr. Cohen means, Alice, is that there have been some recent developments in your case. Mr. Cohen has been working with the district attorney on a plea bargain for you, and today they were able to reach an agreement."

"Okay," I say.

"Unfortunately, the agreement is time-sensitive and expires quite soon. That's why we had to meet this evening."

"Right, thank you," Cohen says. "Yes, the plea bargain. I believe this is a great opportunity for you, Alice. What's so great about this is that you won't serve any jail time. Your sentence will be here at Savage Isle and will be determined by your doctors rather than a judge or jury."

I trace the words on the paper. They blend together in a jumble of legal jargon I don't understand. My fingers land on an acronym. "What does NGRI mean?"

More sweat gathers on Cohen's upper lip, and his mouth fumbles over the words. "NGRI is a legal term and it means that the defendant, *you,* isn't responsible for their actions due to a mental or psychological condition. And, well, since you can't remember your actions that night—we've got a solid NGRI case."

I suck in an uneasy breath. Why is he dancing around the words? "What does NGRI stand for, though, *exactly?*" I lick my lips and stare at Cohen.

Cohen shrinks a little before he speaks. "NGRI stands for 'not guilty by reason of insanity.'"

I push the papers away from me like they're going to burn my hand.

Cohen stops the stack from sliding farther, his hand landing on the sheets like a paperweight.

"I am not insane."

Cohen stutters and his face goes red and blotchy.

"Alice, I think you should consider the plea bargain," Dr. Goodman interjects.

Consider it? How can I? My freshman year in English class we read *The Crucible.* Well, I didn't read it. I watched the movie, the one with Winona Ryder. In one of the final scenes, John Proctor is convicted of witchcraft and contemplates signing a confession. He makes a big speech about his name, about how he's been stripped of everything, and he cries, "Leave me my name!" I am *so* John Proctor right now.

"No," I say matter-of-factly.

"No?" Dr. Goodman furrows his brow.

"I'm not pleading insanity and I'm not signing the plea bargain."

"Alice, I really believe this is in your best interest," Dr. Goodman continues.

"I don't think it is." I stand.

Cohen looks anxiously around the room. Donny takes a step forward, but Dr. Goodman waves him off.

"Please, Alice." Sara speaks, soft and low, and her voice slices through me. I slump back into my chair. Sara slides the papers over to me. Just before I take them from her, she lays her hand on top of mine. I examine her hands, hands that hold the life I could have had. Her nails are clean and her skin is smooth, totally unblemished. Dr. Goodman sits straighter in his seat, but he doesn't draw Sara's hand away like before. "Read them," she says. And I do, because it's Sara who's asked. Because I could have been her in another life.

It takes me twenty minutes to read through the whole plea bargain, and most of it I don't understand. Of course Cellie's named in it. Words like *accomplice*, *accidental*, and *unaware* float up at me. Cohen sweats so much I think he might be getting dehydrated. Once in a while I look up. Sara and Dr. Goodman are watching me closely. I get to the last page, where there is an empty line waiting for my signature. The DA has already signed. I stare at it until my eyes water and everything blurs.

Sara squeezes my hand. "I think it's for the best," she says. "You can put all this behind you, focus on getting better. You'll be eighteen soon, and you can grow so much in a year. It's not too late to start looking at colleges, thinking about your future."

I bow my head and a few tears slip down my cheeks. I wipe them away before anyone can see. *Suck it up, Alice.* "All I have to do is sign?"

"It's your choice, like everything else. *You* have control," Sara says. "If you really focus, really open yourself up, you could be out of here soon. You could start a whole new life."

What she says is tempting. It's like the apple in the Garden of Eden. Except we all know how that turned out. She's promising me the same things Jason promised right before our Great Escape—a future full of paths that lead away from Cellie. All I have to do is sign my name. Confess to a crime I didn't commit. Acknowledge that I played a small but unwilling part in my best friend's death. Admit that I'm unstable and maybe, just maybe, a little bit dangerous.

But Jason was wrong, and so is Sara. There will be no refuge from Cellie. I picture her pacing in her little D ward cell, mumbling incoherently, smashing the flies on the wall and waiting, waiting for her opening, when the door is left unattended or a guard takes his eyes off her. That's when she'll come for me.

My hand picks up the pen that has appeared next to me as if by magic. Signing this document is merely a means to an end, I realize. But not the end Sara, Dr. Goodman, and Mr. Cohen have in mind. I won't get to Cellie while I'm wearing a red wristband or while I'm locked up behind bars. And I have to get to her before she gets to me. My hand hovers over the paper. I bite my lip. Part of me feels like I deserve this. This is the price I pay. I loved her. And in loving her I was complicit. What was it Chase said? *I fear never being able to forgive myself.* Me too.

I scribble my name on the designated line. And just like that, I'm one step closer to Cellie and absolution.

All the air seems to rush back into the room. Cohen snatches the contract up like he thinks I'm going to change my mind, black out my name. He stuffs it into his briefcase, and I can tell he's eager to go home and wash the smell of the hospital from his body. I wonder if he has a family, a couple of kids and a wife. Maybe he'll hug them a little tighter tonight and tell them about the lost girl with the pyromaniac twin who lives in a mental hospital.

Sara hugs me, once again ignoring Dr. Goodman's "no touching" rule. Cohen and Sara leave together, and I resist the sudden urge to wrap myself around Sara and beg her to take me with her.

"You've made excellent progress today, Alice." Dr. Goodman motions Nurse Dummel forward. "I think you're ready to be off restricted status." Nurse Dummel pulls a pair of shiny silver scissors from her lab-coat pocket. She grabs my wrist and the cold metal sinks into my skin.

In one swift motion my red wristband is cut and a yellow one replaces it. Involuntarily I rub where the scissors pressed into me. Doc dismisses me and Donny takes me back to my room.

Amelia lies on her bed. A magazine obstructs her face, and she doesn't lower it to acknowledge my entrance. I crawl into my bed, pulling the sheets up over my head, and let the silence between us grow heavy, full of unsaid things.

Later on, Nurse Dummel knocks. She's brought me a neat, laundered pile of my clothes. On top of the pile is a plastic bag with my little paper zoo and a stack of brightly colored origami paper. She hands them to me and I place them on the dresser. Electing to stay in the ratty scrubs a little while longer, I sit down on the edge of my bed and stare at the stack until the colors run together. For some reason, some reason I can't even begin to describe, the thought of changing back into my clothes, despite their clean, fresh scent, makes me feel dirty.

I'm surprised when the mattress begins to sink under Amelia's weight. She's sitting beside me now. A red band encircles her wrist. I crack my knuckles. "I told them about the razors," I confess. "I'm sorry if it got you in more trouble."

"It's okay." She nudges my shoulder. "Thanks for the mouse." I hadn't been sure if she'd found the gray origami mouse I'd made for her, but I guess she did. She gets up and goes to the dresser, riffles through it, and comes back with the paper mouse in hand.

I take it from her and touch one of the triangle ears. "What should we call him?"

"How about Clovis?"

I laugh. "Clovis is a terrible name."

She scoffs and touches her chest in mock indignation. "Clovis is my grandfather's name. It means fighter." She grins, plucks the mouse from my hand, and turns to the dresser.

"I really am sorry, you know," I say softly.

Her shoulders stiffen and then relax. "It's okay, Alice. Seriously. I don't know what I was thinking stealing those razors." She pauses and sets the mouse down. "I have a bad history with sharp things."

FROM THE JOURNAL OF ALICE MONROE

At exactly 12:01 a.m., the day after our sixteenth birthday, Cellie and I celebrated our "un-birthday" with Jason. He bought us each a pie with a lattice crust and lit a single candle in the middle. As the weather got colder and Mother Nature pulled the curtain from summer to fall, we fixed up the shed in the backyard of Candy's house. We made it into our hangout, putting a little piece of ourselves into it. Jason spray-painted the walls with silhouettes of children holding guns. Cellie collected dolls and stuffed animals from around the neighborhood and strung them up from the ceiling. And I made white paper doves and hung them between the doll heads and muddy Care Bears.

We blew out our candles while Jason lit up a joint. He took a long drag, and the air became supercharged with the smell of marijuana and gasoline. The shed was also where Jason liked to keep his accelerants.

I looked down at my pie. "Shit, we don't have any forks."

Cellie jumped up. "I'll go get some." Ever since she had drowned my cat, she'd been nicer to me, trying to build a bridge across her treachery. I knew her madness well enough by then to know it came in waves. Right then, it was low tide.

As soon as the door shut behind her, Jason offered me the joint. Normally I would have rejected his offer, scrunched up my nose, and turned my head away, but that night I wanted to try it. Wanted to know what it felt like. We exchanged it over the pie, and a little ash fell right into the middle. I held it like a cigarette and took a long inhale, making little *oh*s as I exhaled, as if I'd been smoking for years. I grinned at him. The smoke traveled through my body like a curling vine.

"Classy, baby," he said.

I smiled in a different way and with my free hand dug into the pie. I brought a gooey scoop of blackberry filling and doughy crust to my lips and sucked it off my fingers.

Jason's gaze became heated. He groaned and flopped backwards onto a beanbag chair. I stamped the joint out and threw my head back and laughed. Everything seemed so funny and I felt so light. I crawled toward him, up over his body, until my legs were on either side of his hips.

His eyes were half lidded and his arm snaked around to hold me. "You're an animal," he said.

I laughed again, this time lower, huskier. Then I smeared some of the pie onto his lips.

"You wanna play?" he asked. His mouth curved into a wicked

smile. Then, quicker than a flash of lightning, he flipped me over onto my back so that he straddled me. His hands wrapped around my wrists. "Jesus Christ." He leaned down. His voice became almost reverent. "I love you in the fucking worst way." He licked the pie from my lips and then moved in for a much deeper kiss.

The door to the shed creaked open. Something dropped, a soft clatter of metal hitting concrete. The door banged closed, and then there was the sound of footsteps fleeing into silence.

For a moment, worry made my body go limp. I thought I should go after Cellie. Make her understand that I needed them both. Tell her that I remembered the last bite of cake and I would never forget. But then Jason's lips were on my throat. His hands were in my hair and his body was moving over mine. And the worry melted away under all of his heat. And I didn't care. I didn't care. All I could think was, *I am his. From the east to the west, I am his. I am his.*

———◆———

CHAPTER
16

HIP-HOP AND HAPPINESS

TUESDAY IS FIELD TRIP DAY, AND SINCE I'VE BEEN UPGRADED TO yellow-wristband status, I'm allowed to go. Amelia is still red-banded and she pouts.

"I'll bring you back something," I say. We're in our room, and I've just finished changing out of the ratty scrubs and into my regular clothes.

"This is such bullshit. You cut your hair *after* I freaked. I should've gotten a yellow wristband by now." My guess is that she's serving double time, one sentence for the stunt with Elvis and another for stealing the razors. Even though we talked it through and I apologized, she still seems fragile and not entirely herself. The Quiet Room does that to you.

The red band on her wrist slides down. Her scars look whiter today. She's lost some weight, and the scars stand out against her parched skin, puckered and angry. I can count at least five of them crisscrossing over one another underneath the cigarette burns. Funny, I hadn't noticed them before.

I fiddle with the edge of my hoodie and think about the deal I made with the DA and the relief in Sara's and Dr. Goodman's eyes when I signed the plea bargain. How I traded my name for some sheets of origami paper and a yellow wristband. I tell myself it's for the greater good. I need to keep one step ahead of Cellie, and I can't do that if I'm on total lockdown. Grandpa used to say that sometimes you have to wave a white flag in order to win the war. The plea bargain is collateral damage.

Amelia makes a sound that is part growl, part whimper. She crosses her arms, sniffles, and flops back onto her bed. "It's not fair. I wish my parents would come get me already. They're supposed to be coming, you know."

It's all she talks about now, how her parents are coming. She clings to it. I don't point out to Amelia that even if her parents did come, they wouldn't be able to see her. She wouldn't even know they were here. They would be turned away at the door. Part of me wonders if she has parents at all. They've never visited. And I've seen kids like her before in foster homes. Always talking about how their parents would come soon. They'd watch through the windows for familiar cars to turn down the street and then feel disappointed when nobody came. Jason used to be like that. And yet—I still can't reconcile that hopeful young boy with the twisted man he became.

I sit next to her. "It's not fair," I agree. "If I could, I would give you my wristband."

She smiles, wan and distant. I wish I had the old Amelia back. The one who called Monica a muff eater and said she wore dirty underwear. "Who knows," she says. "Maybe by the time you get back, I'll be gone."

Her words settle into the pit of my stomach. I say goodbye to her, promising one more time to bring back something from the outside. I'm not sure what it will be, since I don't have any money. Maybe a leaf, a speck of dirt, a breath of fresh air?

I meet up with the other patients who are going. We congregate in the rec room. All of us are outfitted with ankle monitors and given very specific instructions about appropriate behavior in public. A guy with dreads makes a lewd jester with his hands. Chase stands a few feet away from me, his big headphones looped around his neck. Dr. Goodman and the social worker intern are going, along with a handful of techs and nurses, Nurse Dummel included. All the staff are dressed in plain clothes.

We get checked out and board a yellow school bus. I shuffle down the narrow aisle, turn into a middle seat, and plop down. Someone has taken a Sharpie and written on the worn green vinyl back of the seat facing me: I PEED WHERE YOU'RE SITTING. My mouth curves into a smile. I put my legs up so my feet cover the majority of the letters. Chase falls into the seat beside me. Monica passes and turns her nose up at us.

"What do you think she's in for?" Chase whispers.

I chew my lip. "I don't know. She probably couldn't stop drawing dicks on everything."

Chase laughs. "You wanna listen to some music?"

"Depends."

"On what?"

"What you got?"

"I'm feeling some gangsta rap today, what do you say?"

"I say the filthier the better."

"I thought you might say something like that."

Chase puts on the headphones but turns one out so it faces me. I lean over and press my ear against the cushioned head. He turns the volume up. A beat starts, and out come the most appalling lyrics I've ever heard. I've never heard the words *mother, balls,* and *toilet seat* strung together in such a creative way. We listen all the way to the botanical gardens. Chase taps his fingers against his leg in rhythm and I lean against him, wishing that this day would last forever. That I could feel the wind through the open window, smell the vinyl seats and pouring rain for all of time. That this calm happiness would never go away, that I could capture this moment for life.

FROM THE JOURNAL OF ALICE MONROE

Cellie, Jason, and I had stopped at a convenience store, some no-name truck stop on Highway 101, on our way to the beach. Cellie loved truck stops. We were skipping school. Or rather, Cellie and Jason were skipping school. I was just tagging along, unable to resist

Jason's sweet smile and the dimple that appeared in his cheek. Plus, I wouldn't be missing that much in class. Jason had called in a bomb threat (Cellie's idea), so classes would be out for a while.

Jason's arm was around me, anchoring me to his side. In front of us, Cellie twirled, laughing. "Whoops," she said as she accidentally knocked a bottle of liquor off the shelf.

Jason chuckled. The guy at the register, who looked like he had spent too many years inhaling gas fumes, frowned. He went to the back, grabbed a broom, and started to clean it up. Cellie stood close to the guy. A little too close. She flirted with him, giggled, and touched his chest. While he was distracted, Jason went behind the counter and stuffed cigarettes, money, and lottery tickets into his pockets. I hung back, closer to Cellie. Even though I felt safer by Jason, I thought the guy was safer with me closer to Cellie. That way I could interfere if she went too far. The guy took off his hat, rubbed the back of his neck. His gas-stained work shirt had the name *Earl* embroidered on it. "You sure you're eighteen?" Earl asked Cellie.

"Almost eighteen." She looked at him with big, wide eyes and twirled a lock of hair around her finger. We had just turned seventeen and were nowhere close to eighteen.

"Well, then . . ." He shuffled his feet. When his head came back up there was something wrong. Tension filled his face and his body went stiff. Cellie noticed. Her gaze followed his. He was staring into the circular mirror that was hung up in the corner of the shop, right above the beer case. The convex mirror gave a three-quarter view of the store, and right in the middle of the image was Jason, hands in the cash drawer, an unlit cigarette dangling from his mouth. Cellie's mouth formed a little *oh*.

"Time to go, Allie." She yanked my arm, pulled me along with her, inadvertently or maybe purposefully putting me between her and Earl.

Even though Earl was a little slow on the uptake, he was fast to react. He grabbed my arm, *hard*. "Where do you think you're going?" he asked, his breath stale and sour. He reminded me of Roman. I winced.

Jason was on him in an instant. He leaped over the counter, overturning the cash drawer and spilling candy in his wake. "Keep your fucking hands off her."

Earl's hand bit into my skin, and the flesh turned a muddy purple around where his fingers pressed. "Jason." I was scared. Big tears formed in my eyes. I wasn't tough like Cellie. If Earl were holding her, she would have spat in his face and kneed him in the balls.

Before I knew it, before I even had time to blink, Jason was on Earl. Cellie, too. She scratched his face and kicked his shins. Earl's hold on me was tight and when he started to waver, to tumble like a tower in an earthquake, I fell with him. All the way down we went. Cellie helped me roll away, and together we scrambled up until we were sitting, backs pressed against the glass refrigerators.

Stunned, we watched Jason pound on Earl. Until Earl's face turned a muddy purple that matched the bruises on my skin. Until

Earl's arms dropped, no longer able to block his face. Until Earl was completely still and Jason's rage was exhausted. The sound of violence echoed. Fist hitting a cheek, breaking bone, crunching like rocks thrown through glass. And then all of a sudden it was quieter than freshly fallen snow.

Jason touched my face and it was wet, from my tears and the blood on his hands. "Are you all right?" he asked.

I flinched and turned away. For some reason all I could see was Roman's face layered on top of Jason's. It was the first time I remember being afraid of him. Afraid and disgusted.

"I think you killed him," Cellie said right beside me. She stared at Earl with hungry curiosity.

Jason glanced over his shoulder at Earl, who lay in an awkward position. "He's still breathing." Jason helped Cellie to her feet. "We should get out of here." He held out a hand to me. "Cops might come." But I didn't take his hand. I stood up on my own, eyes trained on Earl's body.

"He asked for it, Allie," Cellie said.

Does someone ever ask to get beaten within an inch of his life? Jason lit up a cigarette. The blood from his hands smeared on the paper. He smoked it, the red drying—burning up and becoming ash. "We got to go, baby. He'll be all right."

I still didn't move. My feet had grown roots through the tiled floor.

He sighed. "Look, if it'll make you feel better, we'll call 911 as soon as we're down the road, give them the address."

I was frozen. A block of ice settled on my chest, and my blood ran cold. Earl was *so* still. His breathing was *so* shallow.

Someway, somehow, I made it back to the car, slow and stumbling and disbelieving. We drove off. Jason didn't do as he had promised. He didn't stop to call 911. He kept going and I watched the trees blur together, seeing them through a red, watery haze.

CHAPTER
17

THE GARDEN

THE JAPANESE BOTANICAL GARDEN IS LIKE A SYMPHONY FOR the eyes. Even though it's winter, bright colors are everywhere. They layer and bleed into each other, creating a rich palate of every shade of green, red, yellow, brown, and gray you can imagine. The clouds above us are heavy with rain, but for the moment it's dry. A docent meets us at the gate. She's old and seems happily oblivious to the fact that the kids in front of her are from Savage Isle. She leads us on a tour, pointing out plants and the importance of balance and symmetry in Japanese gardens. The techs, nurses, and Dr. Goodman fan out, corralling our group between them. Chase and I hang to the back, closest to Donny.

The rain has touched everything in the garden. Little droplets rest on the leaves and glisten on the gravel path. The docent stops the group to point out something. I stare into a puddle at my reflection. I push the sweatshirt hood off my head. I think about how Jason had loved my hair, loved running his fingers through it. He said it reminded him of dark wood, of the soil in a dense forest. Who'd ever heard of dirt being beautiful?

Outside the garden, beyond the wall, a truck zooms by, a big one, so big you can feel its two-ton weight in the shaking concrete.

"I might be a killer," I say.

Chase cocks a brow at me, but he doesn't look surprised, only mildly interested. He's used to me now, my offhanded comments, the moments when I space out, my dirty mouth.

"Might be?"

We've been given twenty minutes of semi-unsupervised time in the garden. The techs, nurses, and Dr. Goodman carefully walk the walled perimeter.

I secure my hood on my head. "Yeah. I'm not sure."

Chase veers right, leads us over an arched bridge and into a separate garden with a shoji screened pagoda and koi pond. "Well, it would probably be something you'd remember, don't you think? Like getting a tattoo on your face or riding a bike. You never forget shit like that."

I chuckle and don't tell him that I never learned how to ride a bike. I walk toward the pagoda, run my fingers over the fragile shoji screen paper. The pagoda was built over the koi pond, and fish the color of orange and red poppies dart in and out of view. As the fish move through the water, their bodies make tinkling noises that are like the softest lullaby. "They pinned Jason's death on me. They offered me a plea bargain—not guilty by reason of insanity."

Chase screws up his face. "Jesus," he says, and steps into the pagoda.

"I took it." I watch his reaction carefully, waiting for the horror, for the judgment to wash over him.

The shoji screen makes a shadow and plays with his face, so that I can't see how he reacts. "Why?"

I step into the enclosure with him. The pagoda smells of freshly cut cedar, of lemon oil and rainwater. It is blissful, heavenly. "We would've had to go to court, to trial, and Cellie would be there. And I could go to jail. With the NGRI plea, I stay in Savage Isle, and I might be able to get out sooner." Or get to Cellie sooner.

"You think you're crazy?" He takes off his hat and runs his fingers through his hair.

Images flash before my eyes: black-and-white snapshots that bleed color—Earl's still body, purple and mashed. Cellie's wicked smile. Jason smoking a bloody cigarette. "I don't know." A shudder runs through me. "I don't think I'm crazy. But I think there's something wrong with me. I think there's something dark inside of me that attracts the wrong people and then makes me care about them." A tear slips down my cheek. God, how many times have I cried in front of Chase?

"So what does that say about me?" Chase stands still in the middle of the pagoda, hands jammed in his pockets, hat back on. His face is shadowed again, this time by the bill of his hat, so that I can't see what he means, what he's really asking.

"You?"

"Yeah, me. You said there's something wrong with you—and with who you choose to care about. What does that say about me? About you and me?" He's mad. I've seen him angry before, once, in the field when I thought he was Jason, all lit up and electric. He was mad then because he was confused and scared. But this is a different kind of anger, one that is born from hurt.

Voices drift over us, over the plants and through the shoji screen, but they're far away. We're still alone. I back up a step until I'm pressed against one of the wood columns that frame the screens. "I don't know."

He steps closer, into my space. He tilts his head. "Am I the wrong people?"

My nose fills with the sweet scent of fabric softener and something else, something that is uniquely Chase. I think of all the faces of Chase—his calm mask when he came to my room and gave me an awful eighties mix to listen to. His lighthearted expression when he tells the world's worst jokes. I compare them to Jason's faces, his look of desire when he watched Roman's house burn. His hard features that never bent to guilt or sorrow when he almost killed Earl. Is Chase the wrong people? "No," I whisper. Definitely not.

He gives me a half smile, one made of happiness and something else I can't place—guilt, maybe regret, but that doesn't seem right. There are muffled voices a few feet away, the sound of patients talking, a tech's or nurse's confident laugh. But we're shielded in here. No one can see us.

I study Chase's face. His too-white scar, his light eyes, the curve of his cheek, and the line of his lips. We're standing close, so close that I can feel his body heat radiating off him. It's been so long since I've felt warm.

"Tell me about him." He's asking about Jason. "Tell me about how he was the wrong people. Did you love him?"

I lick my suddenly dry lips. I close my eyes, think of Jason, his green eyes and his hair. Try to remember running my hands through his curls. I loved Jason, but the love I cradled for him for so long has worn thin. I always thought he was my knight, keeping me away from a dark path, but now I know — he was just leading me down another, much darker road. Still, I answer the question truthfully. "Yes, I loved him." A part of me might even always love him.

"Do you think you could ever love someone like that again?"

I open my eyes. I don't know if I want to love someone like that again, like a fever, hot and bright. "I don't think anyone could replace him." But Chase is here. Jason is dead and Chase is here. "I also don't think that there's one great love, or that we only get one chance at happiness." I say this because if I believed that — that there is only one great love for each of us — it means I'd probably never love again. Circumstances have forced my hand. I touch Chase's face, trail my fingers over his scar where it is smooth and deep. And finally I ask the one question I've wanted to for so long. "Why are you here? Why are you at Savage Isle?"

His eyes close, in pleasure or pain, I can't tell, maybe both. "I did something to someone. I hurt someone . . . I love. I let someone down." He swallows, closes his eyes tighter. He still hasn't answered my question. He's being evasive. Why so many secrets? He takes a step back and to me, that is all but an admission of guilt.

I step into him and continue to touch his face like a blind person. "Is that how you got this?"

"Yes," he says.

"Did someone do this to you?" I brush the pad of my thumb over his eyelashes and am surprised to feel moisture gathering there.

He sniffles, darts his head away. "Yeah . . ." He wipes at his eyes with the back of his hand, so hard I think he may have hurt himself.

"The person you hurt?"

He nods his head. It's what I thought: he hurt someone, someone who hurt him. And for some reason I am relieved. Chase is broken, like me, but not like Jason. Not like Cellie.

"Where are they now?"

"I'm not sure." He looks at me. Looks at me like I have answers, like I know a secret and he'd do anything for me to tell.

"I'm sorry," I say, because I don't know what else to say, and it seems like I should say something.

He reaches out, touches my cheek, traces my jawline. His hand cups my head, slowly removing my hood. "My little bird with a broken wing."

I close my eyes and try to shut him out, guard myself against his gentle assault. But something is creeping in, maybe it has been creeping in this whole time and I was too blind to notice. It blossoms inside of me like ink through water or blood in snow. Chase moves through me, into the part of my soul that is stained, where there is something wicked and dark. Like Jason, he's not afraid to touch it.

Wetness forms in my eyes and they flutter shut, either to keep the tears in or to force them out. I can't tell. One tear escapes, makes a soft trail down my cheek. Chase brushes it away, first with a finger and then with his mouth.

"Based on the way you ate that mango, I bet you're a terrible kisser, huh?" He lets out a low laugh and touches my lower lip with his thumb. "Yeah, I bet you kiss like an angry Velociraptor." He mock sighs. "I guess there's only one way to find out."

I smile because he's funny and sweet and I appreciate him breaking the tension. Our lips meet, and instead of cinnamon I taste salt and mint. It's refreshing and filled with hope. A light blooms bright behind my eyes. Chase is kissing me like I'm the rain and he's lost in the desert. Like we were always meant for each other, one half calling to the other.

There's a shout followed by the short burst of a whistle. Dr. Goodman's voice trails closely behind, calling us back. It's time to go.

Chase presses his forehead against mine. His heavy breath fans my face.

"We should go," he says.

"Yeah," I say, but neither of us moves for a long moment.

When we finally walk out of the garden, we're hand in hand, but when we come into view of the group, we drift away from each other. We sit next to each other on the bus. Chase plays the Eagles, makes us listen to "Desperado" four whole times. And despite his shitty taste in music, I like him. I like him more than I ever thought possible.

When we've been driving for a while, he pauses the song, turns to me, and says, "You know you can trust me, right?"

I roll my eyes. "Uh, okay."

"No. I'm being serious." He touches my knee. "No matter what, you can trust me. You do trust me, right?"

This question seems vastly important to him, so I consider it. "Yes," I say eventually. "Yes, I do." What Chase doesn't know, what he can never know, is that saying this means even more to me than saying *I love you*.

From the Journal of Alice Monroe

We checked into a motel to clean up. Or rather we slipped into a room after a maid got done servicing it. The room was cheap, the blankets threadbare, and rats or insects or something crawled inside the walls. We holed up in there for a while. Cellie sat down and smoked cigarettes. Jason took a shower. He came out of the bathroom, jeans hanging loosely from his hips. I didn't want to look at him, standing there half naked, drops of water making trails over his tattoos. And I didn't want to watch Cellie light matches and put them out on her tongue. I grabbed for the TV remote, hoping for distraction in cartoons or some reality show, but as I did, I caught my reflection in the black square screen. My face was streaked in blood. How had I not noticed this before? My eyes stood out among all that red—bright white orbs that glowed from hollow shells.

I clicked the power button, changed the channel. But there was no escape. My face was there again, caught in that square screen, now abuzz with electricity and color. Jason, Cellie, and I were all over the news.

"Holy fucking Christ, we're famous!" Cellie cackled.

Surveillance cameras at the truck stop had captured the whole thing: Cellie flirting with Earl; Earl grabbing me; Jason jumping Earl. It played on a continuous loop as an anchorwoman did a voice-over. *"No one knows what precipitated such a vicious attack. The alleged perpetrators seemed to have been robbing the convenience store when it all went wrong. The victim's name is Earl Sanders. Early reports state that he was flown by helicopter after such a brutal beating. Earl is listed in critical condition—his wife and two kids hope he will make it through the night."*

Jason leaned over to block my view of the television and then clicked it off. "Don't watch that shit."

I turned to him as if he were a stranger. "He might die," I choked out.

"He's not going to die. C'mon. I'll help you clean up."

"No." I scooted back so that I was pressed up against the wall, and then I began to pace. "We need to call the cops, turn ourselves in." I closed the distance between us, grabbed Jason by his shoulders, and tried to shake him. But it was like trying to move a boulder. "Maybe if we tell the truth, how he was going to hurt me and Cellie, and that you saved us." I nodded and kept pacing, burning a trail in the carpet. "Yeah, if we tell them the truth." I kept going on and didn't notice how still Jason and Cellie had become, how they looked at me as if I'd gone mad, caught some sort of highly contagious flesh-eating virus.

Cellie brought her knees to her chest and put her hands over her ears and started to hum.

"Stop," Jason said to Cellie. She didn't stop. She got louder, and I kept talking, trying to reason over her humming.

Jason stepped in front of me. "Stop." He shook me. "Both of you, just let me think."

I stopped, so did Cellie; our eyes went wide. "We can't go to the cops," he said.

I opened my mouth but he pressed a finger to my lips.

His voice and eyes softened. "We can't go to the cops. They'll lock you and Cellie up again. I don't care about myself, but you know what they'll do to you. They'll put Cellie in a padded room. And you, too." He put a hand on my head. "Think about it," he pleaded.

I knew then that Jason was right. If we surrendered, we wouldn't be sent back to Pleasant Oaks. We were too old. We'd be sent to Savage Isle, and according to the rumors, it made Pleasant Oaks seem like a day spa.

"Don't let them lock me up, Alice." Cellie's voice was childlike, and something inside of me reached out to protect her.

I straightened and wiped away my tears. "So what do we do?"

Jason smiled, relieved. "Just leave it up to me." He kissed me, slow and steady. I melted into him like snow in a rain puddle. "C'mon. Let's get you cleaned up." He led me to the bathroom and turned on the water in the shower. I got in with my clothes on and watched the blood slide down the drain like a warm red tide.

We couldn't go back to Candy's. It was only a matter of time before the cops figured out our names. We thought we had a couple days to get out of town, start a new life. But we were wrong. It wasn't days. It was hours.

CHAPTER

18

MATES FOR LIFE

AFTER THE FIELD TRIP, WE RETURN TO OUR ROOMS TO AWAIT group therapy. It has started raining again, a light mist that makes me feel as though we're living inside a cloud—or maybe it's just the floaty afterglow of Chase's kiss.

I find Amelia standing by our barred window, gazing out onto the wet, misty world. She turns as the door clicks shut behind me, as soft as a whisper.

She smiles hesitantly. "My parents finally came."

My eyes drift over to her bed and the shiny new duffel bag sitting in the middle of it. "Oh," I say. She links her hands together, making a show of the fact that her red wristband has been removed. I bite my cheek. "Oh," I say again, this time more faintly.

All of a sudden my throat feels itchy and my chest aches. It's like my heart has tripled in size and it's struggling to beat normally inside a too-small cage.

"They're moving me to Green Lake." Green Lake is a private mental health facility where patients are assigned private rooms, designer hospital scrubs, and their choice of gourmet cafeteria food. "It's good, right?" She looks at me hopefully. She needs me to tell her it's okay. That I'll be okay.

"That's good. I hear it's nice there," I manage to say, even though something akin to grief is snaking up my airway.

Suddenly Amelia throws herself on me, and I'm enveloped in another one of her tight embraces. She squeezes and squeezes until I tentatively wrap my arms around her. "We'll keep in touch," she says.

Keep in touch. That's what Jason's mother muttered through wine-soaked lips.

"Of course," I say as we separate.

"I wrote my contact information down." Amelia gestures to a blue square of origami paper on the dresser. "You can call me anytime. They allow cell phones at Green Lake." She bites her thumb and rocks up on the balls of her feet. "My parents are waiting for me. They came a couple hours ago, but I insisted on staying till you got back."

"You should go, then." I glance at the clock. "I should get going, too. Group therapy, you know?"

"Yeah," she says.

The seconds on the clock tick by, but neither of us moves.

"Okay, I'll go first." Amelia slings her bag over her shoulder and squeezes my arm as she walks to the door. "Don't let Monica give you too much shit, okay? And about Chase . . . be careful. I know you're into him. Just make sure he's as into you."

I force the corners of my mouth into something resembling a smile. "Don't worry. Chicks before dicks, right?"

"Always!" Amelia shows me her pearly-white teeth in a smile that's as real as love. I used to smile like that. I smiled like that all the time when I was with Jason. But now, I can't.

I can't even manage to watch Amelia walk out the door.

"Tonight I'd like to discuss relationships," Dr. Goodman says during evening group therapy.

Chase sits next to me. He's not paying attention. The big headphones looped around his neck emit a soft beat, just low enough so that no one can hear it but us. Every once in a while he shifts in his seat and brushes his leg against mine. My body hums, pulses at his light touches. It's been hours since our kiss in the pagoda, but I can still feel him, his lips and body pressing into mine.

I remove the piece of blue origami paper from my hoodie pocket. Flipping it over, I reread Amelia's contact information. Amelia's gone. I'm happy for her. And sad for myself. It's weird how two emotions can war inside you.

But I'm not worried about what she said about Chase. Based on our kiss earlier today, I'd say he's pretty into me. Plus, I've told him things. Things I've never told anyone. Let him have a part of me that I'd kept locked away, even from Jason.

"I want us to examine our past and current relationships," Dr.

Goodman says. "Let's discuss how we behave in them, how we react in them — really study how they define who we are and the choices we make." I start to fold Amelia's note into the shape of a swan.

It's like Dr. Goodman has pulled tonight's group therapy topic from my head. Everything used to be so black-and-white. Cellie was bad. Jason was good. But my memories have taken on different shades lately. I think about Cellie and her terrible love. I think about Jason and how his love was terrible but in a different (and possibly more dangerous) way, only I didn't know it at the time.

Chase nudges me. "You know swans mate for life, right?" he whispers, and plucks the swan from my fingers to look at it.

I stifle a laugh. "How do you know that?"

Chase sprawls back in his chair. "What can I say? I'm a marvel of weird and inexplicable facts. People would pay good money to study me."

"Why do I like you?"

He grins, and a little dimple appears in his cheek. "Because I'm tall and semi-dashing?" He winks at me. I snatch the swan back and tuck it safely in my pocket.

Dr. Goodman clears his throat, effectively bringing our private conversation to an end. "Alice, is there something you'd like to add?"

I shake my head.

Dr. Goodman turns his attention to Chase. "Chase?"

Chase says no more forcefully than seems necessary. He's really got it in for Dr. Goodman, but I don't know why. While Dr. Goodman drones on, I pull out another piece of origami paper (green, this time) and make a second swan.

Group therapy continues uneventfully and Dr. Goodman ends with his usual speech about what good work we've done and how we should pat ourselves on the back for the progress we've made. Chase and I are the last ones in the single-file line to shuffle out the door. As we pass Dr. Goodman, Chase trips. His broad shoulder pushes into my back, and I fall to the floor with an *oomph*. Pain splits my knees and stings my palms as I land on all fours.

"Jeeze, Allie, are you all right? Shit, I'm so sorry," Chase says, crouching down to inspect the damage and help me up, but Dr. Goodman beats him to it.

"It's fine," I say, shrugging out of Dr. Goodman's light grasp. I take a step forward and adjust my sweatshirt.

"Are you sure you're all right?" Dr. Goodman asks, sincere and concerned.

"I'm fine," I say, rubbing my stinging palms together. "Thanks." I make a beeline out the door, my cheeks warm with embarrassment.

Chase catches up to me. "You sure you're okay? You went down like a ton of bricks." He takes off his baseball cap and runs his fingers through his hair.

"Thanks for the observation."

"You're mad."

"Again, another stellar observation by Chase Ward."

Chase puts a hand on my shoulder and stops me. "I'm sorry."

"Whatever." I roll my eyes, realizing that I've overreacted. "What'd you trip on, anyway?"

"Nothing."

"I don't understand."

"Maybe I tripped on purpose."

"Why would you do that?"

"To get something," he says. "To get *you* something."

"You pushed me down to get me something?"

He grins. "Yep, and before I show you, let me give you permission to prostrate yourself at my feet with thanks and gratitude."

I fold my arms over my chest and wait for Chase to get to the point. We're alone again, like we were in the garden, only this time, I can tell Chase isn't going to make a move. He's up to something else entirely.

Slowly, ever so slowly, he pulls something out of his pocket. A white badge attached to a red lanyard dangles in front of my face. Realization sinks in. Chase has lifted another security badge. But this time it's not just any badge. The photograph in the center smiles at me, a thin face with wire-rimmed glasses. Dr. Goodman. Below Dr. Goodman's picture are three of the sweetest words I've ever seen: ALL SECURITY CLEARANCE.

I press the badge into Chase's chest, covering the white plastic with one of my hands. "This might be the best present anyone's ever gotten me."

Chase's look grows serious and maybe a little grim. He lays a hand against my neck. "I want to help you find your sister."

"When?" I lean into his touch, feeling soothed.

He gives his head a little shake. "Tonight. Come to my room." His hand travels down my shoulder, over the bumpy burn scars, then down my arm and right into my hoodie pocket. He comes out with the second swan I folded, the green one. "I'm going to keep this." Then he's gone.

As I walk back to my own room, a voice in my head chants, *Tonight, Cellie, I'm coming for you. Tonight, Cellie, I'm coming for you.* But the voice sounds hesitant and smaller than before. Somewhere between my vow to kill Cellie and stolen kisses in a Japanese pagoda, my resolve has weakened. Chase has gotten under my skin. And I'm not sure anymore if I am willing to trade his warmth for cold revenge.

FROM THE JOURNAL OF ALICE MONROE

I don't know how they found us holed up in that shitty hotel room. But we were surrounded. Someone banged on the door. A voice shouted for us to come out with ten fingers pointed toward the sky. When we didn't cooperate, when we refused to come out, they broke down the door.

Jason and I fell to our knees, hands behind our heads. We were pressed to the ground, cheeks digging into the grimy carpet and hands cuffed tightly, uncomfortably, but Cellie fought. She wouldn't be Cellie if she hadn't. She laughed the whole time, a manic, high-pitched laugh that overrode the cops' voices and the blare of sirens.

They dragged us away, put Cellie and me in one car, Jason in another. As they were shoving him into the back seat, he winked at us and told the cop that It was worth it.

We were taken to the local police station. Once we were processed, Cellie and I were sent to Savage Isle. We peed in cups and spoke with intake counselors who checked questions off a list. I met with Dr. Goodman, who peered at me over his glasses. Cellie screamed from the office next door. He asked if my sister was all right. And I told him no, she had never been right. Cellie's room was just across the hall from mine, and every night she howled.

One day she came and stood in front of me during arts and crafts. She had stopped talking as soon as we were admitted. Her face was gaunt and hollow under the yellow lights. How had I failed to notice she'd become too thin? Dark circles hung under her dull black eyes. She wasn't well, and I didn't know how to help her. I reached for her, wanted to tell her to sit with me. I would make her a paper animal or tell her stories from our childhood, maybe one from Pam and Gayle's house—the house she liked best. But I didn't get the chance. Her hand locked around my wrist and she tried to sink her teeth into my forearm.

Techs had to come and pull her off me. They dragged her to the Quiet Room, where she screamed all night. She screamed until she was hoarse, and the techs had to come and administer a sedative with a long, sharp needle. I watched from the background, even though the techs tried to keep me away. I wanted to be there when they opened the door. Foolishly I thought that if she caught a glimpse of me it would calm her down. But my presence only made her more agitated. She shook and she cried and she whimpered. And all she would say, over and over, was *Everybody's lying. Everyone's lying.*

———◆———

CHAPTER

19

CHASE'S ROOM

I DON'T BOTHER KNOCKING WHEN I GET TO CHASE'S ROOM.
Instead I slide the keycard over the black box, knowing that the
beep preceding the opening of the door will alert him. When I
enter, only the bathroom light is on. It illuminates the space, washes
it in a soft glow, like candlelight. My green swan is sitting atop his
nightstand.

"Hey," I say, shifting uncomfortably in the doorway. Chase lies
on his bed, one arm behind his head, the other tapping a rhythm
on his chest. He gives me a smile. "Where's your roomie?" I ask.
The bed next to his is empty and made.

"He freaked out earlier. Something about how he hates forks.
Started throwing a bunch of shit, hit Nurse Dummel right in the
eye with one of his shoes." Chase scoots over a little and pats the
space next to him.

I bite the inside of my cheek. Why does everything suddenly

feel so awkward? "C'mon," he says. "I have a present for you. I forgot to give it to you on the bus."

I arch a brow and take a step closer. Two presents in one day? This is a record for me. He pulls something from his pocket. I have a flashback of Cellie pulling a unicorn lighter from her pocket and my stomach turns. But when Chase opens his fist, it's not a lighter. A speckled gray rock rests in his palm.

I set the keycard on the nightstand, sit on the bed, and take the rock from him. I examine it. "Thanks." I'm not sure what to say. I know Chase well enough now to know he doesn't do things without a reason. But I can't for the life of me figure out why he would give me a rock.

"It's from the garden. I picked it up on our way out." He sits up so we're face-to-face. "Don't you notice what shape it's in?"

I turn the rock in my fingers. That's when I see what it resembles. "A heart?"

He touches my waist. "It's to remind you . . ." His eyes swim with sincerity. "To remind you that you deserve to be loved."

I close my fingers around the rock. I don't know how to process his words. Something inside me denies it. I lower my lashes. "Everyone deserves to be loved, but that doesn't always mean that they are."

He tilts his head at my cynicism. His mouth curves up into a smile, and his voice is so full of warmth I think it could melt a glacier (or my icy heart). "You will be." He says it so quietly I almost don't hear.

He kisses my lips, so soft and sweet and full of promise I could weep. My arms wrap around him. We kiss again and again, small pecks that turn to lingering open mouths. We grip each other and tumble to the bed. As we fall, a vision of Jason dances before my eyes and I'm taken back to the night on the roof, when Jason and I had our first kiss. I blink, and Chase kisses me long and deep, ripping every thought of Jason away. He kisses my ear, then my cheek, my eyelid, and my pulse—right in my neck where it's hammering. "I promise. I won't let you down, Alice." He keeps murmuring it between kisses. *I won't let you down.*

We break the kiss, mostly because we need to catch our breath. I rest my head on his chest. "That was . . ." I don't know what to say. I don't have the words.

He chuckles, and the rumble I feel under his T-shirt makes me smile. "Ah, Just Alice, you sure do make a guy feel good." He kisses my forehead. "Stay here with me tonight."

I start to pull away, but his arm around me pins me in place. "We can just sleep. I want you to stay here. I'll set my alarm to wake us up before the morning bed check."

We were supposed to go find Cellie, go back to the D ward. But suddenly my desire for revenge is outweighed by my desire to stay in Chase's arms all night. Because this won't last. Whatever is blossoming between us is bound to burn out. I'm still holding the rock, thinking about how the heart shape is now imprinted on my palm from clutching it so tightly. I rub my cheek on his shirt. "Okay," I say. I'll stay. I won't think about Cellie, because maybe everyone does deserve to be loved. If only for a little bit. If only for just one night.

We fall asleep wrapped up in each other. I wake up shivering in a room full of blue light. Dawn is coming. Chase lies next to me on his back, his breathing even and deep. I yawn and shift to move out of the bed, knocking Chase's present, the rock, with my feet as I do. I don't know how it ended up there. Smiling, I bend to pick it up. As I'm stuffing the rock into my back pocket, my eyes catch on something shoved under the mattress. A corner of paper pokes out.

"Alice?" Chase's sleepy voice drifts over to me.

I smile quickly at him and then go back to the paper wedged between the mattress and box spring. "What's this?" I ask.

He follows my gaze, worry sketched all over his face. My curiosity doubles, then triples. "Allie." His voice holds a slight edge of warning. "It's nothing." He lunges for it at the same time I do. But I'm closer and quicker, and I get to it first.

I wiggle it out. It's a thick file.

Chase's eyes narrow. "Give it back, Allie. It's nothing." He moves toward me, ready to snatch it from my fingers, but I step back, file in hand.

I pace in front of him, far enough to be out of reach. Chase runs an aggravated hand through his hair. He kneels on the bed and cusses. I read the name on the file. First I'm curious, then surprised, then confused. I feel the color drain from my face. "Chase?"

He turns his head—in shame? In embarrassment? I'm not sure. Why can't he look at me?

I say Chase's name again. I say it so lightly it barely ruffles the air in the room. I look down at the file in my hand, just to make sure that my vision didn't betray me. But the label on the file still reads ALICE MONROE.

— · ◦ · —

From the Journal of Alice Monroe

In a month, Jason managed to find us. He had spent two days in juvenile detention, then was released into Candy's care to await trial. He would visit every week. And, among the smell of stale coffee and the sound of happy families reuniting with their loved ones, I would weep. I'd cried before, but I'd never wept. Something was broken inside me, and it felt like Cellie was ripping me apart. Everywhere I went I heard the echo of her screams. I came to realize it wasn't really me who was broken, it was *Cellie,* and for the first time, I thought it might be better for the both of us if she were dead. That's what no one will ever understand: the decision to kill Cellie wasn't born of hate. It was born of love. I loved Cellie. But love isn't a straight line. It's curved and kinked, and sometimes it's better if it's cut.

Jason held my hand and made small circles with his thumb. "They've charged me with assault and battery," he said during our first visit. I'd seen his face plastered all over the news (Cellie was right; we were famous), and so I already knew about the charges that had been stacked against him. I turned his hand over so I could see his unicorn tattoo.

"I don't think . . ." I choked. The words were a ten-foot wall I couldn't scale. "I don't think I'll make it in here. Cellie keeps getting worse. She won't stop screaming and . . ." I trailed off again, unable to admit what I was thinking. Soon only one of us would be able to survive.

"What about Cellie?" he asked.

I turned from him, and involuntarily my fingers grazed the bruises where Cellie had grabbed me and tried to sink her teeth into me.

"Alice." He grasped my chin, forcing my gaze back to him. "What happened to your arm?" The black-and-blue marks were impossible to ignore. "Did she do this to you?"

Trying to tell him she'd actually caused me bodily harm was one of the hardest things I'd ever attempted. And in the end I couldn't quite force myself to do it. But it didn't matter. The answer was drawn all over my face. "You don't belong here," he said. He leaned forward so all I could see was his back. The way his T-shirt stretched over his shoulders made me think of the ink scrawled beneath—*God's Will*. He bowed his head. "I can take care of you."

I scooted forward and rested my ear on his shoulder blade. I could feel his heartbeat. I wanted to dive into his certainty, his strength. I thought about those nights at Roman's house, cold hours spent huddled in the dark corner of a closet. How I'd made paper lions. *My lionheart.*

He cupped my cheek and kissed my forehead. "If you could go anywhere, anywhere in the world, where would it be?"

I pushed my face against his chest. Images of my grandfather's house, of gray clouds pregnant with snow, drifted across the backs of my eyelids. "Somewhere warm. Somewhere light."

"We could go somewhere like that."

"Where?" I teased.

Jason forced my chin up and made me meet his gaze. "I'm serious. I can get you out of here. I came in through the visitors' entrance. It's not as secure as you think."

I pictured us living our lives together on the run, and it seemed romantic but not unreal. After all, isn't that exactly what we'd been doing all our lives? We'd been pushed around by the state, by the government, tossed from home to home, living on the fringes. What Jason proposed was taking our lives back. *My* life back. No more group homes. No more hospitals. No more Cellie. The possibility was like a heavy drug in my veins. The feeling was sweet and addictive. "I'd go anywhere with you."

We spent the rest of the time planning our epic escape. I was eager to put our plan into action, to break free that very day, but Jason said he needed more time to make the necessary arrangements.

When he got up to leave, he kissed me goodbye. The heat of his lips spread through me like wildfire. There are many ways to burn. Jason's kiss was one way. By Cellie's hand was another.

CHAPTER

20

CONFESSIONS

"What the fuck, Chase?"

He sighs, rubs the back of his neck, and calmly comes to stand by the bed. "You weren't supposed to see that."

No shit. "What are you doing with my file?"

He shakes his head. "I can't tell you."

"Can't tell me!" I repeat stupidly. "I think I have a right to know. Did you steal it?" The whole time he's been lying to me. He's been reading my file and laughing behind my back.

"I don't—" He stumbles over the words. At least he has the decency to look ashamed. "It was to help you."

"Is that supposed to make me feel better?" I spit out. "Why?" I press the file to my chest, where my heart is breaking, where it's disintegrating in Chase's hands.

He shrugs and stuffs his hands in his pockets. "I can't tell you. You're not ready."

I snort. "You are such a coward." I throw the file across the room and sheets of paper slip out and fan the ground. My glossy mug shot, from when I was arrested as an accomplice in Earl's beating, lands face-up. In the picture I'm crying and, I remember, my hands were shaking so bad, I could barely hold the placard with my name on it.

Chase's gaze locks onto mine, lightning fast. "What?" he says.

I trample the papers, leaving a footprint on the ugly photo, until I'm standing inches from Chase's face. "I said you are a coward, Chase Ward, a dirty, fucking coward. You hide behind your bullshit sense of humor." I shake my head. "I should've known. You can't be honest with yourself, so why the hell would you be honest with me?" I turn to leave.

I don't hear him coming toward me until it's too late. "Wait." He grabs my arm.

I whirl around and try to yank my arm away, but he's got me in a tight hold. "Don't touch me," I say under my breath. "You make me sick." I thought he was so different from Jason. But he's the same. A peddler of lies. A betrayer.

He releases me right away, his hand coming off my body like I've scalded him, like I've hurt him in some deep place, and I can see by his eyes that I have. "You don't mean that," he says in a heartbreaking whisper.

"Of course I do. You're no different than the rest of them." I turn from him and rest my hand on the door. I don't even care if a tech is out there. I just want out, out of Chase's room and his web of lies.

"I may be a coward, but you are, too." Chase's voice stops me cold, reignites the fury inside me. My shoulders stiffen. "You want honesty, Alice? Why don't we start with you, then? Why don't you tell me what you're doing here? Why are you dead set on breaking into the D ward?"

I don't bother to turn around. I lean my forehead on the door, against the cool metal. "I told you, my sister's there."

He snorts in disbelief. "Yeah, I'm sure. You want to get into the D ward to see Cellie? So you can do what?" He waits a moment, and I'm sure he can hear my heart beating in the room. Boom. Boom. Boom. He knows. He must know. He must have guessed my intent from the beginning.

I swallow my anger and resentment and fear. "Fine," I say. "I'll be honest. I want Cellie dead. I want to go to the D ward. And I want to find her and cut her out like the cancer she is." The truth has festered so long inside me that it's a relief to finally say it out loud.

He makes a little noise, like he's being strangled. "What do you think that's going to accomplish? It's not going to bring Jason back."

Finally I turn, hands balled into fists. "Don't say his name."

He takes a step back, and then he erupts. "Oh my God, that's what you think, isn't it? You think somehow if you kill Cellie, it's going to resurrect Jason."

"Don't say his name. Don't say his name." I shake my head back and forth. My heart pounds and blood rushes into my ears. I can barely form breaths.

But Chase is relentless, a dog with a bone. "Jason. Jason. Jason.

Jason's dead, Allie. Jason's dead, but I'm here." He takes one of my hands, and though I try to swat it away, he holds on. He forces my fingers open and lays them against his chest. "I'm here. I'm real." He wants me to let go, run to him, and leave Jason behind. I shake off his soft plea and narrow my eyes at him.

I press my hand into his chest and push him. He stumbles back a little. "Now you be honest too. Why were you sent to Savage Isle?"

He lets go of my hand and I allow it drop to my side. "My sister." His eyes drill into mine like he's daring me to call his bluff.

"Your sister. That's why you're here?"

"Yeah." He jerks his chin at me.

"Bullshit."

"What?" He's surprised.

"I said bullshit. What are you *really* doing here, Chase? What's with the files, the sneaking around?"

"I'm helping you," he tries.

"Why?"

"Because I said I would."

"You're helping me because I remind you of your sister." His words from days ago haunt me. *You remind me of her, you know. My little bird with a broken wing.* "You want to fix me because you couldn't fix your sister. You want to fix me, and maybe I don't want to be fixed."

"You're so wrong," he says. But when he sees my expression, he backpedals. "Maybe that was it at first. But not now. Now it's different."

"Then tell me what you're really doing here, with me." *Why all the help for nothing?*

He dodges eye contact. "I can't, not yet. I promise I'll tell you everything—it's just not the right time." He hangs his head and backs up some more so he's pressed against the wall.

"This is a waste of time," I say. "We're done."

"Please," he says. "There are some things I can't tell you, but I can . . ." He swallows. "I can tell you that I killed someone."

Everything in my body goes cold and my heart slows, stutters, and then stalls. Amelia was right. Chase killed someone.

"Who?"

He looks away.

"Who?" I persist.

"I killed my sister." His voice is small, weak, and wilted.

He's hinted at it before, that he killed someone he loved, but this is the first time I've ever actually heard him say it. "You killed your sister?" I say when he looks as if he's not going to say any more. "How?" I want to know every detail. What dark path brought Chase to the same point as me?

A shudder runs through him. "I can't." He pauses. "I can't say."

I shake my head, not in anger but in hopelessness. He won't share, and I can't give any more. We're at an impasse. Another stalemate. "I think we need to stay away from each other for a while."

His eyes flash to mine. "What? Why?"

I dodge his gaze, the heartbreak and fear in his eyes. "Because we're broken, Chase. We're broken, and we're not going to fix each other."

"That's not what I want."

I chew the inside of my cheek, and resolve settles like concrete in my gut. He's too damaged. I'm too damaged. "It's for the best." I stick out my hand. "Key?" I say. Chase makes a noise of protest. Still, he rummages through his pocket and finds the tech keycard. He gently places it in my palm. I go to the door and open it. When I look back at him, he flinches like I'm poison, like I'm a jellyfish, and that hurts even more than finding my file under his mattress.

As I walk away, I think I finally got what I wanted. I think about when Chase and I sat together in the rec room watching that God-awful movie. How I told him *I don't need you, you know.* I pushed him away. Another mission finally accomplished.

When I get back into my room I sit on the edge of my bed. My breathing is heavy and labored, like I've just run a marathon. Something hiccups in my chest—sorrow and bitter disappointment. I try to convince myself that it really is better this way, to have cut ties before our relationship got out of hand, before someone really got hurt. But the lie won't stick, and I can't stop fresh tears from forming in my eyes. As I curl up into a ball, something digs into my skin from my back pocket. I fish out the rock Chase gave me. With the pad of my thumb I trace the rough edges of the heart. I close my fist around it, and with all my might I throw it at the picture caulked to the wall. I want to hear something shatter. But all that happens is a soft thud followed by the rock dropping to the floor behind the dresser. I don't bother trying to find it. It's lost to me. Just like everything else.

FROM THE JOURNAL OF ALICE MONROE

Jason visited the next week, and he said everything was almost ready. "My piece-of-shit car broke down, and it's going to cost too much to fix. We're going to have to go on foot." I nodded my head and told him that I could run fast. "They moved my court date up to two weeks from now," he said. "I could go to jail. We have to go soon. But I need another week to get everything together."

I nodded again and hugged him tighter. He linked his fingers with mine. Sometime during our week apart, he'd gotten a new tattoo—my name on his knuckles.

"How's Cellie?" he asked. He worried that she was going to attack again. After her stay in the Quiet Room, she'd been admitted back into the general population. We weren't speaking. She watched me from the shadows. We were circling each other like two dogs about to fight. And with every passing week the tension grew between us.

I shook my head and pressed my lips together. "Not good."

His thumb touched my lower lip. "You'll be free of her soon, I promise. That's the best thing about where we're going. She won't be able to find you. You'll be ready to go next week?" I was ready to go then, but I merely nodded and pressed my nose into his neck, trying to gain strength for the next few days.

That night, there was a crescent moon, and I felt as if I was swinging from it. Once, I had told Jason about Southern California, how the average temperature is seventy degrees and the sun stays out until the late evening. I hoped that was where he was taking us. I imagined us hitching rides along the highway, the sand between our toes and the surf in our ears. I could almost taste the salt in the air.

The next week Jason came and said everything was ready.

"Where are we going?" I asked, unable to contain my excitement.

He touched my cheek. "I found the perfect place."

"Is it somewhere we've talked about before?"

"No, it's somewhere new. We've never talked about it. But I think you'll like it. It's better than anything you could imagine."

I could only think of sun-kissed cheeks, coconut oil, and surfboards. All the bright colors of my future. But I trusted Jason. He wanted what was best for me. "Is it far?"

"No. That's the best part. It's not far at all."

"How long will it take for us to get there?"

"Not very long, you'll see."

He kissed my fingertips hard and asked again if I was ready. I took a look at the door that led back to Cellie and her madness. I nodded without hesitation. Yes. Yes, I was ready.

Jason said go. So I went.

———◦—◦———

21

PURPLE

TODAY I FEEL PURPLE. I THINK BACK TO WHEN CELLIE AND I stayed in that group home, the one where we pretended to be prisoners of war and slept in metal bunk beds with thin mattresses. They had this chart in there, and every morning we had to go up to it and spin a color wheel. At the top of the chart it said TODAY I FEEL . . . and then we'd use the spinner and guide it to the color that best reflected our current emotional state. Cellie always felt red (a color I associated with anger and the fires she loved so much), and usually I felt yellow. The yellow on the color wheel was bright and happy. Often I wished it was more of a pale yellow, the color of sickness, of decay. But today, if I had that chart in front of me, I would push the spinner to purple and leave it there.

Chase and I are not talking, the kind of not talking that people notice and wonder about, the kind of not talking that makes everyone else feel a little on edge. And in a mental hospital, that's the most dangerous kind. During breakfast we ignore each other, and

I choke down a few bites of egg even though I'm too upset to taste anything. In group therapy we sit as far away from each other as possible, which in a circle means almost directly across from each other. It's as if we are the opposite ends of a magnet. We're facing each other, but we repel. Dr. Goodman continues his discussion on relationships. He asks Chase to share, presses him, and won't let anyone else talk until he does. But instead of some smart-ass comment or some clever quip, Chase mutters, "This is bullshit," and storms out of the room, overturning an empty chair as he does.

As the day goes on, my purple deepens until it's heavy and covers my shoulders like a shroud. I miss Amelia and wish she were here. It seems like everything has gone to shit since she left. I wonder what she's doing. If she's happy at Green Lake. If she's calling other patients muff eaters or accusing them of wearing dirty underwear.

During dinner the rain is so loud that it's almost disturbing. Clouds the color of bruised and battered eyes fill the sky. The weather puts the patients on edge. It's a trigger for some, makes their anxiety worse. They're still like jellyfish, but now it's as if God's own hand has come down and is stirring the ocean, making a whirlpool. I don't mind the weather because it matches my mood. It's dark, and I'm feeling dark.

When I go to my evening one-on-one with Dr. Goodman, he notices that something is off with me and says he's concerned. He doesn't have to tell me why. It's all over his pity-filled face. *Relapse. Better hide the razors.* I curl my lip in a snarl. I fold three origami animals: an ape, a hippo, and a bird.

When I get back to my empty room and I'm locked in for the night, I set the paper animals out on the dresser. The zoo is coming along. I touch the lion's mane. The bird I made teeters and tips over. *My little bird with a broken wing.* Anger, like a tidal wave, takes me, and suddenly I'm ripping up the little bird, shredding it to pieces.

As I lay down to sleep, staring at my little zoo, I realize that I've gone the entire day without speaking to anyone. This is what purple feels like.

I wake to a crack of thunder and sparks falling outside my window. Then all at once a boom echoes through the building, followed by a whoosh of doors unlocking. I get up, feeling my way along the wall. At night the light from under the door usually guides me. But tonight it's gone. Another flash of lightning fills the room with a neon glow. I can hear patients filtering out of their rooms and into the hallway.

I make it to my door and hesitate. I'm not sure what's out there, on the other side. The power is out. And it seems that the locks on the patients' doors have failed. But then it occurs to me. This is my chance. No locks. No alarms. The C and D wards are totally open. Vulnerable. This is what I should have been focusing on all along. Cellie. And my revenge. Instead I let myself get blindsided by Chase and all his empty promises.

I turn the door handle all the way down and open it just a fraction. I peer out. The hallway is still and empty; even the sign above the emergency exit is out. It's like staring into a never-ending black tunnel. And though it's scarier than hell to think about navigating the darkness, I don't have a choice. An opportunity like this won't come again. Just as I am about to slip from my room another flash of lightning strikes, followed by a quick roll of thunder. I jump and it lands me outside my room. My steps are hesitant at first, but when the hallway stays quiet, I begin to walk faster and then I break into a semi-run. Keeping my hands in front of me, I use them like a blind person's stick, tapping along until my fingers meet the metal bar of the emergency exit. My body twitches with adrenaline as I begin to push the door open. Already I'm thinking ahead. Cellie is stronger than me. I may need a weapon. I'll have to find something along the way.

The flashlight that crosses my feet and the voice that accompanies it might as well be gunfire. "Whoa! Monroe, where do you think you're going?" Donny says.

All that adrenaline I was feeling quickly transforms into fear. I turn slowly. The flashlight shines in my face and I squint and move an arm to block it.

"Shoot, sorry." The flashlight lowers so it rests across my feet again. "Power's out in the building and the emergency generator hasn't come on yet. Doc wants all patients to go to the cafeteria . . ." Donny trails off.

We watch each other across the flashlight's beam. Donny holds a radio, and chatter bursts over it with updates: *"A and B wards secure, C and D wards, patient updates? . . ."* I'm waiting to see what he'll do. If he'll call a code red again, send me back to the Quiet Room. Donny keeps studying me like I'm one of those drawings where if you let your vision blur just enough, another picture appears. I'm just about to melt to my knees and beg him to not send me to the Quiet Room when he speaks. "Sooo . . . I suppose that's where you were heading just now, right?"

"What?" I ask him, confused. Is he playing some game, messing with my head? He's never been so unkind before.

He gazes at me wide-eyed, like he's talking to a four-year-old. "The cafeteria. That's where you were going, right? I assume that because the hallway was so dark you just didn't realize what direction you were headed in."

Unless I've forgotten the difference between left and right, it's impossible for me to make that mistake. But he's giving me an out. I nod my head slowly and lick my lips. "Yeah."

"Yeah," he says, mirroring my slow nod. "That's what I thought." He puts the walkie-talkie to his lips and says something like "Monroe secure." Then he motions for me to follow him.

Patients are corralled in the center of the cafeteria while techs and nurses with flashlights walk the perimeter. The patients seem antsy as the storm continues to rage, and the hospital staff looks so rigid it's as if their spines are going to break in two. I search the crowd for Chase, despite the unpleasant developments in our relationship. I find him almost instantly. He's on the outermost fringe of the crowd, almost leaning against the wall. His hat is pulled down low and his hands are jammed in his pockets. He looks defeated and sad. I want to go to him, but I'm still too mad.

Dr. Goodman leaps onto a table and calls for attention. When that doesn't work, Nurse Dummel blows a whistle. Dr. Goodman frowns a little. "Thank you, Ms. Dummel. Ladies and gentlemen, as you have probably already surmised, the power has gone out." Some of the patients cheer while others begin to cry. "I'd like for everyone to return to their rooms. Techs will be patrolling the hallways along with other staff. I know the storm can make some of you feel anxious. Please see a nurse or tech if you'd like something to help you sleep. That is all."

Dr. Goodman jumps down from the table, and techs and nurses begin breaking patients into groups to be escorted back to their rooms.

Donny spots me. "Yo, Alice," he says, jerking his head for me to come with him. As we make our way out of the cafeteria I look for Chase again, but he's lost in the sea of patients. When I get back to my room, I huddle under the covers. Outside, the storm has quieted. The thunder and lightning have receded. Now a heavy rain falls. I count the drops, hoping for sleep and trying to forget about Chase.

A shrill, wicked laugh filters through my dreams. *Cellie's laugh.* It's been a long time since I've heard it, but it's not the kind of sound you forget. She laughs again, close to my ear, so close I can feel her breath and her cheek grazing mine. *You've been a bad sister, Alice.* I close my eyes tighter and fight against the dream. There's the distinct sound of matches being struck, and the smell of sulfur permeates the air. I toss and turn, throw the covers off of me. I'm hot. I wish I had taken off my jeans before going to bed. I'm suffocating. I can't breathe. Little tendrils of smoke are sucked into my windpipe, and it feels as if knobby fingers are crushing me from within. I come awake in an instant, faster than you can snap your fingers or say *abracadabra*. The room is filled with smoke. Like an apparition, Cellie slips out the door and slams it behind her.

My body spasms and I cough violently, trying to exorcise the black smoke. I try to breathe in, but all I get is more black air that tastes of hot ash and feels heavy in my lungs. The smoke thickens, and it's hard to see. I scramble out of bed, arms outstretched, trying to feel my way out.

There's light, a haunting orange glow that I recognize all too well. Flames. They're suspended in the smoke on top of my dresser. My paper zoo, which I lovingly crafted, folded with my own two hands, is burning.

"No," I choke out. For some reason this seems so much worse than Chase's treachery. Cellie has always known how to cut the deepest. I can't stand to watch them burn, to watch another thing I love turn to ash, wither away under Cellie's wicked hands. I slap my open palms against a burning lion, against a smoldering monkey—trying to extinguish the flames. They bite into my hands and my skin starts to blister, but I can't stop. I keep going, trying to save as many animals as I can. I cough and sputter and snuff out the flames. But they jump, reach out, and connect with one another. I'm not fast enough. I can't save all the animals. Maybe just one then. Just one more.

The smoke thickens, turns a darker shade of gray, and billows up to the ceiling. The smoke alarm goes off. I don't notice the door opening beside me or the flood of technicians. They grab me, but I clutch at the dresser, scraping my nails against the wood, bloodying my fingertips as I am pulled away. I kick. I scream. My voice is raw and hoarse from the smoke.

"One more," I say. "I want to save one more." Patients pour out of their rooms and stand there, stunned. At last the jellyfish are still.

Another door opens, and I am shoved into a dark room. I land on my knees, white padding softening the blow. A whimper escapes my lips and then a word that sounds like a jangled combination of *no* and *please*. I lie on my side and bring my knees up to my chest. Something crinkles in my hand. It's dark in the Quiet Room, but I trace the shape with my fingers. An animal. I saved one. It's the butterfly I made with Chase during group therapy. When I told him all about butterflies, how fragile they are, but how they survive with clever camouflage. When he said he liked listening to me talk. God, that hurts. I press the butterfly to my chest. I squished it while I was trying to save it. Now it's all I have, a butterfly with two ripped wings.

Nobody comes for what feels like hours. I don't even think I'm being monitored. I'm not safe in here, in the Quiet Room. Cellie's found me. She's come. I need to get to her before she finds me again. It's only a matter of time. I was the hunter. Now I'm the hunted. She must have escaped the D ward when the power went out. Probably tried the same thing I did, slipping out through an emergency exit. But she succeeded where I failed.

The door opens, and a tiny crack of light washes over the white room. The power must have come back on while I was stuck in the dark. I put my hand over my eyes and recoil. The person comes in and lets the door close behind her. I scramble to my feet, my heart pounding like a rabbit. I back into the corner and press myself into it. It's Cellie. I'm sure.

The person speaks, and it is the sweetest voice I've ever heard. "Alice."

"Chase!" I hurl myself into his body. He doesn't expect this. His breath hitches and he lets out a little *oomph,* but he catches me all the same, wrapping me up in his embrace. I dig my cheek into his shoulder. "Cellie's here. She got out of the D ward. I don't know how."

"Shhh." He rubs circles into my back.

"She set a fire." I back away from him and open my palm, showing him the crumpled butterfly, but that's stupid because he can't see it in the dark. "She lit my zoo on fire. I saved a butterfly."

"Jesus Christ. I'm so sorry." He brings me in for another hug and holds me even tighter. "This is all my fault. I didn't mean any of it, any of what I said. I'm so sorry. I shouldn't have left you alone." He pushes me away from him and brings his hands to rest lightly on my shoulders.

"It's not safe. I need to get out of here." I step away from him. "I need to find her before she finds me again." She wouldn't have gone back to the D ward. There's only one place on this godforsaken island where she would feel safe. The only place she thinks I wouldn't dare go. I wrap my fingers around the card in Chase's hand. "I think I know where she's gone. But I'll need your keycard." It's the last favor I'll ask of him.

"I don't think you should go alone." His voice is pinched with worry. "I'll go with you."

What is he thinking? He's offering to go with me? He knows now, since our fight, what I'm planning. If I let him help me, he'll be an accomplice. Does he know? Does he understand the consequences? "Are you sure, Chase?" I ask. "You don't have to help me. I can do this on my own."

He finds me again in the dark, runs his hand over my head, catching some of my jagged locks in his fingertips, and for a moment his touch feels so much like the phantom hand of Jason. "I know what I'm doing, Alice. I know what this means. I said I would help you, and I will." His voice is full of resignation. "I think it's the only way."

"It's me or her," I whisper.

"It'll be you," he says, so sure, so confident. "I promise I'll make sure you come out okay. I won't lose you."

He takes my hand and using the keycard, he opens the door, just a crack. He takes a deep breath, determines that the coast is clear. Then we're running. I take the lead. Through the hall, to the emergency exit, and down a zigzag of stairs. The door at the bottom of the stairs bangs open and we're outside.

As we sprint across the grass toward the barbed-wire fence, I know finally what it is that I want. I want what Cellie has done to me to be done to her. I want her to feel the sting of lost love, the icy fear of being hunted. I'm going to cut her heart out.

———•—•———

From the Journal of Alice Monroe

Jason and I burst through the visitor room emergency exit. All at once alarms blared and lights flashed. We took the stairs two at a time. Twice I stumbled, but Jason caught me. When we got to the door leading to the outside, we paused.

"No going back," he said.

"No going back," I repeated.

Together we opened the door to the outside. Our eyes widened against the sudden darkness. All around us alarms continued to shriek, but the searchlights hadn't been turned on yet. For a moment we were sheltered in the safety of the night. Earlier that day a heavy rain had fallen, and the grass we sprinted across was muddy and sodden. It felt like I was running through sand, my legs and lungs burning with the exertion, but Jason kept a tight hold on my hand, pulling me forward almost painfully. Shouts rang out in the distance, techs calling my name, begging me to stop. Earlier, Jason had cut a hole in the barbed-wire fence that surrounded the hospital. He ducked through it.

"C'mon, Allie," Jason yelled. We approached the edge of the forest and kept running. Through the brush and trees we went. Jason did his best to shield me, but branches whipped at my face and cut up my arms.

It felt like we'd been running forever by the time we made it to the edge of the lake, but time moves differently in a dark forest, and it had probably been only minutes. Jason crashed into the water, distorting the reflection of the moon that played across its mirrored surface. He let go of my hand and dived in. As I plunged into the icy water, I had to stifle the urge to cry out. Cold gripped my spine and something slithered against my legs. Jason called to me, treading water in the middle of the lake. I swam toward him, my body weighed down by terror. As soon as I closed the distance between us, he began to swim again, and I followed in his wake.

Jason gave me a frantic kiss as we stumbled from the water. We looked over our shoulders and across the lake, to the other side of the shore, where the techs had paused. Their bright flashlights were swallowed up by the black water, unable to search us out. We were lost to them and finally free. Jason and me.

We walked, our bodies unwilling to do anything but move sluggishly. The temperature dropped and my teeth chattered. Suddenly I was in my grandfather's house again, struggling to stay warm and eating bits of cake. A wave of panic washed over me, and I fell to my knees, unable to go on. It felt as if I'd never be warm again.

Jason was beside me in an instant. "C'mon, baby." He put his arm around my waist and hauled me up. "It's not that much farther."

Together we made it to an old abandoned barn, where Jason had stowed clean clothes and a gas lamp the day before. We would spend the night there.

Jason led me to a rickety ladder, and I climbed up into the hayloft. It smelled like horses and old machines. While I changed clothes, Jason made our bed out of hay and a wool blanket. We didn't light the gas lamp. We were afraid its glow would act like a beacon. Instead we let a sliver of moonlight guide our movements, and soon we lay together. Jason's body was slick with lake water and sweat. He took off his shirt and I traced the line of his tattoos. The unicorn. The set of trees. The letters reading *God's Will*. When he pulled my shirt off and asked, "Do you want to?" I didn't hesitate.

He blew into his hands, warming them, and crushed his mouth to mine. He was desperate that night. I loved him so much then that it exploded out of my skin and manifested as a physical need —a need to be close, as close to him as possible. When Jason moved in me, it felt as if the world was moving, too, perfectly in sync with his body above mine. When it was done, he wrapped me up in a dry T-shirt, kissing my stomach as he did. Then he kissed my eyelids, my collarbone, and the skin right above my pounding heart.

That night I spread all my dreams at his feet, wove them into the hay and the wool blanket and through the wooden slats of the old barn that would burn so easily.

———•◆•———

CHAPTER

22

ESCAPE

CHASE AND I RACE TOWARD THE SKYLINE, TOWARD THE HORI-
zon, where the stars melt into the orange of sunrise. We pass the
D ward, the hole in the gate. The wind whips through my hair,
makes it fly everywhere, so it's hard to see. There's the cry of an
alarm in the distance. Huge spotlights break the dawn and slash
across the lawn, seeking our bodies.

I allow myself one moment to look at the building, the worn
façade and blacked-out windows. Chase stops behind me.

"Alice, you okay?" he asks, and places his hand in mine.

I nod and he gives my fingers a gentle, reassuring squeeze as
we start to run again. At first my legs are sluggish, unwilling to do
what my brain orders them. *Run. Fast. Run. Quick.* And I know
it's not just the physical exertion that's crippling me; it's fear. Fear
of what we'll find. Fear for Chase. Fear of Cellie. It all jumbles up
inside of me, spiking my adrenaline. We come to the barbed-wire
fence. The hole Jason had cut has been patched. Our only choice is

to climb and risk punctured skin. I put my foot through the chain-link and hoist myself over. In my haste I forget that the coiled wire is spiked, and I grab onto it. I let out a cry of pain as the barbs slice into my burned hands. I tumble to the other side. Chase is at my heels. He's managed to dodge the barbed wire. I wipe my bloody palms on my jeans.

Chase gives me a once-over, his face etched with concern. "Your hands okay?" he asks.

"Yeah," I say. I look at my hands. They're still bleeding, but not too much. Not nearly enough to stop me. A spotlight crosses the ground inches from us. "Still with me?" I ask him. It's too late for me to turn back, but it's not too late for him. I want to give him an out, but he doesn't take it.

"I'm with you, Alice."

Then we're running again. The dense forest slows our motions, and it feels as if we've been going for hours, even though I know it's been only minutes. The hospital alarms fade in the distance, and the only sounds we hear are the dry twigs snapping underfoot and the heaviness of our breaths, but this doesn't mean we aren't being followed. When we come to the lake I stop, cold and dead on my feet.

Chase bends and braces his hands on his knees. "Why'd you stop?"

I give a jerky nod to the other side of the lake, where a field stretches and a crumbled, charred ruin of a barn rises from the ground like a tombstone. "I think that's where she went," I tell him.

"Why there?" he asks in disbelief. "Is that where—"

"Yeah," I say softly. "It's where Jason died."

"You don't have to do this, Alice." He puts his hands on his hips and looks at the ground. "I understand if you want to go back."

My eyes flutter shut and I walk backwards into the past. It's like I'm watching a movie on rewind. *Go on, Alice. You have to do this.* "No. She's there. She knows this is the only place I wouldn't go. She thinks she's safe there. This is my only chance."

Before Chase can reply, before I can even see his reaction, I dive into the lake. The icy water shoots a million tiny needles into my skin. The only thing to do is swim, swim to keep warm, swim to stay alive.

I hear the splash of Chase's body hitting the water behind me. He catches up easily, and when he does, we don't say anything. We're too focused on keeping our breaths even, our strokes steady. Finally, mercifully, we come to a place where our feet can touch the rocky bottom. Then we walk, staggering like zombies to the shore. Chase takes my hand, and this time he laces his fingers through mine. We run together, side by side, until the barn gets closer and we can smell its charred carcass. Dew rises from the tall grass, a vapor I almost mistake for smoke, but the building isn't burning. Not anymore. Even if Cellie tried to set it on fire again, I don't think there's enough of it left to burn.

When Jason and I ran here, there was a huge sliding door that he had to push open with all his might. Now the opening is just a big, gaping hole.

I step over the threshold, my heart hammering in my chest. The morning sun filters through the broken and uneven walls, giving the barn a light, ethereal glow. There's a small, childlike laugh behind me. *Cellie.* I whirl around, but it's only Chase, his shadow cast over me. *Shit, baby. I'm burning up.* It's Jason's voice behind me now. I spin around again.

"What is it, Alice?" Chase asks.

Cellie laughs. The noise ricochets off the walls, zooms in a circle. I put my hands over my ears, shake my head. Little droplets of icy lake water spill everywhere. I shiver but not from the outside. Somewhere deep inside me a cold memory is cracking open. "This can't be right," I say, mostly to myself. The barn is empty. Frantically I run farther into the barn until I'm at the ladder leading to the hayloft. I climb it. Chase is behind me. I look around the loft. Cellie's not here. I turn to Chase. "But the fire in my room . . ."

I thought for sure she'd be here.

His eyes soften with sympathy. "There wasn't a fire, Alice. You were screaming and crying, and they couldn't get you to calm down, so they put you in the Quiet Room."

I glance at my hands and examine my palms. They're not blistered, not even pink. There are only the scrapes from the barbed wire and the healed burn—no fresh blisters or scars. "I don't understand," I say to myself, to the barn, to Chase.

"I think you do," he says quietly.

"Cellie's not here."

"You're wrong." He takes a deep breath. "I think Cellie *is* here."

23

THE PERFECT PLAN

Somewhere in the distance, a voice calls me. I can't tell if this is a memory or if it's happening right now.

Cellie stands above me, a slow, quizzical smile building on her lips. She seems sad, fragile.

"Cellie?" I reach out to touch her, but my fingers slice through the air. Her face is only smoke, white smoke that shimmers in the moonlight. I roll onto my knees, and there she is again, standing at the top of the ladder that connects the hayloft to the ground floor. She throws her head back and laughs like we did when we were children, when we'd play all day until we were sticky with sweat and our cheeks smelled of the summer sun. I crawl toward her.

"Allie?" It's Chase behind me. But I ignore him. Now I'm following Cellie from the hayloft, down the ladder, and into a horse stall, where Jason left the gas lamp.

I blink and I'm standing next to the lamp, caressing the glass with a hungry desire to feel the heat and watch something burn.

Cellie's hand hovers over mine. It dips down and melds into my fingers, until it becomes my palm. Cellie is guiding me, but it's my hand that's moving.

I barely remember taking the gas lamp in my hand, holding it aloft, and looking for something flammable. I hear Jason's footsteps coming down the ladder, watch his twisted face as he races toward me.

"Cellie," he whispers, standing outside the horse stall, a seemingly safe distance away. I look at him and see him through Cellie's eyes.

"This is your fault," Cellie hisses, though I'm the one who does the talking.

"You're right. This is my fault."

"You don't love me. Nobody ever does," we say.

"I love you both," Jason says. "How could I love one without loving the other?" He reaches for me, for Cellie, and I let him take my hand. His palm is callused and warm. He squeezes my fingertips, grasps them lightly at first and then more firmly. "I love you both. I always have. I did this for us." He brings his other hand up, cups my cheek, and I lean in. The gas lamp settles next to my thigh, and I don't notice the heat of the flame or the smell of oil, which seems more pungent in this part of the barn. His hand moves down, traces my shoulder, my elbow, my wrist, then wraps around my fingers.

I'm afraid.

Something that is fractured inside me is coming together, like pieces of a jigsaw puzzle. I see myself as a little girl, standing over

Grandpa's body, his skin the color of an approaching storm. Over my shoulder, someone blossoms behind me. A mirror image whose hand feels real, whose touch brings comfort, whose voice brings joy. Someone who takes all the love I never feel, balls it up, and stitches it together inside herself to save me from a lifetime of feeling unworthy, unloved, unwanted. My dark partner. My twisted twin. *Me.*

"It's okay." Jason smiles down at me, bringing his body close to mine. "It's okay," he says, holding me like I am a fragile doll or something expensive made of glass.

"You've known all this time? That Cellie's not real?" I don't understand what is happening. She seemed so real. A part of me is heartbroken that she isn't.

"Of course. I've always known."

It is too hard. I can't swallow what Jason is telling me. "But she terrorized me."

"I'm sorry, baby. You haven't been well for a long time. But I'm going to make it better now." Gently he tries to pry my fingers from the handle of the gas lamp. "Just give it to me." My grip tightens. Something isn't right. "C'mon baby, let go."

I take a step back and he squeezes my fist so hard it is painful. His lip curls. "I said *let go.*"

We struggle, the lamp like the rope in a game of high-stakes tug of war. I swing my arm wildly, trying to dislodge Jason's grip. It works. But I don't have total control of my limbs, and the thin glass shatters against the barn wall. Liquid from the lamp splashes, coating my hand and setting it instantly on fire. I scream at the immediate pain, like hot knives slicing into flesh. The lamp tumbles from my fingers and into the hay, where more fire takes root. I slap at my body, trying to smother the flames. "Help me," I cry. *"Please,* help me."

Jason just stands there, a confused expression on his face. "That's what I'm doing, baby."

"Oh, my God." The pain makes me jump around. "It hurts so bad." Finally I manage to suffocate the fire on my hand, but the fire around us is growing fast. Too fast. No way it could spread without the help of an accelerant. It circles the horse stall and moves to the wooden beams of the barn. All at once I understand. The acrid smell of oil. The fresh, dry hay. A montage of Jason's words spirals toward me.

It's somewhere new.

I think you'll like it better than anything you could imagine.

I found the perfect place.

You'll be free of her soon, I promise.

Cellie is a part of me. There is no escaping her except in death. Jason planned it all. I look at him, a boy whom life has ruined, and I scream. The sound that escapes from my chest is guttural, a war cry. I take one step back and then dart forward. The fire rages, and smoke curls through the barn like some kind of hellish serpent. Jason's hand wraps around my ankle and pulls me back just as a smoldering beam comes crashing down with a loud boom. Jason throws me like a rag doll onto a pile of hay. Some of my hair catches fire and I roll around to put it out. That's when he climbs over me, his legs straddling my hips, his hands pinning me down.

He'd never used his strength against me before. And it is terrifying. Fire bites into my shoulders, but the places where Jason's hands hold me hostage remain unburned.

"It's too late, Alice. Be still." He wants us to burn up together. This was his perfect place. His perfect plan. He throws back his head and laughs. "Shit, baby. I'm burning up!"

Blue and red lights flash outside the barn, and through the cracks I see police cars. The rusty door of the barn screeches open and two police officers step in, their arms shielding their faces against the smoke and heat. Their badges flicker orange in the firelight. They shout something at us, but I can't make it out over the roar of the blaze and my hammering heart. They retreat.

Even so, I see a glimmer of hope. My hands are useless, the whole upper part of my body is useless, drowning in fire and Jason's rage, but my legs still work. I bring one up, jabbing my knee into the place I know will hurt Jason most. He yowls and rolls off of me. I try to stand but the heat bows my back and makes me stoop.

"Alice, please. Don't leave me." I don't know if he is begging for my help. If he regrets his decision, or if he wants me to lie down next to him and let the fire consume us both. I never find out. Spasms rack my body and my legs give way. And then I am falling, gravity is harsh and unforgiving. I land on Jason's chest. Vaguely I recall not feeling any movement underneath me. There is no way out, no escape. Finally Cellie is quiet inside of me. She isn't raging, trying to claw her way to the surface. My eyes drift shut. I try to fight it. But some things are so much stronger than our will or our want. Death is always the ultimate victor. Time passes, and in the darkness I feel myself lifted and carried. Rescue. Fresh air hits my face, but not my lungs.

Someone holds me. It feels as if my chest is being cracked open. Finally, *finally,* I open my eyes. Chase is holding me, holding me like I'm made of glass. But it's too late, I've already shattered into a million little pieces.

CHAPTER
24

FALLING DOWN

CHASE'S HANDS MOVE UP AND DOWN MY ARMS. HIS WARMTH rips away the cold and brings me back to the present. The burns on my shoulders ache, but I can't tell if the pain is real or not. All that time I thought Jason had held me, shielded me from the fire . . . but now I know that I am forever branded by his madness. His betrayal seems small compared with my own.

I toy with my white hospital bracelet, the one with the bar code that rests just underneath my yellow wristband. I trace the letters of my name, *Alice.* They blur together until they rearrange: *Celia.* The truth is a dagger buried in my back. "I'm Celia?" I ask. Though I'm not talking to anyone in particular. Chase bows his head and pulls me into a tight hug.

"I don't understand," I say, pulling back. Even though I feel the truth in my core, something inside of me rejects it. "You said she was in the D ward." My voice is faint, full of doubt.

Chase shakes his head and looks at me sadly, pitifully. "I never said she was in the D ward. You drew that conclusion yourself."

I nod in a sort of vacant way. My mind runs through our conversations. I was the driving force behind each one. *She's in the D ward,* I had said. And Chase hadn't disagreed, but he hadn't agreed either. Silence hides the most damning things, I guess.

I press a hand against my chest. It feels as if my heart has cloned itself and now there are two heartbeats at war with each other. Thousands of images swirl in my mind. *Cellie offering me cake. Cellie stealing food at the Chans'. Cellie setting fires.* No — not Cellie, *me.* Oh God, all the things I've done, all the people I've hurt. How will I ever forgive myself? I stagger back and have to use the wall for support. The surface is charred, and little splinters prick the skin under my fingernails. How could I not have known? "Why didn't anyone tell me?"

Chase takes off his hat and twists it in his hands, so hard that water squeezes out of it. The scar on his cheek twitches. "I thought, in the beginning, when you asked about her, that she *was* real. I didn't know she was . . ." He can't look at me. "I didn't know she *wasn't* until the things you said didn't quite add up, and then I stole your file. And it spelled it out, all in black-and-white. Dr. Goodman noted in it that he didn't think you were ready to handle the truth. He believed that if you were told the truth, it would cause significant and irreversible damage. And I thought that was bullshit." It all makes sense now, Chase's dislike for Dr. Goodman.

But then, all too fast, Chase's lies come back to me. It hurts.

My file must have said everything. He played along with my fantasy. I'm being held together with thread. I sink to the floor, draw my legs up, and hook my arms around them. I'm shaking, but not from the cold. I rock in place and cry. "So what? This was all some game to you? Something to keep you from boredom in the mental hospital?" I spew the words, and they're full of hate.

"No." He shakes his head, almost violently. He melts to his knees and reaches for me, but I turn my cheek and choke back a sob. A cold finger runs down my spine. The world shrinks away, and I just want to find a hole to crawl into.

"Look," he says. "You remember I told you about my sister, how I killed her?"

I don't answer, I just keep crying. Cellie's not real. It's destroying me. I always wondered what it would feel like to be brought to the bottom, and now I know.

Chase squeezes my kneecaps, forces my eyes to his. "Please, I know I don't have any right to ask you this, but just listen, okay? That's all. Just listen? And then if you want me to go, and you don't ever want to see me again, I'll understand, okay?"

I can't manage words so I just nod. He starts talking fast, like if he doesn't get the words out in enough time, they'll burn up in the distance between us. "My sister, Maya. She was sick." He smiles, but it's melancholy. "I told you that you reminded me of her, remember?" He doesn't wait for me to confirm, just goes on. "That was the thing at the beginning—you reminded me of her." *My little bird with a broken wing.* "She had all sorts of things wrong with her, mostly this horrible temper—which you don't have. But my parents, they kept insisting that she was just sad, that there wasn't anything wrong with her. They refused to get her help. And she got worse." He looks at the ground. "Like, a lot worse. One night when my parents were gone, she freaked out and started saying all this shit about how the government was tapping our phones. I couldn't calm her down. She was out of control. She grabbed a knife from the kitchen. When I tried to wrestle it out of her hands, she cut me real bad." He motions to the scar on his cheek. "I locked myself in the bathroom. She finally calmed down and tried to apologize through the door. But I was so pissed. And I . . . I said things I shouldn't have, things I didn't even mean. I told her I hated her. I told her to go away."

The silence builds and then collapses as the final part of his secret spills out. "You don't know how many times a day I relive those final moments. She made this sound like . . . like I was pulling out her heart. *Fuck.* After the house had been quiet for a while, I came out. I found her in the kitchen. There was so much blood. I remember taking off my shirt and wrapping it around her wrists. I screamed that I didn't mean any of it. I begged her to stay. Stay alive. But she died. After that, it was like there was a monster in my chest. I was so angry. Five months later, I wound up at Savage Isle in the D ward for beating the shit out of a teacher who asked me if I was doing okay. I don't even know why I did it. When the cops came to arrest me, I sobbed like a fucking baby. All I could do was rock back and forth, and all I heard was that sound Maya made."

I understand what he's telling me, but I don't have it in me to sympathize. I just don't. I've heard enough. "Chase—"

"Just let me finish, okay? I know what you're thinking—what does this have to do with you, right? So, like I said, you reminded me of her, but then you didn't, and I started to like you in a whole different way. Like, *really* like you. I didn't understand why you were at Savage Isle. So I stole your file and that's when I figured it all out. And I thought . . . *Fuck*." He runs a hand through his hair, leaving a chaotic mess in its wake. He's wild for me to understand, accept, and forgive what he's saying. "I know, what I did was wrong, but I guess I thought if I couldn't save my sister, I could save you."

I was right. He wanted to fix me because he couldn't fix his sister. I don't blame him, but I don't excuse him for it either. He slumps down so his shoulder aligns with mine. I have a sudden flash of Jason holding me, his weight pressing me down. I flinch at the contact and curl away. "Jesus, Alice. I'm not going to hurt you."

I want him to go away. I don't want to hear anything else. I lie down and rest my cheek on the ashy floor. There's movement in the barn and it's not from Chase, he's gone utterly still, just like me. There are footsteps. And then a voice. "Alice, are you in here?" It's Dr. Goodman.

Chase nudges me. It has no effect. He tries again. But I'm frozen. It's almost like one of those horror stories you hear about when people are anesthetized and their bodies can't move but they can feel everything during surgery. I would be lucky to feel such torture. I feel nothing. I'm not even crying now. I'm all dried up inside. Hollow like the wind through dry grass.

Chase stands with his hands up. "She's here."

"Alice, come on out. You're safe now," Dr. Goodman says, and his voice echoes in my ears like I'm standing at the back of a cave.

"She won't move." Chase gasps, and then, based on the noise he makes, he's either crying or sick. Maybe both. "I really fucked up. I think I really fucked up."

"Chase, come on out. We'll get everything sorted. I just need you to step away from Alice for me. Can you do that?" Dr. Goodman negotiates.

Long seconds pass and nobody moves. Finally, the standoff ends when techs storm the stall. Chase is pushed down. I hear the unmistakable sound of handcuffs, and then Chase is dragged away.

Dr. Goodman kneels beside me. "Alice, it's over now. Time to go back to the hospital." I don't move. He draws a penlight from his pocket and shines it in my eyes. I guess my body still works, because I squint and try to withdraw. Someone, a nurse I think, asks if he wants to sedate me. *That's funny.* My limbs are already heavy. Finding out that your twin doesn't actually exist is a kind of natural sedation. He tells her no. The world falls out beneath me as I'm lifted. Donny carries me to a waiting police car. He settles me into the back seat and assists me with the seat belt. Dr. Goodman gets in beside me. I turn away from him. Chase is in the next car. I can't see his face, because he's hunched over. Shudders rack his body.

The doors slam and the car lurches forward, red and blue lights spinning. Dr. Goodman shrugs off his jacket and lays it over my legs. Somehow I forgot that I'm soaking wet from the lake.

"I'm sorry this happened, Alice," Dr. Goodman says. He goes

on to tell me all sorts of things, about how hopeful he is for my recovery. How when I'm ready, he'll be there to listen. He wonders if I know now that Celia isn't real. He says I must have so many questions. I do. Or I did. But right now, they don't seem to matter. "You won't have to worry about Chase coming back to the hospital. I'll find him a placement at another facility." He's trying to reassure me, but it's pointless. I close my eyes. Dr. Goodman keeps talking, but all I hear are the wheels of the police car on wet cement and the sound of Chase taking me to the edge and pushing me off.

25

POSSIBILITIES

I SPEND TWO WEEKS IN SECLUSION, UNDERGOING INTENSIVE therapy with Dr. Goodman. Donny is my babysitter. For a while I can hear Cellie's voice. She talks to me when Donny won't. Dr. Goodman says this is common. That I may sometimes hear her, but the important part is that I now know she isn't real. He says that the brain is a fragile thing and that mine invented Cellie as a mode of survival. I guess he's right. The way he says it, it's like he thinks I'm some kind of miracle. But I don't feel that way. I feel more like a monster. Something that somebody sewed together with leftover parts, and I can only hope one day to be whole.

When I ask the good doctor my questions—*How could I not have known? Why did I remember Celia and other people interacting?*—he is patient and kind and gives me the answers that Chase found in my file. Because of my mental state, Dr. Goodman felt that I wasn't ready to hear that Celia was a waking hallucination.

He said he had tried to tell me before, during my first visit to Savage Isle, but my hallucinations were deep-rooted and became increasingly worse. I had called him a liar and said he was plotting against me. *Everybody's lying. Everyone's lying.*

I had screamed that, not Cellie.

Dr. Goodman hopes that the medication he prescribed will eventually enable me to differentiate reality and fantasy. And that's exactly what Celia was. What she *is*. A fantasy. Someone I invented all those years ago while I waited to be found in a cold house next to a dead body, because my mind couldn't bend toward the truth.

Dr. Goodman and I spend hours reviewing my journal entries and deciphering each one. Together we carefully unlock my warped memories, memories I had twisted and recreated so that Cellie was real. Dr. Goodman is right. The mind is a wondrous thing. My mind rejected so much. The pain of my grandfather's death. Horrible foster homes. Jason's madness. Celia absorbed it all. I'd be lying if I said I wasn't thankful for her. She kept me together for a long, long time.

After two weeks, Celia quiets, and I return to the general population. Time is different in the hospital. It passes slowly, and sometimes the days blur together into one big nothing. Before I know it, three months pass. My red band is replaced with a yellow one, and my privileges are reinstated—which includes use of the telephone.

Lately, Chase has been calling. He was transported to another facility that night. When they questioned me about our escape, I did my best to cover for him. I said it was all my idea, which it kind of was. I was the one who pushed him to help me. I even claimed that I aided in stealing the keycards—and that I asked him to lift my file.

I think the lies worked, because recently Chase was granted outpatient treatment, along with probation. Which in total is the equivalent of a slap on the wrist. I was candid with Dr. Goodman and told him all about the stolen moments Chase and I shared —sneaking up to the rooftop, kissing in the pagoda, spending the night in his room. Since I was still trying to sift fiction from reality, I asked Dr. Goodman what he thought of Chase's motives. And Dr. Goodman agrees with me. Chase's motives, though misguided, were pure, born from good intent. I trust Dr. Goodman now. More than I trust myself. Sometimes when Chase calls, I talk to him, and sometimes I don't feel like it. He always seems to understand. Last time we talked, he asked if he could visit and I said I wasn't ready. But yesterday I was. And today, he's coming.

My mind hums with excitement at the prospect of seeing him again. There's a slight bounce to my step as I make my way to the visitors' area. I spy him right away through the half window in the door. He sits in a brown chair and every line of his body is filled with nervous energy, from his elbows resting on his knees to his hands clasped together, to his feet tapping on the ground. Sara is also there, standing farther back, clutching her purse to her chest.

In no time I'm through the door and standing next to Chase. He looks up as if I've surprised him, like he wasn't expecting me.

"Hey." He stands up, wipes his hands on his jeans, and then grips me in an awkward hug. "I made you something." He reaches down to the table beside him and picks up a bright bouquet of origami flowers. "Here," he says, pressing them into my hands. "I've been practicing. Whenever we talk on the phone, I practice." He takes off his hat and runs his hands through his hair. "I'm sure it's not as good as you would do it."

"They're beautiful," I say. "Thank you."

"Yeah, well, I figure they're better than real flowers. You probably can't have real flowers in here, anyway. Probably some bullshit reason like you might try to eat them to poison yourself."

I laugh, and it breaks the tension. A little. I put my hand on his elbow, and he goes still. "Really, they're wonderful. Thank you."

He relaxes, and then suddenly I'm enveloped in a tight hug. "Christ, I've missed you," he says into my hair. We hold on to each other a touch longer than is appropriate. When we draw away, the tension is back. But this time it's a different kind of tension, full of all our intimate moments. I still find him beautiful, more so than when we first met. Because now there are no more secrets between us.

We sit and he resumes the same position as before. He waits. Dr. Goodman steps into the visitors' room and stands by Sara. They watch me. It's something I'll have to get used to, until I earn their trust. I clear my throat. It doesn't taste like ash anymore.

"How are you?" Chase asks.

"I'm better," I say, and smile at him.

A shudder runs through Chase's lean frame, and he grips his knees. "I'm so sorry, Alice, more sorry than you can ever imagine. The last time I saw you—"

I lean forward and touch his hands. "It's okay." I swallow. "I think I actually have to thank you."

He snorts in disbelief.

"No, I mean it. I don't know how long it would have taken for me to realize . . ." It's still hard for me to say her name.

"Are you really doing okay?"

I'm not doing bad, but I'm not doing great either. Most days it feels as if I'm coasting. Dr. Goodman says that part of my recovery is learning to be truthful with others and myself. But sometimes there's compassion in withholding. I take Chase's hands in mine. "I'm doing great. *Really.*"

Chase bows his head. He trembles and comes apart. I sit on the arm of his chair and hold him. His arms encircle my waist and his head rests on my stomach. His tears are for me, I think, but also for his sister, for himself. I always thought something was haunting him, and now I know it was. The dark specter of his past. He keeps saying he's sorry. I run my fingers through his hair. Like I said before, he doesn't need to apologize. I've already forgiven him. Dr. Goodman says there's grace in forgiveness, the ability to pardon others and ourselves. And I suppose it's true. It was easy to forgive Chase, but it's not as easy to forgive myself. Sara says it will take time.

When it's over, and he's done, and the last shudder has racked his body, he smiles, and it's like the ghost that's been haunting him has finally been called away. Maybe she has.

There's another awkward silence. Neither of us knows what to say next. We've already said so much. Finally we say goodbye, and Chase says he'll come again next week. I tell him I'm looking forward to it.

Donny escorts me back to my room. I hold the paper flowers Chase gave me close to my chest. We pass a couple of techs chatting in the hallway.

"Jeez, it's hot out today," tech one says.

"I know," tech two says, and rubs the back of his neck. "I'm burning up."

I pause mid-step. Donny nearly runs into me. "Alice, everything all right?"

I can smell kerosene and burning hay. I take deep breaths, willing the olfactory hallucination away. Dr. Goodman says this is normal. That it's part of my PTSD, post-traumatic stress disorder. That some things may trigger memories that seem like they're happening right now. The scent dissipates, and I'm back in the hospital looking at Donny's overly concerned face. I smile at him. "I'm okay. Just needed to catch my breath."

He accepts this and we keep going. When we get to my door, I thank him as he opens it. Alone in my room, I lean back against the door and take another moment to compose myself. I don't like being in here alone. I close my eyes and do a deep-breathing exercise Dr. Goodman taught me. Inhale, hold for three seconds. Exhale, hold for three seconds. Inhale. Exhale. I open my eyes, feeling calmer.

Outside the steel mesh window, the sun dips below the horizon and beams of light filter through the trees, reminding me of crooked teeth. The light fills my room, illuminating my paper zoo and spinning dust around the animals, touching each paper leg and folded head with a golden hand. I place Chase's flowers inside the zoo, right in the center, a garden for my animals. In the corner of the dresser is the heart-shaped rock Chase gave me. I found it, a few days after my weeks in seclusion, behind the dresser. Often I think of the day he gave it to me, and I am quietly thankful. I don't know what tomorrow will bring. If I'll get out of Savage Isle . . . if I'll go to college . . . if Chase and I will be together again. But that's the wondrous thing. *I don't know.* I, Alice Monroe, am suddenly full of possibilities.

EPILOGUE

CELIA

AT NIGHT WHEN EVERYTHING IS QUIET, SHE STARES AT THE plaster walls in her hospital room and weeps. Softly I come, from somewhere deep inside, somewhere where her regret and sadness collide.

Allie, I say. She closes her eyes tight and heaves a breath, as if trying to blow me away. *Allie,* I say again. She's fighting me, trying to convince herself of the illusion. But I can feel her clinging. I am her lifeboat, the only constant in a sea of chaos. I am better than nothing, and nothing is all she has.

Her face cracks, and I know she's lost the internal war she's waging. "Yes, Cellie," she answers.

I am sorry, I tell her.

She turns in her bed to face the window. Outside, clouds shift and cover the moon, stealing light from the room. "You've said that before."

I've meant it, every time.

"You're not real."

I laugh at the word, and I feel it ripple through her body. *I am real. You made me.*

"I want you to go away," she says, but her voice is weak. She curls herself into a ball.

Poor Alice. Always alone. She needs me. I risk a touch to her brow and she furrows it. She can feel me moving around inside, filling up all that empty space. *I'll tell you a story.* It's a memory I've been keeping, tucked safely away. I tell her of our day with Grandpa, weeks before he died. How he took us to the zoo and we watched a lion with her cubs. We ate cotton candy, and the sugar melted between our fingertips. Grandpa paid for us to feed the elephants, and one wrapped its trunk around her arm. I remind her of Grandpa's wrinkled face in that exact moment, how it lit up like a thousand lanterns in a dark sky and then erupted in laughter.

My whispers paint a picture in her mind and she smiles, the memory unfurling like a little fire sparking in her belly. Slowly, her tears dry. And I know, I *know*, we'll never be apart.

ACKNOWLEDGMENTS

I owe thanks to so many people.

To my super agent, Erin Harris, for pulling this manuscript out of the slush pile and seeing its potential, for reading each draft and never tiring, and for helping me navigate the wild waters of publishing. This book would not exist without you.

To my editor, Sarah Landis, for her wild enthusiasm, for taking a chance on this dark, gritty book and seeing all the beauty in it. And to Christine Krones, for her kindness and guidance through copy edits and much more.

To the entire team at HMH Books for Young Readers, for a beautiful cover, for awesome marketing support (Hayley Gonnason, Ann Dye, Lisa DiSarro, Amanda Acevedo), and for everything else—it truly takes a village.

To my family, for their unwavering support: Kiya and Mariko, sisters and best friends, for always *loving* everything I write, including a really bad book about Fairies. Nate, big brother, for fun title variations such as *We'll Never Pee and Fart* and *Let's Eat Split Pea Soup and Shart*. Tony, Ev, Liz, Elaine, Aimee, and Jody. Grandpa

Bill, wherever you are, I hope you're smiling. How did I get so lucky to be a part of such an amazing family?

To my mom, for taking me to the library and encouraging prolific reading, for reading my bad poetry in high school, and reading my work now; hopefully it is slightly better.

To my dad, for taking me on walks and looking at the stars, and for teaching me that I could be anything—a doctor, an astronaut, a dancer on a star.

And finally to my husband, Craig, to whom this book is dedicated: None of this is possible without you.

EMIKO JEAN is an elementary school math teacher whose work with children in foster care inspired *We'll Never Be Apart*. She lives with her husband in Seattle, Washington.